STORMY WATERS

STORMY WATERS

Rosemary Aitken

This first world edition published in Great Britain 2001 by
SEVERN HOUSE PUBLISHERS LTD of
9–15 High Street, Sutton, Surrey SM1 1DF.
This first world edition published in the USA 2001 by
SEVERN HOUSE PUBLISHERS INC of
595 Madison Avenue, New York, N.Y. 10022.

British Library Cataloguing in Publication Data

Aitken, Rosemary
  Stormy waters
  1. Cornwall (England)
  2. Domestic fiction
  I. Title
  823.9'14 [F]

  ISBN 0-7278-5728-2

Typeset by Hewer Text Ltd.,
Edinburgh, Scotland.
Printed and bound in Great Britain by
MPG Books Ltd., Bodmin, Cornwall.

To Sally, who has so often
acted as midwife to my stories

PART ONE
January – May 1911

One

Aunt Gypsy's funeral was everything she would have wished for. Not the usual wrought-iron funeral cart, draped in droopy loops of black crepe, decorated with branches of yew and pulled by a reluctant pony from Penvarris. This was a splendid affair, a great polished black carriage-hearse, with gleaming brass handles, drawn by four solemn black horses with funeral plumes and attended by proper professional coffin bearers – exactly matched for size, so they didn't jolt the casket – dignified and doleful, in their mufflers, top hats and gloves.

The church was half full, too, in spite of Ma's gloomy predictions. Couples who had known Aunt Gypsy in Penzance, one or two servants and tradespeople, and, more surprisingly, local people from Penvarris itself were in attendance. Mostly Covers, of course – people from the Cove didn't have a lot to do with Terrace folk as a rule – but there were one or two 'up-overers' from Penvarris village, too.

'Come to stare,' Ma said when she saw them, and she walked into church like a ramrod, with her head held high under her best bonnet with its new black ribbons.

It was hard to know what they had come to stare at. Not at Ma, she looked the same as ever; her diminutive figure rigid in the same black bombazine she had worn ever since her own mother's death, her grey hair dragged back into a neat bun, her gold-rimmed glasses on a chain around her neck. Apart from the new bonnet ribbons anyone might see her just like this any Sunday morning of the year.

They weren't looking at Pa, either, though he was a rarer

3

sight, buttoned into his best suit with an unaccustomed collar too tight around his neck. He didn't often come to the church, for all Ma's fussing. Pa, like most of the fishermen in the Cove, had an aversion to 'white-chokers' and would run a mile if a 'dog-collar' came anywhere near him. He wasn't a fisherman exactly, he was a boat builder by trade, though there wasn't much scope for that in the Cove these days beyond the odd repair, and mostly he ferried stores for a living. But he had a few pots and hand-lines as well, and he *behaved* like a fisherman: wouldn't put to sea without a swift reverent nod towards the tiny seaman's chapel down on the rocks and a handful of crusts in his pocket to appease the Bucca, just in case.

People weren't even staring at Sprat, though goodness knows she felt conspicuous enough in her black silk dress, which was, ironically, a hand-me-down from Aunt Gypsy herself. Made over, of course – no self-respecting sixteen-year-old could be seen out in a dress of that daring cut, especially in the Cove – but all the same, there was no disguising the quality of the cloth. As the last hymn 'Rock of Ages' ceased, and they stood up to follow the coffin to the graveyard, Sprat was deliciously conscious of the silk swirling over her petticoats and swishing around her ankles.

Ma dug her in the ribs sharply, and gave her a ferocious frown. Sprat realised, with a guilty start, that she had been smiling. That was odd. If there was one person, in the whole building, who was most deeply and sincerely sorry that Aunt Gypsy was dead, that person was Sprat Nicholls.

Sprat had adored her Aunt Gypsy. Idolised her almost. Aunt Gypsy had been everything that Sprat was not. Tall and elegant, while Sprat was like Ma, small and wiry.

'Take after your Grandfather, you do,' Aunt Gypsy would say, on one of her infrequent visits, and she would brush Sprat's hair – long, loving strokes with a silver-backed brush – before the carriage came to collect her and she disappeared again in a cloud of perfume and powder, and rustling silk. Afterwards, Ma would go around for days with her face set and disapproving, while Sprat secretly tried to model herself on her beautiful, exotic, dangerous aunt.

They *were* similar in some ways, she told herself. They shared the same fair hair and grey eyes, but while Aunt Gypsy's blond tresses were swept into a fashionable chignon, Sprat's yellow curls were scraped into skinny plaits and skewered with hair pins round her head. Aunt Gypsy enhanced her eyes with something called a 'coal' pencil, just as she – wickedly – used rouge on her cheeks and carmine on her lips. She dressed beautifully, in satins and silks and figured muslin, and soft fine wool in the winter. Sprat knew it was sinful – Ma said so – but she was also secretly aware that Uncle James Jamieson, whom Aunt Gypsy had married, far from treating her as a 'shameless hussy', seemed to like her very much indeed.

And now they were dead, both of them, carried off by the same infectious fever. Uncle James Jamieson had died first – he was old after all; Aunt Gypsy had been his second wife – and then, last week, Aunt Gypsy had finally followed him. All that beauty and vibrant life. It was still impossible to believe.

The mourners were walking out into the graveyard now, and the cold Cornish wind bit at Sprat's ankles under the silk. Aunt Gypsy would have known how to deal with this, how to prevent the silken skirts from billowing up or catching on the grasses as they passed, how to walk with elegance among the toppling gravestones and granite angels. Gypsy – even the name was romantic. Short for gypsophila, Ma said – a kind of flower, but it reminded Sprat of caravans, pegs, lace-making and a life on the road. And now, here was Aunt Gypsy, lying lifeless in that box, which the four coffin bearers were lowering, with difficulty, on four long silken ropes, into the earth.

Sprat caught the vicar's eye in time to step forward and sprinkle a handful of earth on the coffin, then, on an impulse, she tore the ribbon from her hair and dropped that into the grave, too. Ma looked daggers, but it was too late. Others were stepping forward to scatter earth in their turn, and very soon

Mrs Gypsy Jamieson, widow, lately of this parish, had gone to her eternal rest.

Sprat turned away, the tears at last beginning.

'Wilhemina?' A man's voice. 'Wilhemina Nicholls?'

She looked up doubtfully. Nobody ever called her by that name – not in the Cove, or even up-over, in the school or church. 'No bigger'n a sprat,' Pa had said when he first saw her, and 'Sprat' she had been ever since. Sprat didn't mind. Almost all the Covers had a nickname of one kind or another, and besides, 'Wilhemina' was such a peculiar sort of name. Even Ma didn't seem to care for it, so why she had chosen it in the first place, Sprat could never see.

Yet here was this man using it, as if it were the most natural thing in the world. And it wasn't anybody she knew either – one of Aunt Gypsy's gentrified friends from the town. She looked at him, frowning, and blinking back the tears.

'You must be Wilhemina,' he said again, smiling. He was a thin, cadaverous sort of fellow with a nose like a gannet's beak and eyes like awls. 'The late Mrs Jamieson spoke to me about you.'

She stared, saying nothing. The late Mrs Jamieson. It was true. It was over. Aunt Gypsy was there, in that box, and she was gone for ever.

'My name's Tavy. James Tavy, her solicitor.' He was still smiling, a bleak, businesslike sort of smile.

Suddenly Sprat could not bear it. 'Well, she never spoke to me about you,' she burst out, and flung herself, like a child, towards Ma and Pa for comfort. Pa was very good, he didn't ask questions or make a fuss, just took her arm and squeezed her elbow, and even Ma – who wasn't given to demonstrations of affection – patted her hand in the hired carriage on the way home, and gave her a clean handkerchief to blow her nose.

Ma Nicholls sat in the carriage, holding her head high and her face carefully composed, but inwardly she was in a turmoil. There could be a score or more people 'come back to the house' for the funeral tea, and she had only allowed – cold ham, thin-sliced bread and butter, and 'dark' cake – for a dozen.

There were some marinated pilchards, if the worst came to the worst, in the earthenware bussa under the stairs, and a drop of dandelion wine in the store cupboard for when Pa's bottle of special-occasion sherry ran out. But what were people to eat and drink it from, that was the question. Twelve people she might have managed, with a few crocks and glasses borrowed from Mrs Polmean next door, but a crowd like this would have stretched the 'good china' capabilities of half the Cove. And you couldn't let those Penzance folk eat off enamel and tin-ware – not for a funeral. It wouldn't have been 'fitty'.

Besides, whatever would people think? She could see it now – those awful stuck-up servants of Gypsy's looking down their noses and nodding at each other knowingly. After all, they had wanted to do the funeral feast themselves in Penzance, just as they had done Mr Jamieson's – a fussy affair with all sorts of fancy dishes, and 'little bits of something and nothing' you were supposed to eat in your fingers – but on this point Ma had been adamant. It was different for James Jamieson. He was a Penzance man, buried in the cemetery there beside his first wife. Gypsy was born in the Cove, died in the Cove, and was buried – if not in the Cove, at least in the nearest piece of sanctified ground that was soft enough to take a shovel. So it was to the Cove that the funeral party should return for the 'baked meats' – or in this case, the boiled ham.

Ma was, however, beginning to wish she had not been quite so insistent. She had no wish to look foolish in front of a bunch of servants, and as for the 'up-overers', it was well known that they relished any opportunity to sneer at a Cover. The story of her discomfiture would be all over Penvarris in a day or two. Why ever did Pa suddenly have to go inviting everyone back to the house like that?

She favoured him with one of her most formidable scowls, but Pa was thinking of something else, and only gave her a vague amiable smile.

It was just like Gypsy, Ma thought crossly. Brought nothing but trouble living, and nothing but trouble dead. Yet, she had to own it to herself, Ma always did have a soft spot for her pretty, spoiled, younger sister. Why else would she have brought her back, frail and exhausted, from the Fever Hospital at Mount Misery, to ebb out those last dreadful months on a borrowed bed in Ma's best parlour. Proper performance it had been, as well: a sheet dipped in carbolic at the doorway, and Ma running to and fro like a nursery maid, and having to disinfect everything that went in and out of the room – herself included.

Foolish really, when Gypsy had a great house in Penzance, and servants willing to wait on her – but Gypsy had wanted to 'come home' and what Gypsy wanted, Gypsy got, as a rule. In death as in life.

'And after all she's done! Weak as water, that's what you are, Myrtle Nicholls,' Ma muttered inwardly, as the carriage lurched onward.

Sprat, sitting opposite, was looking pale and tearful. Poor little maid. She had thought a lot of Gypsy, though, of course, she didn't know the half of it. Just as well. Ma had done her best, but there was no denying that Gypsy had been an unwholesome influence in that direction, insisting that Sprat should 'stay on' at school to Standard Six, filling her head with nonsense and giving her ideas above her station. And of course, Pa was as soft as putty where that girl was concerned. Well, it was all over now. But it was hard on Sprat. Ma, feeling a sudden surge of sympathy, leaned over and offered another 'blow' on the handkerchief, and then sat back, setting herself again to counting mentally the glassware and wondering how to make it stretch.

As it happened, she needn't have worried. When they arrived at the Cove – a terrible slow bumpy ride down the steep lane, it would have been a sight easier to walk – Mrs Polmean, who had stayed behind from the funeral to 'give a bit of hand' had already been in and there was a tin of corned beef and a tray of hot splits ready and waiting in the kitchen.

8

'Our Peter went up to the church,' Mrs Polmean explained, as Ma stripped off her bonnet and tied on her apron to await the guests. 'Wanted to see the 'earse and the 'orses, with they men in tall 'ats sitting atop of it – and of course when he came home and told me how many people there were come . . . Well, stands to reason . . .'

Stands to reason, she meant, that she had brought her contribution to the funeral feast – and more than that. A second later, there was a tapping at the door, and there was Norah Roberts, of all people, come from the end of the Row, with a plate of rock buns and a half-dozen assorted cups in a basket. And a few minutes later, there were others, too, so that by the time the rest of the funeral party arrived in their fancy carriages – white-faced and shaken after the ride from the churchyard – the little house was bursting with more provisions than a Sunday-school treat.

That was like the Covers, Ma thought, trying to shoehorn yet another visitor into the tiny parlour. Rallying round like this on her account, though most of them had no cause to love Gypsy. It wasn't done for Ma, either – she was clear-sighted enough to realise that: a lot of Covers thought that Myrtle Nicholls 'gave herself airs' because her husband had a trade and didn't rely on fishing like the rest of the men. No, it was done for the Cove itself, and in that spirit she accepted their help. Ma could stand on her own two feet, everyone knew that, but no one was going to stand by and have those townsfolk and 'up-overers' embarrass her by being too many for the wake.

Well, she couldn't stand here idle. She poked up the fire, set the kettle to boil, sent Sprat out to the barrel for another pitcherful of water, and turned her attention to the business in hand.

Sprat was kept very busy all the afternoon. If it wasn't the kettle wanting refilling, it was passing food and bringing back empty cups and glasses to the kitchen for 'a drop more'. Some game it was, too. The crowd had spilled out from the front room into

9

the passage and was threatening at any moment to flood the kitchen as well – so what with all the borrowed best china, and folks in their Sunday clothes – Sprat had to be more than usually careful in balancing the brimming teacups and plates of jam splits through the crush. And when she did spill just a tiny drop, when someone blundered into her, Ma glowered at her ferociously.

'Chin up, Sprat,' she could almost hear Aunt Gypsy's voice in her imagination. 'Remember Cinderella, started as a servant, ended a princess.' Gypsy was always saying things like that – of course, she'd started as a servant herself, in a big house near Penzance. Sprat offered round the plate of splits with her most princessly smile.

She almost dropped the lot, though, when suddenly a hand fell on her shoulder, and a soft voice said, close to her ear, 'I was sorry to hear about this, Sprat. I know how fond you were of your aunt.'

She whirled round, her face scarlet. Denzil Vargo! She hadn't seen him come in! She hadn't even noticed him at the church, though how she had come to miss him she couldn't think. Usually, if Denzil was anywhere in sight, Sprat was embarrassingly and overwhelmingly aware of the fact. But now here he was, smart as Christmas in his dark suit and tie, and (though not even Gypsy could have pretended that he was a handsome prince, exactly) he had such a strong, humorous, intelligent face that it gave her goose pimples looking at it.

'My life!' she blurted, to cover the moment. 'Half scared the life out me, you did. Near made me drop these splits, and what would Ma have said, then?'

Never mind the splits, in fact. They both knew what Ma would say in any case. She was saying it now.

'Sprat? Come here with those splits a minute, here's poor Mrs Roberts dying for one.'

Sprat gave Denzil a rueful smile, and turned away. She didn't have to explain, he understood as well as she did. Ma didn't care for Denzil. Not that she had anything to say against him,

10

exactly – nobody had, Denzil was a real nice fellow and educated, too – but there was something unspoken she objected to. Because he was an 'up-overer' more than likely, instead of 'one of we'. Because he *was* educated, perhaps. Because he was ever so clever. He could typewrite, and knew shorthand, and all sorts – he had a job in a shipping office in Penzance. Maybe that was it: Ma often said office clerks were 'too big for their boots'. But whatever the reason, the outcome was always the same. As sure as Ma saw Sprat and Denzil together – which wasn't often in any case – she found some urgent reason for Sprat to be elsewhere.

Like now. Sprat threaded her way through the throng towards Mrs Roberts, who smiled and took a split – rather doubtfully, Sprat thought, as if she hadn't particularly wanted it in the first place.

'Now then,' Ma said, glancing at the clock on the mantelpiece, 'don't forget you're supposed to be going to see Mrs Meacham this afternoon. I promised you'd call up there today, let her have a look at you, see if you'll suit.'

Sprat's heart sank. She had known this was coming, of course, but with all the bustle and upset of the funeral, she had almost put it out of her mind. But now, suddenly, here it was. Ma had been keen for a long time to find Sprat a 'good position', but what with Ma's own ma fading away in the front parlour and then Gypsy doing the same, Sprat had been useful at home and nothing had ever come of it. But now Gypsy was dead, and before she was even in her grave Ma had been making arrangements. Awful, Sprat thought, going for an interview the very day of the funeral, but Ma said it had to be done – before someone else stepped in and snapped up the position.

Up to Fairviews, of all places! Sprat could remember how the children, going to school, had frightened each other – and themselves – with stories about that mysterious great house on the cliff. Even now her heart gave a nervous skip at the thought of it. But she couldn't say that to Ma. Good positions were hard to come by, especially so near the Cove. Besides, Mrs Polmean's cousin was a part-time cook to Mrs Meacham – that was how Ma had heard about the vacancy in the first place. The tales were just childish nonsense. All the same . . .

Mrs Roberts voiced her thoughts. 'Going up Fairviews, are you? I heard she was looking out for someone. Queer old place by all accounts. Singer or something, wasn't she?'

'Sang opera and all sorts,' Ma said proudly. 'Long time ago now, mind. Poor old soul's bedridden now – that's how she wants someone up there, to fetch and carry and do a bit of shopping now and then. Not really a maid, more of a companion really. She got's a woman there already to wash her and get her up, and Mrs Polmean's cousin goes in to clean and cook a drop of dinner, so there's no heavy work. It's a good position for a girl starting out, and close to home, too.'

''Tisn't settled yet,' Sprat began, but Ma was too quick for her.

'Soon will be, if you make a good impression. They'll be looking out for you by this time. You'd better run along. People will be leaving soon, so Mrs Polmean and me will manage handsome now.'

Typical, Sprat thought. A minute ago Ma couldn't do without her – now, all of a sudden, she wasn't needed at all. She knew why. Because she'd stopped to have a word with Denzil Vargo. But there was no appeal from Ma. 'Let me at least have a split and a cup of tea,' she said crossly, and helped herself before Ma could protest.

'Well,' Mrs Roberts said doubtfully, 'Sooner you than me, m'dear. Queer folk, these theatricals. Still, I mustn't keep you here gossiping. It's been a sad enough day for you and you don't want to make it worse by being late, first off.'

'Mind you comb your hair before you go,' Ma said. 'And give your boots a bit of a rub, they're all over mud from the graveyard. At least you look half tidy in that dress.'

Sprat nodded, her mouth full of split and blackberry jam (delicious, she remembered picking the berries herself). She

swallowed the rest of her split and drained her cup hastily. 'You
sure you can manage?' she said to Ma. 'There'll be no end of
washing-up, and we're short of water with all this.'

Ma made a little grimace. 'Oh, I'll use the garden butt and
boil it – save you walking all the way to the "peath" with the
barrel.' This close to the sea you couldn't sink a well without
having salt in it, and the stream ran red from Penvarris mine.
Everyone had a rainwater butt, but the salt got in that, too,
together with occasional creatures and bird's droppings. All
right for some jobs – it washed your hair beautiful – but mostly
water had to be fetched from the peath up the hill, or – if you
were in funds – bought for a halfpenny a pitcher from the water
woman who came every week with a barrel on a donkey.

Sprat nodded. 'Well. I'll be off then. Bye, Mrs Roberts.' She
made her way back through the crowd, nodding farewells. She
stopped by the hallstand to look at herself in the speckled
mirror. Her hair was tousled and her dress awry from struggling
through the crush. Some Cinderella, she thought. She straigh-
tened her hair, rubbed her boots against the backs of her
stockinged legs and then slipped softly out of the door. She
had hoped to say goodbye to Denzil Vargo, but there was no
sign of him.

Her heart was thumping as she stepped out into the narrow
lane that separated the scattered row of higgledy-piggledy stone
cottages from the sea. The tide was out, and there was a strong
smell of seaweed from below the wall, where the nets were
stretched out for mending.

She stepped past a pile of empty lobster pots, still smelling of
the old fish-heads which the men had used as bait, and skirted
the rocky beach. She could see a half a dozen boats, deprived of
their grace and movement, stranded on the shingly bottom,
keeled over crazily, or nestled on the shore where they had been
hauled up above the waterline. One of them was abandoned:
holed, ruined and rotting – like the pair of roofless cottages at
the end of the row. No seine boat, now – the last big haul of
pilchards had been years ago, when she was a small child. She

could still remember the excitement and the bustle of it but there had never been another, and without that living silver which was its lifeblood, the old life of the Cove seemed to be slowly, but certainly, ebbing away.

Even Pa's repair yard was all but empty now. Only Half-a-leg Roberts' old fishing boat, waiting to have a rotten plank replaced, remained. No money to refit the old boats properly these days, it was all patching and making do. Pa hadn't built a new boat for years, though he'd served six years of apprentice-ship and all. Perhaps, in the end, fishing would stop altogether, and the poor old Cove would be as dead as Aunt Gypsy.

She gave herself a little shake – that funeral was giving her morbid fancies – and picked her way up the steep winding footpath which led up the hill. She took the left-hand fork, through tall grasses and wild flowers which snatched at her petticoats, crossed the tin-stream on a wobbling plank bridge, and so up and over the crest towards Fairviews, the grey granite four-square house, where Mrs Meacham would be waiting.

Two

W hen she reached the house, she didn't know how to conduct herself. Down the overgrown path to that imposing front door, or skirt round to the back? There was a carved wooden hand on a post, pointing the way for TRA-DESMEN ONLY – NO HAWKERS and, in the end, she followed that round to the kitchen door.

She hardly had time to knock – timidly – before the door was flung open by a tiny, sharp-faced scrap of a woman in a mountainous maroon skirt and apron, her wispy grey hair skewered into an awkward bun. 'Ah, there you are at last!' She hustled Sprat into a huge echoing kitchen as she spoke. 'And about time, too. Thought that funeral would never finish. And here I am, waiting to take these letters to the post.'

Sprat gazed around at the racks of gleaming brass saucepans, the tiled walls, the ladles, knives and jelly moulds. There was even an inside tap at the sink. For a moment, she hesitated. Surely this could not be Mrs Meacham? Of course not. Mrs Meacham would not wear a pinny and work in the kitchen – and anyway she was confined to bed. But the woman had such a sharp air about her, like a schoolteacher, and she spoke with a strange accent – it reminded Sprat of some 'summer visitors' from London, who had been once or twice to stay in the Cove. 'I'm some sorry,' she said, and added doubtfully, 'Ma'am.'

'Don't be absurd,' the woman said sharply. 'I'm not madam, I'm Florrie, and don't you forget it.' She glared at Sprat as if the name explained everything.

This obviously was not Mrs Polmean's cousin, whom Sprat

would have recognised vaguely, so presumably it was Mrs Meacham's other help. No further explanation was forthcoming, however, and after a moment's terrible silence Sprat ventured, 'You work for Mrs Meacham?'

'Work for her? I should think I do. I've been with Madam for thirty years. I used to be her dresser, didn't I? Joined her when she was first starting out – Violet Gresham she was in those days, and a voice like an angel – and I've looked after her ever since, Mr Meacham or no Mr Meacham. There's nothing about Madam I don't know, so don't try telling me!'

Sprat, who hadn't the least idea of telling anyone anything, and had always thought that a dresser was a wooden cupboard to keep plates on, could only shake her head meekly.

'And now all of a sudden it's not good enough,' Florrie went on. 'Packed off out of the house into a little cottage in the grounds and asked to give way to a crowd of strangers, who know nothing about Madam and her ways. I blame that doctor of hers, always thinking he knows best for everybody! Getting too much for me, he said – just because I had a bit of a turn last year. Too much! As if anything I did for Madam could ever be too much. But there you are – exiled, that's what I am, and now I suppose we'll have to put up with you sticking your nose in. As if that cook woman isn't enough already.'

'Madam must think a lot of you, to give you a cottage,' Sprat said. She was only speaking her mind, but it was the right thing to say. Florrie's face relaxed a little and she gave Sprat an approving nod. 'And,' Sprat went on, with a flash of inspiration, 'I can see how you don't want to leave her with strangers, but I could go up and talk to her while you go and post her letters if you like. Keep an eye on her for you.'

It was already dawning on her that, in spite of her impatient greeting, Florrie didn't really want 'to be off' anywhere. Mrs Meacham had suggested this arrangement, Sprat guessed – probably in order to hold the interview in private – and Florrie resented leaving 'Madam' in anyone's hands but her own.

'Well, all right,' Florrie said. 'I won't be long. You can take her tray up when you go.' She had whipped off her apron and was struggling doggedly into an ancient black coat. 'Though I'm ashamed to send it, aren't I? That cook woman! No more sense than to make the mistress a salmon mousse for her tea. Far too rich. I've put it on the tray, of course – more than my life's worth not to – but I've cut some nice cucumber sandwiches, just the way she likes them, and put out a bit of chocolate cake I made. That's what she'll eat, see if she doesn't. You can take it up to her, but be sure you move the tray when the doctor comes, or he'll be fussing her about her food again. As if a treat now and then was going to do her any harm, poor lady.'

She plonked her old-fashioned high bonnet atop the grey bun, and stood for a moment with her hand on the door handle. With her long, black coat buttoned tight to her knees and her voluminous skirts bunching out under it, she looked, Sprat thought, like an indignant coal shovel.

'Well, you'd better get a move on,' Florrie said, as if Sprat had been doing all the talking. 'I've got her up, haven't I, and she's waiting. Up the stairs, third on the right. You can't miss it.'

Sprat gazed at her, open-mouthed. Whoever heard of going in for an interview like that, unannounced. 'But . . . aren't you . . .?'

Florrie shook her head. 'You don't need me for that. She's expecting you, and the sooner I take these letters, the sooner I'll be back. We don't stand on ceremony in this house.' And, seizing her letters, she was gone.

Sprat stood for a moment gazing around the kitchen. Mrs Roberts was obviously right about 'theatricals'. It was a queer old place, all right. Though, oddly, instead of feeling dismally remote from life, as she had been all afternoon, she was suddenly sharply curious to know what this strange Mrs Meacham would be like.

She picked up the tray and made her way up the stairs.

* * *

17

Once Sprat had left the funeral feast, there was really nothing to keep Denzil there. He had lost his heart to Sprat years ago, when she was a child in pigtails at school, and he had come today solely in the hope of seeing her. He would have followed her out when she left except that Ma Nicholls had her gimlet eyes upon him, and seemed to be able to read his thoughts. She had been scowling at him ferociously all the afternoon, but the moment he made a move to pay his respects to Pa and sidle away, she elbowed her way towards him and cornered him in conversation.

'Well, Mr Vargo!' she said, producing her most meaningful smile and pinning him against the wall with it, like one of the butterflies in the frame over the fireplace. 'Nice of you to take the trouble to come. Should have thought you'd be wanted down that fancy office of yours.'

Denzil forced a smile in return. 'Had a half-day owing,' he said. He didn't add that he'd worked late every night for the week, in lieu. He had his explanations ready. 'Thought I'd come by, to pay my respects. Mother's working this afternoon, but she was very fond of Gypsy when they were young.' That was all literally true, though naturally his mother hadn't the least intention of coming.

'Very nice of you, I'm sure,' Ma retorted, in a tone of voice which implied something else. 'Though I daresay it's very well for some – nothing to do all day but sit at a desk and push a pen about. Not like we Covers. Take an afternoon off and lose the catch more than likely. Tide won't wait.'

It was nonsense, of course. Her husband didn't depend solely on fishing and in any case the tide was out this afternoon. But Denzil didn't argue. He *was* lucky, compared to most men round here: in an office, not at the mercy of wind and weather like the farmers and fishermen, nor working in dirt and darkness till the sweat ran, like the men down Penvarris mine. It had been his mother's dearest ambition for him, 'An indoor job, regular hours, in clean clothes like a gentleman, not pushing a tin tram till your back's red raw, like your father used to do.'

18

Denzil could remember his father, just. An untidy bear of a man who seemed to fill the house – with bellowing laughter and extravagant presents when times were good, and equally bellowing fury when, more usually, they were not. There was a smell about him, a smell which Denzil still associated vaguely with roaring and slamming, but which he had learned long ago was the smell of beer. The memory had been enough to make him take the pledge once at the Band of Hope, though he and Mother were 'Church' rather than 'Chapel' – if they were anything.

One day, when Denzil was small, Father had got more ale in him than usual and 'stood up to' a shift leader at the mine – meaning that he'd knocked him down – and shortly after that he'd gone to Canada to join his brother and 'look for a new life'. Presumably he had found it for he'd never come home again, although he was always threatening to do so in his letters. There was talk, at first, of Mother and Denzil going out to join him but somehow they'd never done that either, and life had settled into a quieter, more ordered routine. Father still sent money home. Enough for the rent (luckily the cottage was privately owned and wasn't tied to the mine) and a little bit over, but not enough to keep Denzil at school, even with the scholarship, nor to pay for evening classes in typewriting and book-keeping. That had been Mother's doing – scrubbing, lifting potatoes, cleaning the church at St Evan – and Denzil could only guess at the scrimping and saving it had cost her to manage it, even then.

'Mother was working this afternoon,' he said again.

Ma Nicholls was still smiling at him intently. 'How *is* your mother?' she asked, though he knew it was more to keep him there than anything else.

'She's well, thank you.' He seized his opportunity. 'She'll be home and waiting for me by this time. I'd best be off. Afternoon, Mrs Nicholls. Mrs Polmean. Fine funeral. I'll see myself out.'

It was cold outside after the stuffy warmth of the overcrowded parlour and he was glad of the coat and hat he had retrieved from the hallstand. There was no sign of Sprat, Ma Nicholls had seen to that, but he briskly set off up the path glad of the exercise to keep off the chill.

Besides, Mother really would be waiting. Although, of course, she'd be furious when she knew where he'd been. Bullivant's office was almost sacred in her eyes. She was always telling him, 'You don't know when you're well off, Denzil. I know the pay isn't a lot to start with, but you just apply yourself, and I'm sure you're as good as any of them. Mr Bullivant should be glad to have you. Aren't so many offices down Penzance can boast a proper type-writer like you. Makes him look up to date.'

Of course, it wasn't as easy as that. Ma had inflated ideas about the importance of type-writing. There was one type-writer in the office already – senior to Denzil – and it was only letters that were typed, in any case. All the book-keeping was still done by hand, in copperplate, and anyway it took more than a few certificates to make an office worker. Denzil knew that, if she didn't. There was his speech, for one thing, though he was working on that – even at school he had understood that 'speaking proper' was almost as important to the visiting inspectors as getting the answer right.

But there were other, more subtle things. He had found that out on his first day, proud as punch in the trousers and jacket that Mother had bought him from the second-hand shop.

No one else from Penvarris went to work in collar and cuffs and he thought himself very grand, until he stood too close to the fire in Mr Bullivant's office, waiting for the post, and burnt all the hairs off his trouser leg. He didn't notice at first, the material was stiff and hairy and stood away from his calf like corrugated cardboard, but suddenly there was a dreadful stench and he felt heat on his leg. When he looked down there was a great brown scorch on the back of his trousers. It still showed, even when he shaved it with the office scissors, and he spent the rest of the day standing with one leg awkwardly behind the other, like a mannequin in a clothes shop.

What completed his humiliation was Tom Courtney, the senior clerk, saying loudly to a delivery boy who had wrinkled his nose at the smell, 'A case of spontaneous combustion I should think. Poor old trousers were ashamed to be seen in a public place. Pity the same thing didn't happen to that awful coat.'

Denzil had visited the tallyman that very day – shilling down and sixpence a week – and bought himself a new working outfit, modelled closely on Tom Courtney's, complete with overcoat and hat. He said nothing to Mother, and she never asked, but she must have noticed. She must have guessed that it cost him every farthing of his wages over and above what he gave her, and that he went without at dinnertime to save a few pennies, because there was always extra for him when he came home – another slice of bread and cheese and more than his share of jam. Once or twice when it was raining she'd even offered him twopence for the horse bus 'to save his clothes' so he knew he was forgiven, even if he'd hurt her feelings.

When he was working, copying endless tedious letters beginning 'We acknowledge your esteemed instructions of the fifteenth ult.', he mentally sorted them into piles: these for the trousers, so many for the coat. It gave meaning to the day, and helped him to keep a tally of how much he had repaid. It wasn't much, but it was steady.

Perhaps, when he had managed that, he'd get himself a place in Penzance, and save himself miles of walking morning and evening. He'd have to do it some day, if he wanted to get on. Mr Bullivant 'had his eye on' Tom Courtney for a senior job, and Tom had to call at his house night and morning to carry Mr Bullivant's briefcase to the office and home again. 'Training' he called it. Denzil wasn't likely to be picked out for advancement yet, but if the opportunity did arise, he would have to be ready.

He'd reached the gate by now, and unconsciously changing

his accent to the one he used at home, he called out, 'You back, Mother? I'm 'ere!' and let himself in.

The house through which Sprat was gingerly carrying the laden tea tray, was eerily empty and echoing. Clean and polished (doubtless Florrie and Cook vied with each other to see to that) but chilly and unused. Open doors gave on to cheerless rooms, where even the grates stood empty. It *was* like something in a story-book. Sprat was beginning to feel quite creepy, and she would have been only half-surprised if a wizened old man had suddenly appeared from nowhere and put a spell on her.

But nothing happened, only her footsteps echoing in the silence. She came to the third door on the right. She stood outside for a moment, swallowing hard, and then tapped timidly.

A voice said, 'Come in.'

Sprat pushed opened the door – and almost gasped aloud. For there, suddenly, was the soul of the house. The room was full of warmth and flowers, and packed to overflowing – not least with Mrs Meacham herself, the woman lying on the divan and the pictures of her that jostled each other on the walls. Sprat goggled.

'Nice face she's got, but she's a large woman,' Mrs Polmean's cousin had said. It *was* a nice face, plump and pretty in spite of the years, but 'large' wasn't really the word for it. Mrs Meacham was vast: a human mountain of soft, perfumed flesh. Yet somehow she was delicate too – like one of those milk-jelly shapes which Aunt Gypsy called a 'blummonge'. And pink – everything about Mrs Meacham was pink, from the satin pillows and potted azalea to her fat little velvet-slippered feet.

'Ah, there you are! Nicholls, is it?' Mrs Meacham said, and Sprat realised she had been staring.

'Yes, Ma'am,' hastily. After all, she could hardly expect Mrs Meacham to call her Sprat.

'Well then, put that tray down somewhere and let's have a look at you.'

Sprat stood looking about for somewhere to put it. It wasn't easy. Every surface was cheerfully crammed with books, lamps, potted palms, powders, inkstands, perfumes and every other commodity that Mrs Meacham could possibly require, all within reaching distance of her outstretched hand. In the end, Sprat moved aside the gold-backed brush set and made a space on the dressing table. Aunt Gypsy had a brush set just like that . . . or, used to have one. Sprat remembered the terrible sound of earth falling on the coffin, swallowed hard, and tried to concentrate on something else.

That portrait over the divan, for instance. It was Mrs Meacham, obviously: though it was hard to imagine her as the young woman painted there – elegant and vivacious in a dove-grey evening gown, with a music sheet in one slim hand and feathers in her hair. Some things about Mrs Meacham hadn't altered, though, when you came to look. Her eyes were still the same amazing blue – almost violet like her name – the chin (under its cascading folds) had the same determined jut, and she still had the same twinking smile.

'Hmm,' Mrs Meacham said, 'you look presentable. Neat figure, nice hair, good features. And you stand well – something could be made of you. Not one of those dreadful dough-faced, clodhopping creatures I was afraid of. Tell me about yourself. What makes you want to come and work for a useless old woman with still more useless legs?'

Sprat hardly knew how to answer, but she mumbled something. Mrs Meacham listened vaguely, and then began a series of questions while she busied herself with the tray (the cucumber sandwiches *and* the salmon mousse). Sprat found herself wondering whether Mrs Meacham's legs had failed her before she turned into a blancmange from years of lying in bed and eating, or whether it was the other way about.

'So,' Mrs Meacham said at last, helping herself to the chocolate cake, 'your mother thought it would be a good opportunity, did she? No doubt I've been the talk of the town?'

Sprat flushed. There had, in fact, been a lot of gossip in Ma's kitchen. Not outside of it – Mrs Roberts would semaphore news around Penvarris quicker than a flagship – but plenty of gossip among friends. Mrs Polmean could remember the Meachams when they first moved into Fairviews – 'He was a proper gentleman. Banker from the City, come to Cornwall because of his health. And she was a fine-looking woman then. But when her husband died, she shut herself away – pining I s'ppose. I don't think she's set foot outside of that house since.'

'Only that you used to be a singer,' Sprat said, simplifying the truth.

'Yes,' Mrs Meacham said. She sighed, a great deep sigh that set the blancmange wobbling. 'I missed that terribly, you know – still miss it. The lights. Music and greasepaint. And all those young men at the stage door, with their flowers and presents.'

It all sounded a bit wicked. Sprat glanced at her uncertainly.

Mrs Meacham saw the look and smiled. 'All perfectly proper in the end. That was how I met my husband. Poor Rupert, how he loved the theatre. In the early days of our marriage, anyone who was anyone in theatre dined at our table. So you can see, it was difficult for me, coming here to this.'

'The Cove's all right,' Sprat said, forgetting herself sufficiently to speak without being spoken to. 'Always something to look at, with the sea. And the people, too – too funny to laugh at, some of them.' She bit her lip. Was she speaking out of turn again? Pa always said she spoke her mind first and used her brain afterwards.

But Mrs Meacham merely said, 'Well I can hardly see it all, can I? You see what I've come to. I'm 'up' as Florrie calls it – meaning that I'm lying here fully clothed with a blanket over my legs, instead of being in bed, in a nightgown. That's the only difference. What makes your mother think working here would be an opportunity? More of a living grave, I should call it.'

Sprat might have explained about it being close to home and no heavy work, but she was suddenly struck by the enormity of it – that beautiful young woman on the wall, imprisoned here in this milk-jelly body, unable to walk. 'Must be terrible for you,' she said, 'stuck here in one room, like a trapped lobster in a pot. Haven't you got . . . you know, people who would come and visit you. Cheer you up a bit.' She had been going to say 'friends' until she thought better of it.

Mrs Meacham looked at her stonily. 'You forget yourself, Nicholls. If I choose not to invite people here, that is my concern. Don't be impertinent!'

Sprat felt her cheeks flame, and fervently wished herself dead. Impertinence was the worst of sins. Mrs Meacham would never have her now. Ma would be furious. 'I'm sorry, Ma'am,' she muttered. 'I didn't mean to be forward. It's just – I was thinking how it would be, that's all. Especially after a life like yours – all that glamour and travelling . . .' She was making it worse, she could see that, and she broke off in confusion.

Mrs Meacham slowly helped herself to a marshmallow. 'That seems attractive to you, does it? Travel?'

'Always been my dream,' Sprat said simply. ''Course, it's nice here, but sometimes when I see the bluebells in the lane, or the waves coming in with the wind whipping the tops, I think to myself, I wonder what it's like other places. There's a friend of Pa's used to be a sailor, though he's old now and so short and fat you'd think he was a crab in a greatcoat. But the places he's seen! You should hear him talk – wonderful it is.'

Mrs Meacham was smiling. 'So, you would like to travel, would you? An unlikely ambition, for a girl of your sort.'

Sprat flushed anew. 'I suppose it's stupid, Ma'am, but you grow up here, you can't help thinking about it. All the men, now, they're always off places, what with the boats and all, but there's women in the Cove never been further than Penzance in all their lives. My Aunt Gypsy, the one who's dead, she used to say you didn't know how lovely the Cove was until you'd seen what other scenic places were like. Always promised she'd take me somewhere when I was older. Plymouth perhaps, or Exeter. But she's gone, and I don't suppose I'll ever do it now.'

'Ah, yes. The funeral. How was it then?'

The question took Sprat totally by surprise. Mrs Meacham seemed to have a way of saying whatever you least expected, when you least expected it. She blurted, 'It was grand, thank you. Black horses and all . . .' Her voice faltered.

'It was lose-your-salvation terrible,' Mrs Meacham said, matter-of-factly. 'Funerals always are.'

Somehow the blunt truth made Sprat feel better than soft words would have done, but she felt the tears stinging behind her eyes.

'Well, don't stand there sniffing,' Mrs Meacham said. 'Sit down. If you are to come here I want you to be my eyes on the world. You have a way with words, I'll say that for you. "A crab in a greatcoat", indeed. I like that. Now, this funeral. I want to hear all about it. I want to imagine it. Tell me about the hats.'

Somehow, once she started, talking was a great relief. Sprat was still telling about it, '. . . Aunt Gypsy's housekeeper, sitting up so prim and straight you'd think she'd swallowed a bowl of starch,' when Florrie came back.

'Florrie, this girl's been making me smile,' Mrs Meacham said, as though Sprat wasn't there. 'Not the sort of companion I had in mind at all. I was going to advertise in the quality papers. But she's done me good. Worth a trial for a week or two? What do you think?'

'I think the whole thing is nonsense,' Florrie said, seizing the empty tray with vigour, 'but at least she isn't pushy like that cook. If we have to have someone extra in, I daresay she'll do as well as anyone. Afternoons. I can manage on me own mornings, can't I?'

And with that, Nicholls had the job. Six hours a day, six days a week. Three and six a week and lunch provided. It was handsome. Ma made a point of telling Norah Roberts, and it was all over the Cove by nightfall.

Three

Mother *had* been waiting for Denzil when he came in. As soon as she saw him, she stopped sweeping the kitchen floor and put down the broom with a clatter.

'You went then?'

'Yes.' A pause. 'I told you . . .'

'I know what you told me. Hoped you'd thought better of it, that's all.'

He stood there hopelessly, not knowing what to say.

Ma said nothing either. She put on her I-am-saying-nothing face, picked up the broom again, and began brushing noisily, as if she were sweeping Gypsy Jamieson away with the dust – supposing that there was any. Mother always kept the cottage spotless, and it would be a brave speck of dust that dared settle in her kitchen when she was in this mood.

'Ma Nicholls was asking after you,' he said, at last. It was true, after a fashion, and it did the trick.

'Myrtle? She never was, surely?' But she put down the broom and began filling the kettle from the ewer by the hearth. That was a good sign. 'Mind, I never had anything particular against Myrtle – as Covers go. But that Gypsy . . .' She set the teapot on the hob to warm.

Denzil, encouraged by the kettle, helped himself to a jam tart from the plate on the table. 'I thought you and Gypsy were supposed to be thicker than thieves when you were young? I remember you telling me about it – scrumping apples, and knocking on door knockers and all sorts.'

Mother snorted. 'Well, so we did, but we was just bits of girls in those days. And I aren't sure I should have been friends with her even then. Led me into all sorts of scrapes, she did. She'd talk her way out of it, always could, and it would be me got the jawing if anybody did. Always was a charmer, was Gypsy. And I'd fall for it every time.' Mother was swilling a drop of hot water around in the pot, but she permitted a reminiscent half-smile to cross her face.

Denzil took advantage of the smile and ate another jam tart. 'Still like that to the end, from what I gather.'

Ma's smile faded. 'Didn't mind who she charmed, either, that was her trouble.' She put the tea into the pot: leaves carefully dried and hoarded from a previous meal. 'Many people there?'

'Dozens. Several folk from up-over, showing a bit of respect. I wasn't the only one.'

'You didn't go for respect. You went to see that girl, Sprat or whatever they call her. And don't say you didn't 'cause I know you. I've warned you, Denzil, no good will come of it. She's a Cover for one thing, and you know what that means!'

Denzil did, or at least he knew what *she* meant by it. The last man from 'up-over' to court a Cove girl was set upon by her brothers one night, wielding pickaxe handles, until he thought better of it. 'Oh, come on Mother, that was fifteen years ago, or more.'

'Well, folks round here've got long memories. And she's a Jenkins, besides – or at least her mother was. There's things I could tell you about that family would make your hair curl.'

Denzil paused in mid-bite. 'What, for instance?'

Mother flushed the sort of deep red which meant that she didn't know, or couldn't say. 'All sorts,' she said crossly. 'Any trouble between us and the Cove, there's always a Jenkins mixed up in it. Your father'd tell you, if he was here.' She seemed to realise that she was losing the argument, and she went on, 'Got a letter from him this morning, by the way. Behind the teapot, if you want to see it.'

The silver-plated teapot, she meant – one of Father's impulsive presents. It wasn't used; it was set up on the mantelpiece for show and was full of bits and pieces – buttons, needles and darning wool.

Denzil picked up the letter. 'Coming home, is he, as usual?'

'You can read it yourself,' Mother said. 'When you've brought in some more wood for the fire. And don't go eating all those jam tarts – I'll be needing those for tea. Didn't they feed you at that funeral?'

So he had a chance to tell her about it, after all.

Sprat was settling in nicely. Once she got used to Florrie's sharp tongue and learned to keep out of the way of Mrs Polmean's cousin, she found she was beginning to enjoy herself. There was, of course, more 'heavy work' than Ma supposed – Florrie was too sharp to miss the chance of a pair of strong young arms to scrub floors and carry coals – but much of the time Mrs Meacham would simply have her sit beside the divan and tell tales about the Cove and Covers, or, if all else failed, to read to her from one of the many volumes on the shelves.

There were not many books in the Nicholls house, apart from the Bible, the attendance prizes from Sunday school, and a collection of fairy tales that Gypsy had once given her, so this reading was a delight to Sprat. She made the acquaintance of the heroines of Mrs Aphra Benn, and the poetry of rather daring people of whom she had never heard and whom Mrs Meacham called 'fandisee-eckle'. She didn't mention that at home, but there was another secret which, in the end, she simply had to share.

If there was one thing Mrs Meacham liked more than any other, it was to fetch down the heavy Moroccan-bound albums from the shelves and reminisce about her early days. The people she'd known (and she'd known titled people), places she'd been and the songs she'd sung. But one thing quickly became clear.

Mrs Meacham, banker husband or no banker husband, was not at all the sort of respectable invalid widow that the Covers took her to be. It was a wonder to Sprat that no one had ever discovered it – Covers were very good at knowing everything

29

about everybody as a rule – but there it was. Of course, Mrs Meacham kept herself to herself, she had a small private income, and the memory of elderly Mr Meacham with his frock coat, bowler hat, and respectable side whiskers suggested the soul of propriety.

Yet there was no denying it. Florrie and Cook would go to the stake rather than breathe a word, and even Mrs Polmean had no idea. But Sprat had not worked at Fairviews a week before she realised that the 'singing' for which Mrs Meacham was famous in her youth was no classical operatic recital. The portrait over the divan showed a demure evening dress, but in the albums the costumes were sometimes positively daring. Violet Gresham, to put it plainly, had 'worked the halls'.

Sprat was both impressed and scandalised – so scandalised that she dared not mention it to Ma, or that would have been that. But she was dying to tell someone. (She might have confided in Aunt Gypsy, if she were alive, though Gypsy would probably have thought it a great joke, and told everybody.) She did, in the end, pluck up courage to tell Pa, one day when she saw him out in the yard with Half-a-leg's boat.

He was on his own, for once – Half-a-leg was out in a borrowed dinghy laying lobster pots, and Pa was working slowly, lovingly caulking the new seams with oakum and covering them with pitch to keep them watertight. Sprat picked her way over to him, revelling in the familiar smells of wood and old rope, paraffin and tar.

He stopped, in the act of unravelling the hemp rope, and looked at her. 'Hello, young Sprat. What brings you here this hour?'

She told him. She half expected him to whisk her away from Fairviews at once, but his response surprised her.

'Poor woman, she won't be singing again in a hurry, or dancing either.'

'Imagine,' Sprat said, breathlessly. 'Mr Meacham, marrying a music-hall turn. And him a banker and all!'

'Well,' Pa said, turning back to the hull and laying the caulk between the new boards. 'Bring a bit of glamour to his old age, and give her a bit of security for hers. I daresay it worked out very well.'

'But,' Sprat persisted, 'there's pictures of her singing, showing her petticoats, and her arms all bare and everything. I don't know what Ma'd say.'

Pa put down his awl and looked at her long and hard. 'Well, don't you go telling her, my handsome. Nor anyone else neither. There's enough gossip in this Cove without either one of us adding to it. Mrs Meacham isn't about to do you any harm, I don't suppose. Woman's got a right to live down her past, and Ma'd say the same – if she didn't go off half cocked first and blurt something out without thinking.'

Sprat wasn't sure that Ma would say anything of the sort, but she nodded.

'Glad you told me, all the same,' Pa gave her arm a squeeze. 'Only, you leave Ma to me. You be off home now, tell her I'll be in for my tea directly, it's getting too dark to work anyhow.' And Sprat went, vaguely comforted.

The next day, however, something happened which she did not even share with Pa. It was entirely an accident.

Mrs Meacham seemed to have renewed her correspondence suddenly, and Sprat was wanted to take some letters to the mail.

Florrie was deeply suspicious. 'Not bills, are they? I don't know what's got into her, writing all these letters all of a sudden. She'll be inviting people to come here next, and I'll have an invasion of visitors to cope with. She's not up to it.' Florrie scowled and fretted and found a hundred reasons for delay, but in the end, of course, Sprat had to go.

It was quite late by this time, and Sprat was beginning to recognise that she had missed the post altogether and would have to come back tomorrow, when the horse bus rounded the corner, and who should get off it but Denzil Vargo.

He came to meet her, beaming with delight, and she explained about the letters. 'Too late now,' he said, and he walked beside her, a long leisurely stroll along the lanes, away from Ma or anyone else's prying eyes.

Not that there was much said. Denzil told her about Bullivant's and how Tom Courtney was driving him demented with his taunts; she told him about missing Gypsy, and about Florrie and Fairviews, though she minded what Pa had said, and didn't confide Mrs Meacham's shameful secret even to him.

She told him everything else, though, as if they were children in school again. He was so gentle, so encouraging, and he looked at her so lovingly that, when he stopped suddenly beside the stile and asked shyly if he could hold her hand, she agreed at once. It was a bit daring, in public, and rather awkward walking along – keeping their distance but with fingers linked – but it gave her a tingle of pleasure, especially when Denzil began to get closer and closer. Any minute now, she thought delightedly, he would have his arm around her waist.

And then they saw Mrs Roberts. It was terrible bad luck – Covers didn't come up on the top road as a rule. But there she was, coming over the stile from Crowdie's farm, with her shawl round her shoulders and a basket full of eggs.

Sprat and Denzil leapt apart, and he even called a daring, 'Evening!' but Mrs Roberts simply nodded and hurried past them with folded lips.

'Think she saw us?' Denzil asked.

'Soon know,' Sprat said gloomily. 'Be all over the Cove tomorrow if she did. And then won't Ma give me what for.'

But, as it happened, by that time Mrs Roberts had other tales to tell.

When the post boy came Ma was out in the wash-house. She hurried round to the front, scrubbing her hands dry on her apron.

There'd be a letter from Mrs Mason, Ma thought, saying when she and her daughter would be coming down from London. The girl suffered with her breathing and her mother brought her down every summer to get some sea air into her lungs. They'd gone elsewhere the last few years, while there was illness in the house, but now Gypsy was gone Ma was confidently expecting a letter any day. It would mean Ma and Pa giving up their bedroom and sleeping in armchairs for a week, and a lot of extra work, but Mrs Mason's few shillings made a big difference to the annual budget.

Ma wondered if she ought to tip the delivery boy, but he didn't seem to expect it, so she took the letter in fingers still red and swollen from hot water and washing soda and said, 'Ta very much, then' as if the arrival of post boys at the door was an everyday occurrence in the Nicholls' household. It wasn't until he had gone toiling off up the hill on his bicycle that she permitted herself to glance at the envelope.

It wasn't from Mrs Mason. She knew Mrs Mason's writing. That was painstaking, letter by letter, so that you could almost imagine her tongue moving as she wrote the words. This was addressed to her and Pa, in black ink, in a fine, flowing copperplate. Drat. If the whole letter was like that she'd have to get Sprat to read it. Ma could read most things if they were printed, but joined handwriting was apt to be difficult, unless you knew in advance what it was likely to say, like 'Mr and Mrs Albert Nicholls,' on the address.

Whoever could be writing to them? She ran a finger under the red sealing wax on the back of the envelope and took out the letter. The letter-head was in fancy printing, too, but she could make that out: James Tavy, Solicitor and Attorney-at-law.

Tavy! What did he want, of all people? Ma felt herself turn cold. She was almost sure that he knew the family's secret – look at the way he'd spoken to Sprat at the funeral. It would be just like Gypsy to go blabbing everything. What if he did know? What if he let the cat out of the bag? The Nicholls would never hold their heads up again!

She looked at the letter again. Suppose it said something – how would she know? How could she let Sprat read it to her? Pa was no use, either; he could estimate anything by eye alone, and reckon a bill in his head faster than some folks could do it on paper, but he was no scholar at reading. Ma squinted at the paper again, as if by willing it she could make the writing straighten up and lose its curly bits.

She was so busy staring at it that she didn't see Norah Roberts till she was at her elbow.

'Morning,' Mrs Roberts said, rubbing her tarry hands as if they stung. She must have been out spreading the nets and seen where the post boy was going. That was the trouble with Norah – eyes like a sea hawk, and better at spreading gossip than the Penzance Town Crier. 'Nice day.'

Ma thought of thrusting the letter into her apron pocket but her pinny was wet with washing and she couldn't afford to have the ink run, not before she'd read it. She clasped the envelope to her chest and forced herself to smile. 'Yes, might get the sheets dry if the rain keeps off. I'm in the middle of washing.'

Norah didn't take the hint. 'Pincher and Half-a-leg will get soaked, else. Saw them go out to the pots an hour ago.'

Ma nodded. 'Pincher' was Pa, to anyone in the Cove, from his habit of calling out 'Pinch 'er up to the wind a bit!' to whoever was sailing with him. Half-a-leg Roberts was Norah's own husband. He had the same number of limbs as anyone else but had earned his nickname as a child from sitting down careless on a Sunday-school chair. 'They'll be home directly, wanting their crowst and I've nothing in the house until I've done a bit of baking. Best get these sheets out and make a start.'

But Norah was not so easily put off. 'Leastways you'll have something to tell him. I see you got a letter. From Mrs Mason, was it?'

Ma took a deep breath. She wasn't one, as a rule, to tell other people her business, but the news of a letter would be all over the Cove by dinnertime in any case and folks would invent anything. If Norah was going to gossip, she might as well gossip the truth.

'It's from Mr Tavy, Gypsy's solicitor,' Ma said, trying to sound casual. 'Well, more of a friend than a solicitor. Used to visit her quite often. You might have seen him at the funeral.

34

Tall thin fellow who sat at the back.' She didn't take to Tavy, eyes cold as codfish and no more flesh than an eel, but there weren't so many people hereabouts whose sisters hobnobbed with lawyers.

Mrs Roberts was gratifyingly impressed. 'Solicitor, you say? There! Think of that. I knew he was something. Half-a-leg reckoned it was Gypsy's butler, but I knew he wasn't a servant by the coat. What did he want then, in this letter? About the will, was it? Gypsy's estate?'

'Can't be,' Ma said, thinking aloud. 'There is no estate to speak of.'

'Oh, yes. Didn't I hear that James Jamieson left everything to his son by his first marriage? House, money, everything?'

'That's right,' Ma said. That was no secret, it had come out when James Jamieson died. 'But Gypsy had a life interest.' It wasn't as good as a proper inheritance, of course, but it sounded rather grand.

'All the same,' Norah said. 'She'll have left bits and pieces. Clothes, that sort of thing. I was talking to a girl at the funeral, one of Gypsy's maids, and she said that she'd been promised the fur wrap. All the staff were to have something, she said.' She leaned closer. 'Here, I hope it isn't like that woman over St Ives. Left ten pounds to each of her servants and the rest to her daughter – only, by the time it came to *her* there was nothing left over but debts! Anyway, if Gypsy's left bits and pieces they'll have to read the will. That's what the letter is, for sure.'

'Perhaps so,' Ma said, irritated that Norah seemed to know so much about inheritance. 'I haven't had time to read it yet.' Before Norah could say any more, Ma added, 'And I shan't neither, not until Pa comes home.' If the letter was only about reading the will – and now she thought of it, that did seem likely – she'd be able to get the gist of it, and it would be safe enough for Sprat to read it properly when she came home.

'Talking of letters,' Mrs Roberts said, 'I saw your Sprat up Penvarris Road the other day. Going to the post, by the look of it, and hanging on the arm of that Vargo boy from up-over, in broad daylight bold as brass. I aren't one to make trouble, but I thought you ought to know.'

But Ma was thinking about other things today. She gave Mrs Roberts a dismissive smile. 'Now, I really must get on, or I shall be surrounded by wet sheets like a Chinese laundry. I've had that much extra to do, with Gypsy ill, you wouldn't believe. If I don't get this lot dry it'll be Monday again, and I'll never catch up with it.'

She went indoors, put the letter behind the clock, and then out the back to put the sheets in the bluing. By the time Pa came home, they were already flapping in the wind, and the house smelled of boiled cloth and baking.

Four

S prat knew that something was up from the moment she walked through the door. Ma was unnaturally silent, and Pa was twitchy and irritable which usually meant that Ma was upset about something.

It never did any good to ask, so it was almost a relief when, after the tea things had been cleared away, Ma suddenly said, 'What's all this I hear about you and Denzil Vargo walking out on the Penvarris Road?'

Mrs Roberts, Sprat thought furiously. Now there would be Old Harry to pay. Aloud she said, 'Ran into him by accident, off the horse bus. Some nice fellow he is, walked me halfway home and helped me over stiles.'

She expected an outburst, but Ma just said, 'Well, see it doesn't happen again. And don't think I won't hear. There's more eyes in the Cove than a potato field. And, talking of eyes, there's something I'd like you to look at.' Sprat looked at her in surprise. 'Me and Pa have fathomed it out, more or less, but we'd like you to read it all the same, just to make sure.' She handed Sprat the letter.

Sprat opened it. Good quality parchment paper, like Mrs Meacham used. A short formal note. If Mr and Mrs Nicholls would present themselves at Mr Tavy's office at eleven a.m. on Thursday next, they might hear something to the family's advantage.

'Yes,' Ma said. 'that's what we thought.'

'Just us two?' Pa said. 'You're sure of that? It doesn't mention you anywhere?'

Sprat shook her head. 'Not that I can see. Why should it?'

'Nothing. Only Half-a-leg says that people who are mentioned in a will get asked to the reading.'

'I thought it was all the family, if it was anyone.' Ma said.

'Well,' Sprat said, 'what does it matter? Aunt Gypsy didn't have much to leave, she told us so. But it sounds as if you are mentioned in the will. The letter talks about an "advantage".'

'Yes,' Pa said, but he didn't sound convinced. 'Thing is, Sprat, we always thought she'd leave her bits and pieces to you. She told Ma she was going to.'

'She'd leave her things to you, Ma,' Sprat said. 'You were her sister, when all's said and done. And she'd know, if there were dresses and that, you'd give them to me in any case.'

Pa and Ma exchanged glances. 'Well,' Pa said. 'Perhaps you're right. Come to much the same in the end, I've no doubt. We ought to go, I suppose?'

'Of course you ought to go,' Sprat answered, and then realised that it wasn't really a question.

'If we're going,' Ma said, suddenly bucking up, 'we're going to go looking something like. That means your best suit and collar, Pincher Nicholls, and don't argue. You can't visit a solicitor looking like a human shipwreck. And don't forget your armband, since we're supposed to be in mourning. Thank goodness I trimmed my black dress new for the funeral. There's two horse buses Thursday, with it being market day, so that'll suit us nicely. I aren't walking all that way in my best clothes this time of year. We'll be mud up to the eyebrows.'

'I could—' Pa began, but Ma interrupted him.

'If you are going to suggest going round in that boat of yours, Pincher Nicholls, you've got another think coming.' Ma had been out once, famously, around the bay and had resolutely refused to do it again, though Pa occasionally 'took out' visitors like Mrs Mason, and Sprat had loved the water as a child. Not out to his creels of course, women were bad luck in fishing boats, but in the little paraffin-engined dayboat he used for

38

ferrying coal and paraffin, and she could row the pram dinghy like a boy.

Pa looked as if he might open his mouth again, and Ma said firmly, 'If God had meant us women to go out in boats he'd have given us fins.'

'Things with fins don't go in boats, as a rule,' Pa observed, with a twinkle. 'Not without you catch them first. 'Course, I did catch you once, didn't I?'

'Pincher Nicholls, you want locking up,' Ma tried to look severe, but the anxiety was over.

Sprat wasn't surprised. She knew it would be all right from the minute Ma called him Pincher.

When Thursday came, of course, Pa made a song and dance about wearing his good clothes. Grumbled that he felt like a lobster in a shell and stood about helplessly with his stiff collar in his hand until Ma had to attach it for him.

'Hold still,' she said, wiggling the back collar stud into place so fiercely that he winced. 'There! Now lift up your chin and let's see the front. And you can take that knife and run it under your fingernails when I've finished. We're going to Penzance looking like Christians, or my name's not Myrtle Nicholls.' She wrested the second collar front on to the stud and stood back to admire her handiwork. 'There, that looks something like. Now put on your necktie and try to look a bit dignified. We'll have half the Cove peering at us behind their curtains.'

'Your fault, that is, telling Norah Roberts we were going!' Pa grumbled, but he went off meekly enough to dust his boots, though they were already polished shining. A few minutes later they were both ready to Ma's satisfaction.

'Better shut the door,' Ma said. 'There's a wind getting up and I don't want to come home and find a passage full of sand. Now, have you got that box I gave you? I'm going to deal with that first thing.'

'I still don't think you ought to,' Pa muttered. 'Not till we've seen Mr Tavy, any road.'

39

'Will you give over fussing, Albert Nicholls! Gypsy gave me that ring, fair and square when she was here lying ill in her bed. You heard her. For Sprat, she said, and that's what it's going to be. I'm not having any lawyer take it away, just to pay some old bequests to servants.'

'But surely . . .'

'We've been through this all before. You heard what Norah said – that woman over to St Ives. They made a list of everything the poor soul left behind, and dished it all out before the daughter got a look in. Well, I'm not having it. I'm taking that ring in this very morning, and then there's no argument. Gypsy gave me a ring to sell and we sold it – they can't make a list of what they haven't got.'

Pa opened his mouth to say something, and shut it again. He had been difficult to persuade on this one – he always was a stickler for doing things 'right' – but if he'd seen the sense of it, she must be doing the right thing.

'Well,' Ma said, 'can't stand here all day. Are we going, or what?'

They walked down the Row and up the lane, slowly: Ma holding her gloves, straight as a mainmast, with the fringe on her black shawl and the feathers on her bonnet stirring in the wind. If people were going to peer, she would give them something to gawp at. Pa, though, seemed uncomfortably aware of the box in his pocket, and he sat all the way to Penzance as if he had hot bricks in his trousers.

Ma had already selected the shop where she would take the ring, a proper jeweller at the bottom of Causewayhead. Not the pawnbroker. Someone might see her go in, put two and two together and make five. Besides, it wasn't as if they wanted to buy the ring back – on the contrary, the sooner the dratted thing was disposed of, the better. Anyway, the ring was Gypsy Jamieson's, and that meant a bit of class.

Her heart did fail her, though, when they came to the shopfront. Easy enough to talk about it when you were safely home in the Cove, quite another to walk boldly up the three semi-circular steps to that great mahogony front door with the name in gold paint on the door glass. The man dusting the merchandise made her quail as well: all dressed up in a black suit with a cutaway coat and a gold watch-chain across his chest – more like a doctor than a shopkeeper.

There were little glass cases on either side of the doorway, where a few small pieces were displayed: repeater watches in turnip cases, a fancy clock with fat gold cherubs on it, and on the bottom shelf, two or three rings displayed on an artificial hand. The price tickets were handwritten and very discreet, but when Ma leaned closer – pretending to adjust a boot button – the price she saw almost sent her scuttling back to Pa again.

Twenty-seven and six! My dear life! You could half furnish a house for that! She looked back at Pa, undecided.

'Well, go on if you're going,' he said.

She was about to retort that it was all very well for him, when who should come round the corner, too smart for his own good in his overcoat and hat, but Denzil Vargo, with a pile of letters in his hand. Going to the post for Mr Bullivant, obviously.

It was too late, he had seen her and, after a surprised stare, was already raising his hat with a polite, 'Morning, Mrs Nicholls.'

Drat the fellow. Always turning up like a bad penny just when he wasn't wanted. Well, she wouldn't give him the satisfaction of seeing her dither. Ma lifted her head, and – pretending not to see him – marched steadfastly into the shop.

In fact, it was easier than she expected. It must have been her finery that did it, the jeweller didn't ask her a single question, although she had a great many answers ready. Instead he screwed a glass thing into his eye, lit a lamp under a reflecting plate and looked at the ring for a moment.

'How much do you want for this?'

That was one question Ma hadn't been prepared for, and for a moment she was struck speechless. She thought back to the rings in the window. Twenty-seven and six. This one was bigger, although of course it was second-hand. Must be worth half as much at least.

Greatly daring, she said, 'I won't take less than fifteen.'

'Fifteen pounds,' the man said, and she realised with amazement that he was going to agree to that.

'Guineas,' she said, just in time, and the deal was done.

Even when the money was in her pocket she could hardly believe it. Fifteen pounds fifteen shillings. More than a year's wages for Sprat. And all for a bit of a ring. It didn't seem right, somehow, carrying a great sum of money like that about, and she gave it to Pa for safe keeping.

'What are 'ee going to do with it?' Pa said in a hushed voice, as they walked towards Tavy's office.

'Put it by for Sprat,' Ma said.

He nodded. 'I've been thinking,' he said. 'Pay for a year's apprenticeship that would. Something really nice. You know how keen she's always been on making something of herself. That's what Gypsy would have wanted.'

Ma took a deep breath. 'An apprenticeship? What does she want with an apprenticeship? She'll be off and married before you can say "fish". And that money would set her up handsome when she gets wed.'

'I suppose so,' Pa said. 'Bit of a waste, perhaps. Although look at the Cove now – hardly a family can make ends meet without the woman works extra to bring in a penny or two.'

'Salting fish?' Ma said. 'Or walking miles for the pleasure of scrubbing floors? Don't need an apprenticeship for that.'

Pa looked at her mildly. 'Yes. But get a trade behind you, and you can't go wrong.'

Ma knew she was losing the argument. She tried a different tack. 'Besides, give her an apprenticeship, and where will she end up? In Penzance for sure, making eyes at that Denzil Vargo.' She glanced at Pa, knowing that she'd hit his weak spot. 'I don't know how you'd like it, her going so far away. You'd miss her, something chronic.'

Pa said stubbornly. 'Perhaps we should ask her what she thinks.'

'Oh, for heaven's sake,' Ma said. 'You know what she'd say. She'd go like a shot. Getting up to who knows what. No, better to have her near at hand, in a household you know, and keep an eye on her. A closer eye than we've been doing, if Mrs Roberts is to be believed.'

Pa ignored that thrust. 'Anyway,' he said, brightening, 'she's only just started with Mrs Meacham. But in a year or two perhaps.'

Ma sighed. Pa was making difficulties already, and they hadn't had the money more than ten minutes.

'Time enough to make plans, then,' she said, and by that time they'd arrived at Mr Tavy's.

Denzil gazed at the jeweller's door in disbelief. Mrs Nicholls, he was sure of it, dressed up to kill in her Sunday hat and pretending not to notice him as he passed. That did not surprise him, Ma Nicholls made no secret of her disapproval, but there was Pa too, skulking round the corner. Pa was usually affable, but this morning when he saw Denzil, he too pretended to be in a hurry to get to somewhere else.

At a jeweller's too. Some business of Gypsy's, more than like. Unpaid bills perhaps – that would explain the embarrassed scuttle. Normally Ma Nicholls would relish being seen going into a high-class shop like that.

Anyway, it was no business of his. His business was to get these receipts into the post, and get back to the office with some sealing wax and string. It was nice to be out for a moment, away from the dark little corner of the back room where he had his desk. His own desk at last – Mother had been ecstatic when she heard that. Goodness knows what she imagined – some grand, imposing roll-top table like Mr Bullivant's perhaps, with himself sitting behind it in a carved-back chair? Certainly not the tall, cramped, ancient thing he worked at, with its narrow writing ledge and peeling varnish and the hard, high, wooden stool on which he perched like a schoolboy.

He had spent an uncomfortable hour there already, double-checking a list of payments received, while Mr Bullivant read the sums aloud. It was tedious work, but you had to keep your wits about you: Mr Bullivant would sometimes read it wrong, on purpose, to see if you were awake. Tom Courtney had been caught like that, more than once. Denzil was more careful, as Mr Bullivant had seemed to notice, once or twice.

Tom Courtney had noticed, too, and he didn't like it. He was two years older than Denzil, and dreamt of promotion in a year or two when Mr Taylor, the other senior clerk, retired. He was likely to get it, too. Mr Bullivant 'had his eye' on Tom, as he was fond of saying.

Of course, Tom had been the junior until Denzil arrived and now, very conscious of his new status, he enjoyed finding the new boy menial jobs to do. And naturally, as junior-clerk-cum-office-boy it was Denzil's place to do them: mixing the ink, fetching the coal, or taking Mr Bullivant his tea tray. But lately Tom seemed to be doing it deliberately, always wanting his pencil sharpened or his blotter changed – anything to keep Denzil from his desk. Denzil had worked through his lunch hour several times to keep up. He didn't mind – it was warm in the office and until the tallyman was paid he had no lunch to eat in any case. But the more he did, the more there was to do. Here he was now, for instance, sent out with a pile of letters which could have gone first thing, while there was a pile of papers to typewrite waiting on his desk.

He was a better typewriter than Tom, that was part of the trouble. And Tom knew it. Denzil didn't complain – there was nobody to complain to. Mr Bullivant didn't care for 'tittle-tattle' and apart from that there was only Mr Taylor in the front office, who was so elderly and starchy that you might as well save your breath. Anyway, Mr Bullivant knew Tom's father and all that sort of thing. In fact, if Tom was to be believed, he had actually been invited to tea with the Bullivants soon, as a family friend. It wasn't the least bit of use to complain.

He had a long wait for the letters and a longer one for the string, and it was fully half an hour later before he got back to the office. The pile of papers on his desk seemed to have multiplied two-fold, but he settled down to it and had most of them typed by the time the office closed.

'Still at it?' Tom Courtney said, putting on his coat and scarf to accompany Mr Bullivant and his briefcase. 'You're slipping. I finished all mine ten minutes ago.' He gave Denzil a self-satisfied smile.

Denzil said nothing. Rising to the bait would mean that Tom had won. He had a door key (it was his job to lay the fire in the morning) and he battled on until he'd finished, though by that time the last bus had gone.

It was blowing half a gale on his way home, and then the lightening started. When he got to the house – in spite of his overcoat – he was drenched to the skin.

Five

I t was almost full tide as Sprat made her way down the path from Fairviews towards the shelter of the Row. The wind was across the water, and lifted the crest of each wave into a plume of lace as it surged forward, while at the end of the wall and at the head of the Cove, great plumes of white – creamy as sheep wool – reared up and dashed themselves on to the rocks below.

Sprat shivered. Beautiful, but it was to be hoped none of the fishermen had been caught outside the Cove tonight. The stiff breeze had veered and strengthened quickly, and it would be near impossible, once the tide turned, to get a boat in against both wind and water.

Pa was in, at any rate. She saw him through the open door of the store shed, measuring out something in an enamel jug for Mrs Polmean. Paraffin for her lamp, more than likely. She, too, would be expecting a stormy night. You didn't trust to candles in a gale, if you could help it: an unexpected draught could blow one out in no time.

Ma was in the kitchen, where a supply of furze, coal and logs was already piled up by the hearth and the settle moved away from the wall and huddled to the fire to keep the draughts out. She looked up as Sprat came in.

'Ah, there you are. Glad to see you home, and no mistake. Another half-hour and you'd be blown away, coming down that path. Pa's been watching the weather since we got home, and he says it's brewing up a real blow. So, sit you down and get some of this inside you. Bit of rabbit, it is, that Half-a-leg gave

Pa in exchange for a few coals, and it's made a nice drop of stew.'

'Smells handsome!' Sprat slid on to the settle and took the steaming plateful gratefully. Her breezy walk had chilled her to the bone. 'Well? How did you get on with Mr Tavy, then?'

'Ah!' Ma said, and sat down beside her. 'Some smart office he's got there, I'll tell you that.'

'But what happened?' Sprat persisted. It was all right, whatever it was – Ma was in her story-telling mood. If there had been trouble, Ma would have been tight-lipped and blurted it out at once.

'I'm telling you, if you'll listen,' Ma said. 'We got there, Pa and me, with time to spare. Great door, with his name on a gold plate, grand as you like, and a great brass handle like . . . like a jeweller's. We rang the bell – proper little bell-pull – and this man came out. Wasn't Mr Tavy, but he looked important himself, all in black, and such a stern sort of face. I said we had an appointment, and he let us in – a "vestibule", he called it, all wood panels and leather chairs and a great big aspidistra in the corner, bigger than Gypsy's by a mile.'

Sprat grinned. He aunt had been very proud of her aspidistra.

'Anyway, we sat there. Place was that quiet it gave you the creeps – all you could hear was the chair squeaking every time you moved. After a bit Mr Tavy came in – nice as pie he was, you'd think we were royalty calling – and took us to his own office, all over books like a reading-room. He read us a legal thing – I didn't understand the half, but the upshot of it was, James Jamieson left Gypsy outright everything that didn't actually go to his son. All her own clothes and ornaments and things. She gave some things to her servants before she died, and she left me her gold watch, but everything else – her clothes, her brooches, everything – she left them to you, Sprat. For natural affection, Mr Tavy said.'

'To me?' Sprat was almost too surprised to speak.

'Pa and me get to keep it for you', Ma said, 'until you're

twenty-one. Rings, brooches and some necklaces besides – Mr Tavy says there's an "infantry", or some such, up at the house and he'll advise us "how to proceed" he says. So there now, what do you think of that?'

Sprat found she was eating her stew almost without tasting it. 'The clothes'd be nice,' she said, 'but what would I do with rings and brooches?' She had a sudden vision of herself, like Mrs Meacham in her costumes, glittering with jewels.

'Sell, them, of course,' Ma said, bringing her down to earth. 'And, Sprat, it could be pounds and pounds. We sold one ring already – Gypsy gave it me before she died. It was her best one, I know, but it fetched fifteen guineas, on its own. Goodness knows what the whole lot would fetch.'

There was a pause. Ma seemed to be waiting for her to say something. Sprat pushed her plate away. 'I wonder,' she said softly, 'if there would be enough money for me to go for a bit of travel?'

'Don't be daft,' Ma said. 'Have some more stew.'

Sprat found it almost impossible to sleep that night. She lay under her patchwork cover, trying to imagine herself travelling. In England, of course. She'd seen the pictures of 'abroad' in school – *Lives of the Great Explorers* – and she didn't fancy that. Impossibly steep mountains, jungles with tigers lurking at every step, and knock-kneed camels among endless tracts of sands.

Of course, England wasn't like that. There were mountains – she remembered colouring the maps – but she was certain there were no tigers. She tried to picture London, as Gypsy had told her about it – dozens and dozens of shops all together, like a hundred Causewayheads, gas lights in the streets, and houses that went on for miles. She lay awake for hours thinking of it.

If excitement had not kept her from sleep, the storm would have done.

It was quiet enough at first. With the wind in the north, the Cove was half protected by the hill behind, except where the wind could funnel down the valley made by the tin stream, but

48

the gale was veering and soon it was rattling the window panes and whistling around the chimneys. Sprat, listening to its moaning and the fierce hammering of the rain and the hail on the roof, could hear the crash of the sea on the rocks at the Cove entrance. There were bangs and thuds as the wind picked up anything that had not been tied down, and tossed it down again. Pretty soon there were voices in the lane – men shouting over the gale, their voices whirled away in the wind.

Sprat knelt up on her bed and lifted back the curtain edge, but her window was at the side and she could see nothing from it, so she took her night light and, shielding its flame from the chilly draughts which swept the house, tiptoed down the stairs to see. It was pitch black in the Cove, and with the rain lashing the window she was hard put to see anything, even from the front room, until a jagged flash of lightening lit up the scene for a moment, like a magic lantern slide.

Half the cove was out. Men in sou'westers and oilskins leaning against the wind and rain, struggled with ropes and guys, outlined like black silhouettes against the grey of the wall. No one was out fishing, weather like this, but they were all busy with the boats, hauling them further in, or dragging them further out – to the 'flats' where the incoming tide would not pound them so cruelly against the stones. Every stick and rag of rigging that could be moved had already been stowed away, and men laid out extra ropes and anchors, while the wind howled round them and their faces ran with rain.

There were women, too, sodden skirts snatching in the wind, clutching drenched shawls over their dripping shoulders and holding hurricane lamps for their husbands in hands that trembled with cold. Creels and nets had been battened down or brought in long ago, but a solitary crab pot had escaped and was being bowled by the wind like a skeleton football with Half-a-leg in pursuit.

The back door flew open and Pa and Ma came tumbling in through it, panting with cold and effort. It took both of them to close and bolt it against the strength of the storm, although the wind still wailed and howled around the doorpost, like a wolf seeking a way in.

'My life,' Ma said, lifting up the lantern as Sprat came out of the parlour. 'What are you doing, wandering about in your nightgown? You'll catch your death.'

'You will,' Sprat said. Ma had thrown on an old oilskin of Pa's but she was obviously soaked to the skin and perished to the bone. 'You go and get those things off while I stir up the fire and get a kettle going.' And then, as Ma hesitated – 'Go on, or *you'll* be in Mount Misery with a fever, and then where should we be?'

The memory of Gypsy must have done the trick. Ma took the candle and went upstairs, still grumbling. Pa sat on the kitchen settle and pulled off his boots, making a little Cove of his own with the water dripping off him.

'My lor',' he said, 'it's some night out there! I'm wet leaking, and I only went with your Ma to see to *Sea Spray*, and tie a few stones on the furze rick. Never worth it, either. There's slate tiles blowing everywhere – take your head off if you're not careful. Mrs Reid's got half her chimney down, besides. It isn't worth the trouble going out, weather like this.'

Worth the trouble for the furze rick, he meant. He'd have fought a hurricane to save his boat. He was probably right, the furze rick wasn't necessary, exactly. A lot of people didn't have one – didn't have room and didn't bother. But Ma liked to keep a bit of gorse dried and cut into 'tashes' for the fire. There wasn't a bakehouse in the Cove, and no cooking stoves either – food was baked on a bake-iron on the hearth, or boiled on a hook over it. And nothing, Ma said, baked better than a bit of furze.

Sprat took a tash of it now and put it on the fire, which roared up instantly. She put the kettle on the trivet and by the time Ma came down the kettle was bubbling nicely. They sat like that for a long time, all three of them, while the storm raged. The first pale light was breaking by the time the wind eased and they went wearily back to bed.

* * *

Denzil arrived at Bullivant's whistling, the morning after the storm. He'd been waiting to take the horse bus, with his money ready, when Crowdie had stopped beside him in the farm cart and offered him a ride for nothing all the way. So here he was, for once in a while with the prospect of a hot penny-pie dinner-time, and he had dried out, too, pretty well – Mother had ironed the worst of the wet from his clothes and hung them on the kitchen line overnight. And if he looked quick about lighting Mr Bullivant's fire, he could have a warm up in front of it before anyone else arrived.

He was still whistling cheerfully as he unlocked the door and made his way down the hall and through the showroom to the back office where he left the scuttle. The sound died on his lips, however, as soon as he opened the door. The room looked as if a hurricane had hit it.

As perhaps, it had. One of the posts in the yard had blown down, and taken a window with it. The whole floor was strewn with rubbish – not only the glass and wood, but leaves, papers, bits of stone – all standing in a filthy pool on the linoleum where the rain had driven in. There was worse to come, when he came to look.

Those papers strewn against the skirting or swimming limply in the chaos by the window were not just brought in by the wind, or even from the waste basket blown over under the table.

Denzil stooped, picked up one sheet, and held it dripping between his fingers.

'Peter Emms esquire, two dozen crates ex-Newport six shillings and sixpence . . .' These were yesterday's vouchers from the front office! A lot of people came in on market day to collect small consignments in person, or to arrange the shipping of goods and packages to and from Falmouth, Plymouth, London and beyond. For collections, Mr Taylor took the consignment note, stuck it on a wooden block with a spike up the middle, and gave the customer a ticket for the warehouseman in the yard; and for new orders he wrote a 'voucher' which was filed on another spike. These were brought in last thing ready to be entered up in the order book next day.

Yes, there was one metal spike, lying in a pool of water, and the other on its side in the corner, a single remaining voucher flapping forlornly from the point.

Denzil put the wet 'file' carefully on the desktop, where it drooped damply, and feverishly started to collect the nearest documents. It was very nearly hopeless. They seemed unreadable, and it was impossible to hold more than one or two in your hand at the same time – the wet ends clung together and made matters worse. In the end, he had to be systematic.

He found a piece of cardboard and drawing-pinned it over the missing pane. That was better already, the draught didn't move the scattered papers as soon as you turned your back. He found a broom and began to sweep up the glass and leaves into an empty bucket. The bristles left wet muddy tracks on the linoleum, but he persevered, picking up the papers and laying them out one by one on the shelf as he went. He was still doing it when the front door opened. Mr Bullivant and his briefcase had arrived.

What followed was the longest day of Denzil's life. Mr Bullivant was inclined to be furious, at first, at finding the mess on the floor and the fire unlit, but when he knew what had happened he changed his mind. The broken glass was wrapped in a newspaper, and Denzil was sent out for soap, a scrubbing brush, and a glazier, while Mr Taylor pinned a notice to the door saying the office was 'closed until ten o'clock owing to storm damage'. Then they began the painstaking business of sorting through the papers.

There were not only yesterday's vouchers, as they soon discovered. There were one or two from the day before as well, and half a dozen 'invoices owing', awaiting a reminder to send something on account. It was obviously work that Tom had left unfinished, despite his taunts of the night before, because he suddenly came over helpful and insisted that Denzil should help Mr Taylor deciphering the driest papers, while he picked up the remaining soggy ones himself.

Retrieving the lost vouchers took most of the day – they fell apart or turned brown as they dried – but with the help of the warehouseman they managed to piece it together in the end – all except one consignment note. That didn't seem to tally at all, and in the end Denzil put it on Mr Bullivant's desk for him to look at tomorrow. Mr Bullivant himself had been obliged to man the outer office for the day. It was a busy afternoon, too, because a lot of assignments had been held up in the gale, and all the new day's typing and copying landed on Tom Courtney's desk.

Tom was edgy, kept wanting to come and help Denzil in a most unusual manner, but Mr Bullivant told him to stay where he was. Tom was having to do his share for once, Denzil thought with a grin, and he was still hard at it when it was time to carry home the briefcase. Denzil couldn't restrain a smile. Next morning, he knew, most of that unfinished pile would be waiting on his own desk, but all the same he was hoping he might run into Sprat again, and tell her all about it, especially when Mr Bullivant said, on his way out, 'A good day's work there, young Vargo. Well done.'

Denzil was locking up before he realised he'd never had time for his pie.

Up at Fairviews, the storm might never have happened. Mrs Meacham's bedroom was on the middle floor, and while wind rain and hail had lashed at her windows, it seemed she had slept peacefully through it all. She was, though, interested by what she saw from her divan.

'What are they doing, Nicholls? All those people poking around in the seaweed like that? Are they looking for something?'

Sprat smiled. 'Yes, Madam. That is, not for anything in particular. But they always go out after a storm – check the boats first, of course, and then have a look to see what the tide's brought in. All sorts you can find, after a storm. There was a load of boots washed up, one time – no use to the women but all the men in the Cove had a pair. Barrels, tins, sacks – you never know what's in them till you look. Pa found a three-legged stool once, and there's many a nail and rope in the Cove has been a gift from the sea.'

'Boots?' Mrs Meacham said. 'Is that legal?' But she was twinkling.

'Nothing illegal about it, so far as I know. The shops couldn't take them like they were – all stained and stiff with being in the water for days – but folks round here were glad to have them all the same.'

'Well, I want you to take a letter to the post,' Mrs Meacham said. 'You'll just catch it if you hurry. An old friend of Rupert's has written. He has been very ill and is obviously angling for an invitation to come here to recuperate. No doubt you would approve – visitors might "cheer me up", I think was the phrase.'

Sprat blushed. Mrs Meacham had often referred to those unfortunate words at the interview. Though, perhaps in the long run, it had done some good. Mrs Meacham did seem to be taking more of an interest in things lately.

'I shan't rush into anything' Mrs Meacham said. 'But I've written back to him. It was nice to hear what was going on in London – I've got so out of touch. We couldn't have him on his own of course, but I could suggest he brings his Aunt Jane with him – she's a dear old soul, she entertained Rupert and I in London. She must be eighty, if she's a day, but she was always good to us. I'd love to see her again. Florrie would no doubt fret, but we should be very quiet, and the doctor says it would do me good to have a change. So, we shall see. In the meantime, you can post this for me.' She blew on the ink to dry it and sealed the envelope with red sealing wax before handing it to Sprat. 'And when you've done that, you can go down yourself and see if the gale has brought you any more boots. An ill wind, they say, that blows no one any good. But remember, I shall want to hear all about it tomorrow.'

Sprat smiled, but in spite of her loitering she didn't see Denzil, and by the time she got home the tide was in and it was too dark for beachcombing anyway. Ma, though, had found a 'handsome lot of wood' and a good felt hat, which was drying off by the fire.

But there was better news than that.

'No damage in the Cove,' Pa said. 'At least, not to speak of. But a fellow came from St Evan today on purpose to see me. His old father had a boat hauled up the creek, round the other side of Penvarris head. No great shakes but he used her now and then to see to a few pots. Broke loose in the storm and fetched up on the bank with her side stove in. Thing is, his son is Fred Zackary, got that big store down Penzance, and he wants me to build him a new one. Twenty-two foot lugger, counter-stern, only three-foot draught on account of the creek.'

'Some work in that!' Ma said, but you could tell she was delighted.

'Might bring the timbers round by sea,' Pa said, happily. 'Raft them up and tow them round behind the engine boat. Flat calm, we'd do it easy. Too much struggle getting them down the lane with a horse and cart. Remember last time?'

'I aren't so sure,' Ma said. 'You wouldn't be at the mercy of the weather with a cart.'

'Course you would,' Pa retorted. 'And rafting would help season the wood.'

So they bickered contentedly about it all evening. Mrs Meacham was right, Sprat thought. It hadn't been such an ill wind after all.

Six

M r Tavy sent the 'infantry' as promised. This time it was raining, so Norah wasn't there to see it come, and Ma was able to open it straightaway. It had been typed, too, which was a mercy, so she could make out what most of it said. But what she understood made her gasp in dismay.

'What is it?' Pa said, the minute he came in the door. Drat the man, he could read her like a book.

'Nothing,' she said, raking out the fire to put the baking sheathe down.

'Must be an important nothing, then, you're as white as that dough,' Pa said. 'And grimmer than a graveyard. Don't be so wet, Myrtle. Won't seem half so bad when you've said about it, whatever it is. You'll see. What is it? Somebody said something to Sprat, is that it? Told her the truth about Gypsy?'

Ma shook her head. 'Not so bad as that. See for yourself. Up there, behind the clock. It's a list of them things that Gypsy left to Sprat. Brooches and things – lot of money some of them – two pounds, three pounds each, it adds up.'

'Well,' he said. 'What's the matter with that? Should have thought you'd be pleased. Set her up lovely, that would. So, what's the problem?'

'It's just – look at this,' Ma said. 'The bottom of this list. I aren't much of a reader, but I can read figures when I see them. See what it says there? The last item, "one ruby and di-a-mond ring". I'm sure that's what it says. That's the one Gypsy gave me – the one I sold to the jeweller. See. Thirty pounds, it's down

56

as. And I got fifteen guineas. No wonder the fellow was in such a hurry to pay it.'

Pa said nothing – not even 'I told you so.' For some reason that was more infuriating than any words.

'So now you know,' Ma said, slapping the bread down on the bread iron, and slamming the cover over it. 'So don't tell me it's better when I've told you, because it isn't. Won't be better either. I walked all the way to Penzance and back this afternoon, but the fellow won't sell it back. Says he's "sold it on" already. I bet he has. For thirty pounds – which should have been Sprat's by rights.' She heaped the furze and embers up around the baking cover as though she was burying the jeweller along with it.

'Who'd have thought,' Pa said, after a pause, 'that Gypsy'd have a ring worth half so much as that?'

Ma looked at him for a minute, furious to find her lip trembling. 'I'm sure I didn't! What did she ever do to deserve it, that's what I don't understand.'

'Oh yes, you do,' Pa said, 'you understand that!'

You could bless Pincher sometimes, he knew when to make you smile. 'You!' she said, but she was feeling better, though she didn't tell him that. 'What am I going to tell Sprat, that's the only thing. Should have been hers, that money.'

Pa took her by the shoulders. 'You aren't going to tell her anything. She knows you got fifteen guineas and she's thrilled to death with that. You meant it for the best, that's all that matters. There's lots of things that Sprat doesn't know, one more isn't going to hurt, so wipe that scowl off your face and try and look a bit normal when the child gets home for her tea. And that furze is burning. If you don't rescue that baking, there won't be any tea to come to.'

He took the letter upstairs to hide it, with everything else of importance, under the mattress in their bed.

Sprat was starting to enjoy her afternoons at Fairviews. The tasks which Florrie set her were no more arduous than the jobs she did helping Ma at home, and here she was getting paid for them. She loved the hours spent with Mrs Meacham, poring over the old albums, and even when she was doing a job she hated – like the morning ritual of collecting limpets for Pa – she escaped inwardly, by remembering this photograph or that, making up a story to go with the costume and imagining the audience applause.

Besides, she was beginning to understand why Florrie and Cook, for all their disagreements, were so devoted to their mistress. Madam had a good heart under all those folds of flesh, and if she was self-indulgent, she indulged her servants, too. Sprat was developing a taste for luxuries like salmon sandwiches and even chocolate cake, when occasionally there was any left over!

She gave no more thought to her legacy. In fact, since that first news of it, Ma had seemed unwilling to say any more about it, except to hint darkly that nothing came to Sprat direct until she was twenty-one. Perhaps it was just as well. Ma's idea of 'going somewhere' would be to find an apprenticeship miles away up country, to take her away from Denzil.

Denzil – Ma and Pa seemed more against him than ever. She couldn't for the life of her fathom out why, but every time his name was mentioned Ma looked like a human thunderclap and even Pa shook his head and said 'it wouldn't do'. Just because he was an 'up-overer'. It was enough to make you weep.

Still, while she was at Fairviews, there was always the possibility of seeing him. It wasn't disobedient, she didn't make arrangements exactly, but you couldn't help chance, and if Mrs Meacham sent her up to the post, it wasn't a crime to walk back the long way. So several times lately she had run into Denzil coming off the horse-bus, and he had walked her part-way home. Managed to evade Norah Roberts, too, although they hadn't held hands again, just in case.

It hardly mattered. Walking along the lane beside him, Sprat could almost feel the tingling pressure of his hand in hers, although they never touched. Perhaps it was especially because these meetings were a secret – almost, but not quite, forbidden. It made the pleasant excitement more exciting still. Even now, standing by Mrs Meacham's bedside with the tea tray in her hands, she could feel her heart quicken at the memory.

'Well, Nicholls,' Mrs Meacham said, breaking into the dream, 'it seems you may get your wish after all. That will save you a few trips to the post.'

Sprat came back to the present with a jolt. 'My wish, Madam?'

Mrs Meacham looked up from her muffin. 'Yes. James Raeburn. That friend of Rupert's from London that I told you of. I've invited him to come here – with his aunt. Of course, I haven't heard yet, but I rather think he'll say yes.'

Sprat was so suprised, she could only nod.

'If they do decide to come,' Mrs Meacham went on, 'I shall want you to go in and meet them. I shall arrange a carriage from the station, of course, but you could pick it up and accompany him here, to show the driver the way. It would be too much for Florrie and I can hardly ask Mrs Pritchard. You could manage that, couldn't you? You know where the station is?'

'In Penzance?' Sprat said, unbelieving.

Mrs Meacham laughed. 'Of course in Penzance. What other station could I mean? Don't look so thunderstruck. You have been to Penzance?'

'Once or twice,' Sprat said doubtfully. In fact she had been scores of times, on market day or Corpus Christie fair. But only ever with Ma and Pa. The idea of going there all alone was quite daunting when it came to it.

Mrs Meacham gave her wicked twinkle. 'It's no good looking like a startled rabbit. You want to travel – and you won't get far if you can't manage Penzance! Oh, and don't worry about James Raeburn, if that's what you are thinking. I wouldn't send you unaccompanied to meet him on his own. James is an old friend and I'm very attached to him, but I wouldn't trust him alone in a carriage with Mrs Pankhurst, let alone a pretty young thing like you. He'll have his aunt with him, and his manservant too. He never goes anywhere without Fitch.'

Sprat found the wit to say 'That's all right then, Ma'am' and found herself colouring. In fact, she had been so concerned about the idea of going to the station and finding a cab that she had given very little thought to the outcome.

Mrs Meacham saw the blush, and chuckled wickedly. 'Though if they do come, I should want you to live-in for a while – to look after the aunt. Of course, he may have made other arrangements, and it may come to nothing. Now, you can take this tray downstairs – tell Florrie to give you that sandwich for your tea – and then you can fetch me down my blue album.'

Sprat hurried off downstairs, but she was thoughtful. Living in at Fairviews with a strange gentleman in the house! Whatever would Ma say? Just as well this old aunt was coming or Ma'd have her out of there in a trice – and that would be the end of meetings with Denzil and slices of chocolate cake. Still, it wasn't definite. No good looking for trouble. Better to say nothing until it was settled.

She scuttled upstairs again to get the album, and even contrived to be on the top road by the time the horse bus arrived.

'Denzil,' she said, as they parted at the stile so that she could come home across fields, away from prying eyes, 'who's this Mrs Pankhurst when she's home?'

He looked at her with surprise. 'Where did you hear about that?'

'Something Mrs Meacham said. But I never heard of her. Who is she?'

He knew, of course, as she was sure he would. 'A lady, up London, wants to have votes for women. So they can vote for parliament.'

She stared at him, laughing. 'Whatever for?'

But Denzil was serious. 'She might be right, at that. Your old Ma's got a tongue sharper than a cheese grater, but I'd sooner have her opinion than my father's, any day of the week.'

'Your father isn't here. And Ma doesn't know anything about parliament.'

'No, but she could,' Denzil said. 'That's what Mrs Pankhurst thinks. Her and her followers. Suffragists, people are calling them. Mind, I don't hold with their methods. Up to all sorts, they are.' And he told her all about it. Respectable women throwing stones and assaulting policemen – you never heard the like.

'And then, of course,' Denzil finished, 'some of them got arrested and put in jail, and now they're refusing to eat – "hunger-striking," they call it – and the government's in an embarrassment. Shocking it is, really.'

Sprat nodded dutifully, but somehow she couldn't feel as horrified as she should. It was almost like one of Gypsy's stories – helpless women bravely refusing to be bowed. Pity she couldn't tell them about it at home – only they'd guess where she'd heard it from.

By the following evening, though, she did have something to tell them.

James Raeburn looked at his reflection thoughtfully. Not too bad, he thought, for a man of middle – not to say mature – years. True, the thick black hair was greying now, and the athletic grace of his youth had given way to a certain cautious dignity of gait, but his stomach was still trim enough, if he remembered to pull it in a little. At least he was not – he sought for a word – portly.

What would Violet think, he wondered, when she saw him? That he had aged, perhaps? There were a few wrinkles around the slate-grey eyes. Yet lines gave a man's face character and, besides, he had been ill. She would have to understand that. But if he chose his wardrobe carefully – his smoking jacket, for instance, and the blue cravat – she could, surely, not fail to be impressed.

Of course, dear little Violet had been ill herself. 'You will find me much changed,' she had written. Some problem with her

61

legs. Not life-threatening, of course – not like his fever. Why, for forty-eight hours he had been quite at death's door. In fact, if it had not been for his man coming in to find him, and calling for a doctor at once, why . . . He shuddered. The world without James Raeburn was too horrible to contemplate.

He ran a hand over his pomaded, thinning hair. Well, he would go. It would be good for Aunt Jane, too – she so rarely saw anyone these days. She'd want to travel first class, of course, at her age, and with a bit of luck she'd stump up for both the tickets. Indeed, she would probably be flattered – he had rather neglected Aunt Jane these last years.

Of course, it would mean he missed the Coronation. But perhaps that was no bad thing. If the last time was anything to go by, London would be full to bursting with vulgar people, and still more vulgar bunting, and it would be impossible to buy a decent meal at the club. Besides, London was not the place it was. After all that dreadful business at Sidney Street – armed policemen and anarchists – the city was getting more like Russia by the day. Yes, decidedly, this holiday was a good thing all round.

He would have to take everything with him, of course. Rupert Meacham had been dead these ten years, and one could hardly expect his widow to think of all the accoutrements a gentleman might require – shaving soap, brilliantine and bay rum. To say nothing of his liver pills, bile beans and hair restorative.

He would take Fitch of course. Violet didn't have a man-servant in the house, according to her letter, though she offered to get one, but in any case he preferred Fitch. Fitch knew him. Knew how he liked his clothes laid out and how to be discreet after a night in town: 'Mr Raeburn is indisposed this morning.' Not, of course, that there would be any nights in town when he was with Violet. No, indeed, that was the reason for going, to give his system a rest, as the doctor suggested. That dreadful experience had taught him a lesson. James Raeburn was not, after all, immortal.

Yes, that fever had frightened him. And he was still not himself. How dreadfully easy it would be to end one's days like Aunt Jane – frail and unvisited, to be taken out and dusted only when needed, while one's heirs waited for one to die. He did not want to end up like that, forgotten and alone. Especially not alone. He remembered those nightmare hours of delirium, tossing in helpless terror until Fitch returned from his evening off, only just in time. No, especially not alone.

So, it was time to take stock. Time for bracing walks beside the sea and a long look at life.

And sweet little Violet, what had happened to her? She was alone, too. Alone, and in poor health. They had – they had always had – so much in common. Such a pretty young thing, and such an exquisite singer. Well, he would soon see. He would go and see Aunt Jane first thing in the morning, and then send Violet a telegraph accepting her invitation. In the meantime . . .

'Fitch?' He adjusted his tiepin and cuffs, and picked up his top hat and gloves. 'Ah, there you are. My coat, if you please, and you can call me a cab. I'm going to my club for an hour.'

The young man coughed, 'But Mr Raeburn, sir, the doctor advised—'

'I know what the doctor advised. I'm taking his advice. We are going away very soon – to a little place where there is nothing but sea and seagulls – for a long holiday. But before we go, I have a few last days in London. I'm going to my club. And while I'm gone, you can fetch down my trunk and start preparing my things. My smoking jacket, I think, and the blue cravat.'

'Very good, sir,' Fitch said, but James distinctly heard him grumbling on the stairs. 'Sea and seagulls indeed. It'll drive him crazy within a week, and me with him.'

Well, James thought, that remained to be seen.

PART TWO
May – June 1911

One

'Well!' Ma gave the fire an irritated stab with the poker. It seemed as if everything was conspiring to vex her this evening – first Sprat had come home with this news and now even the embers were refusing to draw. 'It's all very well for Mrs Meacham, I daresay, suddenly deciding she wants you up there full-time, but how am I to manage, that's what I want to know?'

This was her own fault, she told herself. She had wanted Sprat settled somewhere near to home, where they could keep an eye on her and keep her away from that Denzil creature. And now this! Living-in up at Fairviews, indeed. Anyone with half an eye could see what would happen. Sprat would be finding excuses to be up on that road, all hours, meeting the horse bus. Well, she would have to drop a hint to Mrs Meacham, that's all. If she knew Sprat had a follower, she'd soon put a stop to it. Or would she?

There were times, these days, when Ma wondered whether working up at Fairviews had been the sobering influence she'd hoped it would be. Sometimes Sprat seemed to be more independent-minded than ever.

'I thought you'd be glad of the room,' Sprat was saying, placatingly. 'What with Mrs Mason coming, and everything. And it'll be extra money in your pocket – you won't have me to feed. I thought it was good of Mrs Meacham, offering live-out rates when she's keeping me as well.'

This was so obviously true that it irritated Ma still more. '"Live-out" rates, is it? I should think so, too, it won't be just afternoons you're working now, young lady. None of this

67

sitting round reading daft books half the day. If you've got these London folk staying, there'll be real work to do. I hope you know what you've let yourself in for. That's all I can say.' She gave the coals another savage poke, and put the flames out altogether. She gave an exasperated snort. 'Now look what you've gone and made me do!'

She reached for the ash bucket and shovel and set to work to re-lay the fire, rattling the kindling noisily and refusing to look at Sprat. She was being unreasonable, she knew that, and the knowledge made her madder than ever. It wasn't the child's fault that Mrs Meacham had suddenly asked her to live in. Ma sighed. She should have listened to Pincher. Even an apprenticeship in Penzance would have been better than this. She puffed at the timid flame with the bellows and at last saw it blaze up cheerfully, catching the log. She raked some coal around it and set the kettle on. But she was so vexed that not even the prospect of a hot cup of tea could make her feel any better.

'Well, it's too late now,' she said. 'You've made your bed, you'll have to lie on it. No doubt you'll think yourself no end of a swell – cavorting around the house all day and night with a gentleman living in the place. A London gentleman, too, and you know what city folk are. Whoever heard the like?'

'I won't be looking after him,' Sprat said, answering back. 'He's bringing his manservant with him. Only I've to go into town Monday, and bring him home in the cab. Somebody's got to do it, and Mrs Meacham can't.'

'Well, it's a pity someone can't do the same for Mrs Mason. Poor woman, and her with a sick daughter, too.' Ma got to her feet, heavily. Getting drenched in that storm hadn't done her rheumatics any good. Her knees were killing her. Perhaps it was that which made her go on grumbling. 'No riding around in fancy hansom cabs for her, she'll have to come on the horse bus, struggling with her valises, too. And walk down the hill when she's got here.'

Sprat had lost patience, as Ma half knew that she would.

'Well, that's not my fault, is it?' she burst out. There were angry tears in her voice. 'What do you expect me to do? Tell Mrs Meacham that I won't go? It was you wanted me up there in the first place.'

Ma whirled around, catching her a slap to the face. 'How dare you speak to me like that!' She saw the mark reddening on Sprat's cheek, and instantly regretted it, as she always did. There had always been this occasional friction between them, and it always ended in the same way, with Ma feeling guilty. Lord knows she didn't mean to put upon the child. But Sprat never seemed to realise when you were fussing for her own good.

Ma fished into the pocket of her pinny and fetched out a handkerchief. 'Here,' she said gruffly. 'Stop snivelling and use this. Then you can warm the teapot and we'll have a cup of tea.'

It was a kind of apology, and Sprat knew it. She took the handkerchief and blew her nose awkwardly. 'Tell you the truth,' she said wanly, 'I aren't really looking forward to picking him up myself. Shan't know what to say, travelling all that way in a cab with a strange gentleman!'

Ma humphed. 'Well, I suppose I did speak a bit sharpish. But I meant what I said. Who's going to go out and get limpets first thing, if you're up to Fairviews in the mornings? Pa'll want his bait whatever, and I shan't have time if I've got the Masons here.'

In fact, she knew she would simply have to do it herself. It was a job she hated – bending over the rock pools with a stone, knocking off limpets into a pail, until your back ached and your fingers were red raw with cold and wet. But even that was not as bad as setting the wriggling things on the hooks, or helping bait the pots. Crab pots weren't so bad – just a fish head and a tail jammed on to a stick – but lobsters wouldn't touch the bait until it was stinking, and then you carried the smell of it with you half the day if you weren't careful. Pa didn't seem to mind it, but Sprat had scrubbed herself with carbolic every morning for years – just as Ma had done before her, and now, presumably, would have to do again. Just as every woman in the Cove had always done.

Except Gypsy, Ma remembered with a little flash of irritation. Gypsy always looked willing as a girl but somehow, when it came to it, she mostly managed to be somewhere else when it was limpet time, or when the lobster creels were being baited. Though there had been times, when the fishing was poor, when winkles were a welcome and necessary addition to the larder, and then everyone had been out picking them – Gypsy included.

Now, what on earth had started her thinking about Gypsy again? These days she seemed to think of nothing else. That ring business must be on her mind.

'When are they coming?' Sprat said, startling her. It took her a moment to work it out.

'The Masons? Friday week, I think. Letter came this morning. Perhaps you can just read it over and make sure?'

Sprat took the letter from the mantelpiece and read it aloud, the quarrel between them forgotten. Ma *had* got the gist of it. Mrs Mason and her daughter were coming Friday week, on the overnight train, and would catch the horse bus to Penvarris '. . . "unless we hear otherwise",' Sprat finished. 'I don't know what that means. Maybe they were hoping Pa might collect them after all, in the engine boat.'

Ma shook her head. 'No hope of that. Pa's expecting that wood next week. Zackary's decided to do it the old-fashioned way, buy the wood himself and just pay Pa to build the boat. Pa's not best pleased – says he'd sooner choose the timber himself – but I can't say I'm sorry. There isn't the outlay, so we won't be worrying whether Zackary will pay something on account before we can afford to buy flour. Having it all shipped down to Plymouth, he is, and then by train to Penzance, and paying the waggon to have it brought out here. Put a stop to Pa's daft ideas about rafting it round. Only, of course, Pa'll have to be here when it comes, Mrs Mason or not.'

'Who's doing the shipping?' Sprat said, with an innocent air.

70

'No idea,' Ma said sharply. 'Now, are we having this cup of tea or not?' But, of course, she knew perfectly well who was handling the shipping. It was Bullivant's, naturally.

Denzil, too, had been having a difficult day. It had started badly, with Tom preening himself over this invitation to tea, and Mr Bullivant in a grump taking over this new National Insurance the Government was bringing in. Cost him three-pence a week for every man in the place, he said, but Denzil was more concerned with the fact that there would be fourpence docked out of his own pay packet. Take him for ever to pay off the tallyman at that rate.

But worse was to come. One of the carters brought word that the unrest which had been bubbling at the Liverpool Docks for weeks was getting worse by the hour, and the men were talking about striking. 'Had it from my cousin, who works on the coasters. Not just Liverpool, he says. Half the docks in the country'll come out. And if they do, mark my words, it'll be the railways next, and then where will we be? Go back to carters, see if they don't, and I can't be taking loads up to London, not at my age.'

All this was not good news for shipping agents. Mr Bulli-vant's mood darkened still further. Then old Mr Taylor, who had not been himself for days, and who had come in all week looking the colour of chalk, was taken bad halfway through the morning and had to be sent home again. Got soaked, he said, walking home in the storm, and it had gone to his chest. If National Insurance had come in, Denzil thought, the poor old fellow could have stayed in bed to recover without losing his pay, so perhaps that fourpence was well spent after all. Now Mr Taylor might be off for days, and Mr Bullivant had to take over the front desk himself, which did not please him either.

Tom did offer to do it, but for once even he had been barked at. And then, of course, Tom had got into a sulk and taken it out on Denzil.

Matters went from bad to worse when Peter Emms, one of

71

their regular customers, came in to collect his consignment. Denzil was working with Tom in the back office, but once the argument began they could hear every word.

Mr Bullivant raised his voice first. 'Says two dozen here, Mr Emms, clear as daylight. There it is in the order book. "Two dozen crates ex-Newport, six and sixpence." See for yourself.'

'I don't care what it says in your blessed book,' Peter Emms' bellow was a match for Bullivant's any day. 'Three more crates there should be, belonging to me. Additional consignment it was – should have been added on. I came in here myself. Where are they to, that's what I want to know.'

'Nothing here about additional consignments.' Mr Bullivant dropped his voice, but the two type-writers had both stopped tapping to listen.

Denzil looked at Tom. These late changes to consignments did happen – and it was always a bother. The paperwork had to be changed and the books made up. He didn't remember seeing this one. Tom, too, was looking anxious.

'Should have come with the same order,' Peter Emms persisted.

Denzil had a sudden memory. 'Wasn't Emms one of those vouchers in the flood?' he said to Tom. 'I seem to remember . . .'

Tom got to his feet, his face clearing. 'Course it was,' he said. 'That'll be what it is. Must have been one of those vouchers we couldn't read, and it didn't get entered up. I'll let Mr Bullivant know.' He started towards the door.

'Going in there now, are you?' It would have taken wild horses to drag Denzil into the front office now, with a customer present and Mr Bullivant in this mood. But Tom obviously didn't care. He hurried off into the front office, and must have shut the middle door behind him. Denzil could hear no more.

It was fully quarter of an hour before Tom returned. He ignored Denzil's questioning look, and turned back to work with unaccustomed gusto. He looked pleased with himself.

He looked even more pleased a minute later, when Mr Bullivant came in, his bad temper forgotten. 'Well done, young

72

Courtney. Clever of you to realise that the problem was one of the flood vouchers. Funny thing is, Emms said he came back later on the same Monday. Should have been entered up the same day.'

Tom stopped smirking and coloured gently. 'We do get a bit behind sometimes,' he said, meekly. 'Denzil does his best, but . . .'

Bullivant looked at Denzil's desk. As usual the pile of waiting papers seemed to have grown during the morning – when Tom had sent him down to fetch fresh ink and envelopes. Tom's own desk seemed clear by comparison. And, of course, most of the completed letters had been signed and sent – there was no tell-tale pile in the out tray to show who had typed what.

Denzil opened his mouth to protest. It was Tom who took all the letters in for signature. Goodness knows what he told Mr Bullivant. Probably made out that he'd typed everything himself.

'I—' he began, but Mr Bullivant forestalled him.

'No excuses, Mr Vargo. We'll say no more about it this time. I haven't forgotten that it was your quick thinking rescued the vouchers that we did save. But you'll have to pull your socks up in future, I'm afraid, or we'll have to reconsider whether you are suited for the position. We're being rushed off our feet with people wanting things shipped in time for the Coronation celebrations. I know Tom here will help you all he can, but you should be pulling your weight by this time.' He broke off as the counter bell rang. 'Good Lord, there's another customer. Let's hope Mr Taylor gets back to us soon – can't run an office with half a staff.' And, without waiting for an answer, he stumped back to the front office.

Denzil was furious. That remark of Tom's had been an act of deliberate spite, and now he was grinning with satisfaction, which made it worse. But there was nothing Denzil could do. No use to defend himself to Mr Bullivant.

'That wasn't fair!' he said heatedly to Tom.

Tom did not even favour him with a glance. 'All's fair in love and war,' he said with a sneer. 'Anyway, Mr Bullivant's right. You don't fit in. Never did, and never will. But since you are here, you can make yourself useful. Bring me some more blotting paper – and fill the coal scuttle while you're about it.'

For a moment Denzil was tempted to sort it out with him, fair and square – drag him outside and punch him on the nose – but the lessons of history restrained him. That, after all, was how his father had lost his job. Denzil went off to fetch the coal, muttering. No doubt when he came back there would be at least one extra letter in his pile.

Well, he vowed to himself, he would keep a watch on Tom. He was fairly sure who was responsible for the error in the books. If he could find some way to prove that Tom was shirking, that would be a different matter. Mr Bullivant was a fair man. Perhaps, when Mr Taylor came back . . .?

But Mr Taylor did not come back. Before the end of the week, the news came to the office. Mr Taylor had been found by a neighbour, dead in his bed.

Sprat was at the station early. She had moved into Fairviews the day before, and for the first time in her life had spent the night away from home – in a dear little bedroom tucked up under the eaves, with a little iron bedstead, a washstand and a hanging corner all of her own. It was such a pretty room, with its knitted coverlet and sprigged curtains, that it was a wonder she had got to sleep; and so snug, with a little fire in the tiny grate and a rag rug on the floor, it was a greater wonder that she had ever woken up again.

But wake she did, and after washing – in her own jug of cold water and a wash bowl – she slipped on the brand-new gingham dress which Florrie had 'run up' for her, and made her way down to the kitchen. Mrs Pritchard and Florrie were already hard at work, arguing about the best way to poach an egg, but Mrs Meacham's tray was ready. Sprat took that up, but after clearing it away and eating her own meal – a whole egg on toast, just for breakfast! – she found to her amazement that there was nothing to do. No pots to bait, no water to fetch. She tried to give a hand upstairs, where Florrie was dusting Miss Raeburn's room for the umpteenth time, but was shooed away. Mrs Pritchard didn't want her in the kitchen, and even Mrs Meacham was preoccupied, trying on a dozen different necklaces one after the other, and insisting on waiting for Florrie to help.

It was odd. For days, Fairviews had been in turmoil. Every room had been scrubbed and polished, fires lit and linen aired. Mrs Meacham seemed to have renewed life, sitting up properly and taking an interest in everything – not only in her own things, but in Mr Meacham's, too, brought down from the attic where they had been stored. Yesterday, Sprat had spent half the afternoon polishing the silver brush set and mirrors for the lady's dressing-room, and the other half helping to decide which of three china wash-sets would be most suitable to put out for Mr Raeburn on the marble washstand.

It wasn't only Sprat. Florrie had been fetched in from the cottage, to her undisguised triumph, and reinstated in her old room upstairs, though her moment of glory was rather spoiled by Mrs Pritchard announcing that she was coming in every day, too, 'for the whole of the gennulman's visit, so there!'

Yet now, there was nothing to do but wait. In the end, Sprat gave it up and took the early horse bus to Penzance, though it got her there an hour too soon, and in the rain as well. She half hoped she might see Denzil somewhere, out on an errand, but there was no sign of him, and she found herself alone in the town for the first time in her life. And with sixty minutes to spare.

It was exciting, despite the drizzle. No traipsing round after Ma today, going from shop to shop in search of the cheapest elastic or three yards of flannelette; no loitering in chandler's doorways while Pa made mysterious purchases of cork and cordage for his pots. Today she was a visitor in her own right, and for half an hour at least (she must make sure she was in good time for the train) her afternoon was her own.

She walked all the way up Market Jew Street on one side and

back down on the other, sheltering under every doorway and gazing into the windows, mentally ordering a dashing red hat with a feather from this window, or a pair of dainty cream button boots from the next. Just like Gypsy might have done, she thought. She glanced up at the market clock. Good heavens, how the minutes had flown. Time to go and find that cab – she had taken a message to the post office yesterday, and they had telephoned – so there should be one waiting. Then she would have to find Mr Raeburn's party.

It was easier than she had feared. Mr Raeburn, in fact, found her. She stood under the clock as arranged, and he came bustling up – a little plump, a little balding, but very dapper and bay-rum-smelling. He was followed by a manservant, a thin faded lady with an ivory cane, and a porter laden with luggage.

'My dear girl, you must be Nicholls. Here you are, Aunt Jane, they've sent the cab for us.' He assisted the coachman to help the old lady up, and turned back to Sprat. 'And how is poor little Violet? I hope she hasn't put herself out too much on my account?'

Sprat, thinking of 'little Violet' and the upheaval at Fairviews, could only shake her head.

'Cat got your tongue?' he said heartily, chucking her under the chin in a way she didn't care for. 'Mustn't be shy of me. Oh dear no. Pretty girl like you. I'm sure we shall be great friends. Don't you think so, Fitch?'

The man he called Fitch was loading baggages into the cab. He looked at Mr Raeburn (rather disapprovingly, Sprat thought) and said, 'If you say so, sir,' in such a lugubrious tone of voice that Sprat almost giggled.

'A smile,' Mr Raeburn said. 'Now that's something!' He reached out and patted Sprat on the hand. 'Smile like that, you ought to be on the stage. Surprised Violet hasn't told you so. Now then, in we get. Does this driver chappie know where to go?' And off they bowled toward the Cove.

Sprat had never been in a carriage before, and she was so

taken up with it all – the leather seats, the little mirrors, the leather straps to hang on to – that she could not have spoken if she'd a mind to. But it hardly mattered. Mr Raeburn chattered all the way, while the old lady smiled and nodded from under her carriage rug, and the journey back seemed to take no time at all.

When they got there, everything was so busy and so strange – with dinner served in the dining-room and Miss Raeburn to be attended – that it was hours before Sprat gave another thought to the Cove.

Two

J ames Raeburn sat in his hip bath and soaped himself thoughtfully, while Fitch poured in another jug of hot water at his back.

It was absurd, of course. Insupportable almost. He would have to make his peace with Aunt Jane, and go back to London as soon as it was decently possible. This great old-fashioned house, perched out on a cliff, with nothing for miles but fishermen, and not even a modicum of creature comforts.

The dinner had been edible enough, but so plainly served, with never a sauce or a garnish in sight, and that child hadn't the first idea about attending at table. Not that anyone else appeared to care. Violet, it seemed, had not been downstairs for years, and treated the whole thing as a huge adventure. Aunt Jane had seemed perfectly content, too, smiling and nodding aimlessly as usual, but he was not accustomed to having to serve his own gravy and having the vegetables passed from the wrong side.

Even that might have been forgiven, but when he had suggested a bath he had not bargained for this! An old-fashioned enamel hip-bath in front of the dressing-room fire, by candlelight, with Fitch carrying hot water up from the copper by the pitcherful, so that by the time it reached him it was already half cold! It was positively primitive. Hadn't people down in the country heard of such things as gas lamps, running water, bathrooms and hot-water geysers? Apparently not. And there was a worse indignity lurking under the bed. He could still hardly believe it. This was the twentieth century!

His own apartments had possessed a proper water closet for years.

And there was nothing at all for a man to do. He had only discovered this at dinner, when he had spoken aloud of his half-formed plan to pop into town and visit a club or two. Town, it seemed, was that miserable village the train had delivered him to, and that was a hour away down unlit winding tracks of puddles and potholes. 'Roads' Violet called them, as if she had never seen a paved surface in her life. There was no telephone, no transport. And even if one did somehow contrive it, there were apparently no clubs to be had. No theatre, no opera, no 'shows', no entertainment at all except a male-voice concert and a Sunday school pageant in the Educational Hall. Violet had been quite amused at his suggestion.

Then Violet! What on earth had she become? He cast a discreet glance at his own stomach, bulging whitely at him from the tepid waters, and pulled his muscles in sharply. But Violet! His delicate little nightingale had turned into a fatted goose, unable to stand up in case her legs snapped off. It was grotesque. And to think he had even begun to entertain hopes . . .

No, altogether this visit had been a terrible mistake. And he had virtually invited himself into it. He sighed. A week – he could hardly get away with less – and then he could return to London. It was to be hoped that this wretched Welsh miners' strike didn't drag on so long that the railways ran out of coal before then. Yesterday's paper had been quite gloomy on the subject.

'All right, Fitch,' he said, heavily. 'That will do. My towels, please, and my robe.'

The towels were warm, which improved his mood a little, he rubbed the patent 'reducing cream' into the widest portions of his anatomy, and a few minutes later he was sitting in the bedroom, beside the fire, draped in a warm robe with a glass of whisky in his hand while Fitch emptied the water into buckets and took the bath downstairs. At least, he thought, it was a decent whisky. He would have to content himself with that over the next few days.

There was a timid knock at the door.

His night tray perhaps. There had been talk of one – a little selection of sandwiches, cold meat, fruit and Vichy water. He called, 'Come in!'

It was not the tray. It was that little maidservant who had met him off the train, carrying a brass warming pan with a long handle. Attractive little thing, trim ankles, neat waist, curves in all the right places. Quite a stunner if she didn't have this habit of turning brick-red every time she uttered a word.

She was brick-red now. 'I'm sorry, sir, I didn't realise you were here. I thought you were next door in the dressing-room. I'll come back later.'

'No, no,' he said. 'Come in.' He did not share the commonly expressed view that housemaids should, ideally, be invisible. Quite the contrary, especially if they were good-lookers like this one. He gave her an understanding smile. 'What did you want?'

She turned redder than ever. 'Florrie sent me, sir, to warm your bed.'

He smiled. 'Did she now? That was uncommonly thoughtful of Florrie.' But the innuendo was lost on her. She simply stood there motionless until he said, 'Well, you'd better do it then.'

'Thank you. Excuse me, sir.' She said no more, but came and knelt by the fire and filled the pan with warm embers. Deuced tempting little bottom, it was, perked up in the air like that as she stretched forward with the coal shovel. If this was London, he thought, and a maidservant had bent over beside him and presented her bottom with such apparent artlessness he would have known how to interpret it. He would have pinched it at once. Here, though, he was not so sure. Besides, Aunt Jane would not approve.

Well, he would have to be careful. Being careful did not prevent him from looking, however, and he watched her appreciatively as she turned back the covers and ran the hot pan carefully over the sheets to warm them.

80

He was quite sorry when Fitch came in with the night tray, and obliged him to drag his attention away to egg sandwiches and Vichy water.

With one thing and another, it was very late by the time Sprat got to her room that night and, although the little bedstead seemed as welcoming as ever, once the candle was out and she was tucked up under the knitted cover she found she simply could not sleep.

There was too much to think about. Mrs Meacham, breathless and panting, actually struggling the dozen paces down the hall from her room to the dining-room. It had taken the combined efforts of Sprat, Florrie and Mrs Pritchard to get her there; seating her had required a special arrangement of two dining chairs, an old door and a pile of pillows; and if it had not been for Fitch, they would never have got her back again – but there it was. Mrs Meacham was as thrilled as a child with a May horn: she had been 'up' for dinner – the first time she had left her room for three years, Florrie said. It was almost as much of a miracle as having Florrie and Mrs Pritchard actually cooperating over anything.

Then there was the misery of serving at table. She had never done it before, since Mrs Meacham always had her tray, and when the idea was mentioned she had very nearly panicked and run home to Ma there and then. She had never even seen a serving salver – at home Ma simply put your meal out of the pan and on to your plate and there was an end of it. Of course Mrs Meacham had told Sprat what to do, but there was so much to remember, what with trying to keep your fingers out of the soup and not spilling the peas, she was sure she had forgotten half of it. Several times she had caught Mrs Meacham's eye and been corrected by a little shake of the head.

In fact, Madam had been very good – not a word of complaint afterwards. 'Not bad for a first attempt, Nicholls. You'll come to it in time' – but goodness knows what the other two had thought. Mr Raeburn was looking daggers.

Sprat wasn't at all sure that she wanted to think about Mr Raeburn. He made her feel uncomfortable. He had been very pleasant to her on the way home – imagine saying she was pretty enough to be on the stage – but though he had been very polite at dinner, he had somehow managed to look put out all the evening. Then, when she went up to warm the bed (when he might have been annoyed at the interruption) he was as nice as pie again.

Like Ma said, you could never tell with city gentlemen.

His aunt seemed nice, though. Sprat had been sent up to attend her when she went to bed, and Miss Raeburn had been so kind – telling her exactly what to do, and smiling all the while – that Sprat hadn't even felt odd about it when the old lady was in her shimmy and directoire knickers. Her eyes, though, were surprisingly sharp and shrewd, and she knew what she wanted, when it came to it.

'Hairbrush,' and Sprat had run the silver-backed brush through the thinning silver hair, while Miss Raeburn sat watching in the chair-back mirror to see that Sprat did it right.

Still, she was a nice lady, with her faint smell of lavender water and camphor balls. Though when she was tucked up in bed, her little white cap atop her white head, against the starched white of the pillowcases, and her white hand lying on the crisp sheets, she looked to Sprat – who was taking away the washing water – suddenly as pale and fragile as a little wax doll.

Altogether, Sprat thought, it had been a funny day. If only she could share her excitement with Gypsy. Still, Saturday was half-day, and she could at least go home and tell Ma about it.

And comforted by that thought, she fell asleep at last.

When Sunday came, Tom Courtney arrived at the Bullivants' house betimes. He had been on tenterhooks all day, though he would not have admitted it to anyone: fidgeting his way through the sermon and toying impatiently with his cold beef and pickle – a meal which he hated anyway, but which was

standard Sabbath fare in the Courtney household since Sunday
was the cook's day off. He could hardly wait to be out of the
house.

Even now he was so early that he had to walk around the
block so as not to arrive before his time, but he didn't altogether
mind that. Mr Bullivant lived in one of the big stone houses
close to the Promenade, and there on fine Sunday afternoons,
you could usually find half the young women in the town.
Admittedly they were generally with a party, if not a chaperone,
but they came all the same, to walk up and down making a
'promenade' in their fashionable frocks, in order to see and be
seen. Even today there were a number of them braving the
bluster. Tom knew he cut a particular dash in his best Sunday
suit with its cutaway coat and high collar and his good boots
polished sparkling, and he was tempted to undo his greatcoat
casually, so that the girls could get a good look at him.

At two minutes past three precisely, he buttoned his coat
again, took off one glove and his hat and rang the doorbell at
number forty-three. A maid came to the door and took his
things, which rather disappointed him. His own family might
only keep a cook and a maid, but at Bullivant's he'd hoped for a
butler, at least.

The girl led the way down the hall and into the drawing-
room, while Tom gazed about him. He had called at this house
for months, every morning and evening, but it was the first time
he had set foot inside it. Normally, he scarcely had time to ring
the bell before he was handed the briefcase, and then they
would be off to the office – Mr Bullivant striding out in front,
and Tom trotting obediently behind. And in the evening it was
the same thing in reverse. So now Tom found himself looking
around with the liveliest interest.

The drawing-room was satisfyingly spacious. There was a
piano, a long-case clock, an aspidistra, a pair of portraits on the
wall over the fireplace, and a generous profusion of large china
ornaments. The whole impression was one of gratifying solid-
ity. Preparations had clearly been made for his coming. There

was a small round table in front of the fire, and on it had been set a lace tablecloth, a seed cake and a selection of dainty sandwiches.

'Mr Courtney . . . Tom . . . my dear fellow. Come in, come in.' Mr Bullivant was upon him, bounding out of his chair to wring him warmly by the hand. 'I think you know Mrs Bullivant?' He nodded toward his wife, a stout upholstered woman like an easy chair, who twinkled at Tom over her chins.

'Of course. A pleasure, Mrs Bullivant,' Tom said, bending over her hand as he had seen his father do when introduced to ladies.

'And this,' Mr Bullivant said, indicating the further corner with an expansive gesture, 'is my daughter, Olivia. Olivia, my dear, this is Tom Courtney, the young man I was telling you of from the office.'

'Enchanted,' Tom said, contriving to take a serious look at the young woman as he pressed her hand. Here, he knew, was the real reason for this afternoon's invitation. Mr Bullivant had made no secret of it, talking to Tom's father. 'I'd be pleased to give that boy of yours a chance, Dick. I've no son of my own, and I don't mind telling you, I'm looking for a sharp lad who might take over the running of the place when I'm gone. And – who knows – to keep an eye on Olivia, too. Everything will come to her one day.'

Tom looked at Olivia and his heart sank. She was dressed in a kind of white sprigged dress with pink ribbons and bows that would have suited a girl half her age and, though she looked good-natured enough, even her father, surely, could not think her a beauty. Yet he had introduced her with such a proud flourish, like a magician producing a rabbit from a hat.

She was rather like a rabbit, in fact, once you had thought of it. She had a small, pointed, face, her brown hair was looped up on either side (for all the world like a pair of drooping ears) and there was a gap between her two large front teeth. Tom would have sworn that her nose twitched.

All the same she was Bullivant's daughter, and some sort of

effort was obviously called for. He knew how to be charming. He enjoyed, in his own estimation, a certain success with the ladies. (Admittedly he'd only put this to the test once, when he'd put his arm around one of the fish girls in the street, and stolen a kiss on the area steps. It was not as exciting as he'd hoped, since she smelt strongly of herring, but she seemed to like it.)

He gave Olivia a warm smile and lingered over her hand a little. 'Enchanted,' he said again, and saw her flush with pleasure.

'Well,' Mr Bullivant said, ringing the bell to summon the tea, 'sit down, young Tom, and give us your news. How is your family?'

And so the visit began. It was an awkward, uncomfortable afternoon punctuated by sudden embarrassed bursts of conversation, and equally embarrassed silences. Tom did his best to give an impression of effortless social ease, but it was difficult. Mr Bullivant attempted to be hearty and kept asking him unexpected questions, while Olivia shot him shy glances from under her rabbit's ears, and Mrs Bullivant plied him with sandwiches and cake. But at last, when it seemed that the afternoon had already lasted a week, he could reasonably take his leave.

'Well, then,' Mr Bullivant boomed, getting to his feet, 'it's been nice to see you, young Courtney. And Olivia has enjoyed it. You must come again.'

Tom nodded, with forced enthusiasm. 'I should like that, very much.'

'It shall be arranged,' Bullivant said and, after Tom had said farewells to the ladies, his boss ushered him to the door. 'By the way, Tom, there's something I wanted to ask you. Informally, as it were. How is young Vargo getting on?'

Tom took a deep breath. A carefully chosen word or two now, and he could have Denzil out of that office for ever. Serve him right. Too clever by half, that one. But it was important not to let Mr Bullivant know how he felt. Better to drop the merest hint, and sound regretful about it.

'Well . . .' he said, adopting a rueful smile. 'He has been a little . . . slow, sometimes. Though he does try.'

Bullivant shook his head. 'Pity. Otherwise, with Mr Taylor gone, I might have put you in charge of the front office, and taken on a new junior to be office boy. The company is in trouble as it is, with these dock strikes breaking out. We'll have to send everything by rail. It all costs money, and if this coal shortage starts affecting the railways, it'll hit us really hard. Losing Taylor has come at a bad time.' He patted Tom's shoulder. 'I always meant to give you a chance, but if what you say is true, we could hardly expect Vargo to cope on his own, especially at a time like this. I suppose I shall have to move him on, leave you where you are, and get another senior man in. When this strike nonsense is over, we can think again. But it all takes time. It's unfortunate.'

Tom felt his rueful smile fade on his lips. Damn, damn, damn. Why hadn't he kept his big mouth shut. This should have been his big chance. Out of the clerk's chair and into the front office where there was real responsibility. A far more senior job, and doubtless far better paid. At his age! And here it was slipping through his fingers – all because of that damned Denzil.

'I'm sorry about Vargo,' Mr Bullivant said. 'I had hopes of him. I'll try to give him a recommendation somewhere. I don't suppose there has been any improvement since I spoke to him? I hoped perhaps a word of warning . . .?'

Tom ran a tongue around his lips and rearranged his smile. 'As a matter of fact, sir, that was just what I was about to say. There has been a remarkable improvement these last few days.'

'Wasn't pulling his weight, eh?' Bullivant said. 'That's not much use, either. Can't rely on a man like that, he'd be slacking as soon as your back was turned.'

'I don't think it was that, exactly,' Tom said, doing his best to sound judicious. 'More that . . .' He thought quickly, and inspiration came to him. 'More that he didn't want to let you down. I mean, there isn't a tradition of education in his family, and he spent a lot of time double-checking. I think he just didn't trust himself to work more quickly, until you said what you did.'

Bullivant nodded. 'Being over-cautious. Yes, that could be so. You know him better than I do. And he always seemed willing enough.' That sounded more hopeful, and Tom was beginning to breathe again when Bullivant went on, 'Pity he didn't prove himself earlier. We can't ask him to take on extra responsibilities if he already lacks confidence.'

Mentally Tom was cursing Denzil to purgatory and back again. He found himself saying, through gritted teeth, 'I think you should give him a chance, sir.'

'I'll give it some thought,' Bullivant said. 'It has certainly made difficulties, losing Taylor just now. Awkward, too. I was going to put out flags for the Coronation, but it hardly seems fitting now. You will be at the funeral on Tuesday, of course? Armbands will suffice, I think. No need for full mourning in your case. Poor fellow. I shall have to do something for his widow. Well, I'll think about what you've said. And come again, my boy. Next Sunday, perhaps. Olivia likes you, that's clear.'

Tom walked home thoughtfully. So, he was obliged to court a rabbit, to argue in favour of Denzil, and to mourn a man whose death was nothing but an advantage. What strange things one was forced to do in order to progress.

Three

On Monday, Denzil heard more about the visit to the Bullivants' than he really wanted to know. Tom, who usually had hardly a word to spare for Denzil, suddenly came over all talkative: how charming Mr Bullivant had been, how welcoming his wife was, and what an undoubted success Tom had scored with the daughter. And every single item in the office seemed to remind Tom irresistibly of some detail about the Bullivants' house.

'If you think that coal scuttle's heavy,' Tom was saying, as Denzil struggled in with the wretched thing to replenish the fire, 'you should see Bullivant's. Solid brass, by the look of it, and embossed all over. Shouldn't think you've ever seen anything like it in your life.'

On the whole, Denzil preferred Tom in his silent mood.

'Never mind. Perhaps you'll have a chance to, one day soon,' Tom said, with an air of ferocious patronage. 'I could put in a word for you.'

For a dangerous moment, Denzil seriously considered hitting him. It would have been enormously satisfying to wipe away that supercilious smirk with one good uppercut to the jaw. But office positions were hard to come by. Denzil unclenched his fists, and the moment passed.

Tom seemed not to have noticed. 'When I go on to the front desk . . . did I tell you that Mr Bullivant wanted me to take over from Taylor at the front desk?'

'Several times.'

Tom gave him a scowl. 'You needn't look like that, Vargo. It will make a difference to you, too. When I'm promoted, he will want you to start training in my place. Big step up for you, that would be.'

This was an aspect of things which had not occurred to Denzil. Of course, if that was true, it would mean calling at Bullivant's house and delivering the briefcase twice a day – and that would make a big difference, not only to his pay packet. It would mean at least an extra hour every evening – what with waiting for Bullivant and then accompanying him home. That, in turn, would mean missing the horse bus and what would be the chance of seeing Sprat then? It was a long walk home and the nights would soon start drawing in so it would be pitch dark into the bargain. Come winter, he might even have to leave Penvarris altogether. 'You're sure about this?'

'Of course I'm sure. Mr Bullivant was talking to me about it yesterday. Asked me what I thought. So pull your weight around here, young Vargo, and I'll see what I can do for you. You can fetch me some more ink for a start.' He must have seen Denzil's face, because he added quickly, 'I've put in a word for you already, believe it or not.'

Denzil *didn't* believe it, but there must have been some truth in it, because he was still mixing the ink when Mr Bullivant summoned him.

Denzil rarely went into Bullivant's private office except to light the fire and he had always found it forbidding. It was large and dark, with heavy furniture, and polished floors. Even the walls were panelled in dark-brown wood and there was a pervading smell of dust and beeswax. Mr Bullivant was sitting behind his desk – the big roll-top one which Denzil so admired – and he motioned Denzil to sit down in the high-backed chair opposite.

Denzil did so, rather nervously.

Bullivant looked at him sternly, over the top of his spectacles. 'Now then, Master Vargo. I wanted to speak to you.'

There was nothing to be said in answer to this, and Denzil prudently held his tongue.

There was a short silence, during which Denzil felt that his ears had never been pinker, then Bullivant said suddenly, 'Are you liking it here, boy?'

Denzil swallowed down a tide of panic. Perhaps Tom Courtney *had* been talking about him! Making trouble no doubt! 'I . . . ah . . .' he managed, foolishly, 'I do my best to give satisfaction, Sir.'

Bullivant tutted impatiently. 'That wasn't the question, boy. I asked you if you were liking it here. Speak up, lad, what do you say?'

A hundred thoughts raced through Denzil's brain. The humiliation of the singed trousers, the missed lunches, the tedium, the thousand little miseries which Tom arranged. But he knew better than to say so.

'Yes, Sir, I . . . that is . . . Yes, thank you, Sir.'

Bullivant harrumphed. 'So I should hope. And Courtney tells me that you are finding your feet at last.'

Denzil experienced a strong desire to 'find' his feet sharply in contact with the seat of Tom Courtney's trousers, but he said, 'I hope I have done so, Sir.'

'And so do I, young man, so do I. I know you have made a slow start, but I haven't forgotten your quick thinking after the storm. You have your wits about you in a crisis. So, I'm willing to give you a chance. I'm thinking of putting Courtney in the front office – he's young, but he's willing. That young fellow's got through more work in a day than any other clerk I've ever had. You'd do well to take a leaf out of his book, young Vargo.'

Young Vargo thought savagely that he'd dealt with a good many leaves off Tom's desk already, but he said nothing.

'And so, Mr Vargo, I'm going to give you a chance at Tom's post. Six weeks or so at first, just as a trial period. And if you bring it off, well – we'll think about making it permanent. That would mean an extra pound a year. And that's only a beginning. Of course it would mean extra responsibilities – my briefcase and so on. What do you say, Mr Vargo? What do you say?'

A pound a year, Denzil calculated wildly. It was a handsome
rise, but it would be difficult to move to Penzance on that. An
extra fourpence halfpenny a week was not going to cover the
rent, even for a little room, let alone pay for candles and coals.
And there would be food to find, and the tallyman to pay – and
he ought to send something home, if it was only a shilling or
two. On the other hand, he could scarcely settle for living at
Penvarris indefinitely. Well, he would have to manage somehow. And mother would be so proud.

What else could he say, but yes?

'You never are?' Sprat said, with horror, when she heard the
news. Denzil took her hand gently. They were sitting together
on the stile at the fork of the road. Norah Roberts might see
them, but Sprat was too upset to care. 'Thinking to leave
Penvarris?'

''Tisn't certain yet, Sprat. 'Tisn't even certain that I'll get
the job, permanent: I've got to prove myself this next six
weeks.'

'You'll do that,' she said, with miserable certainty. 'Do it
better for not having that Tom Courtney round your neck all
day. And then you'll be moving to Penzance. Or even if you
don't, you'll be that late coming home that I'll never manage to
see you.'

'I know,' he said, softly. He sounded as glum as she felt. 'But
the thing is, Sprat, it's an opening for me. Bullivant's been very
good, offering me the opportunity. I can't turn it down just
because it's awkward. There's dozens of chaps in Penzance
would leap at the chance.' He squeezed her fingers, suddenly,
and gave her a sidelong smile. 'Besides, I got to think about the
future, haven't I? Can't think about settling down without I've
got a decent job behind me.' His ears, Sprat noticed, had turned
very pink.

Sprat's heart, which had been somewhere down among the
groundsel at her feet, suddenly gave a most unladylike little
lurch and went soaring off among the seagulls. She felt her own

91

cheeks turn scarlet as she said, as casually as she could, 'You thinking of settling down, then, are you, Denzil?'

He tightened his grip on her fingers and looked at her affectionately a moment, then released her hand with a laugh. 'I daresay I shall do it one day,' he said, raising one eyebrow wickedly. 'When I meet the right girl, that is.'

She chuckled, catching his mood. 'And what would this "right girl" of yours be like?' she asked.

Denzil picked up a strand of her fair hair and wound it thoughtfully around his finger. 'Oh, dark-haired, of course,' he grinned. 'And plump and dull and unimaginative and not on any account from the Cove. Nothing in the least like you at all. What did you suppose?'

He was teasing her, saying the opposite on purpose. She gave him a playful little push. 'You!'

His grin broadened. 'Got a girl in mind, to tell you the truth, and I think she likes me, too. Only,' he added, more seriously, 'her parents don't think a lot of me. If I had a proper position, now, and could support a wife, perhaps they'd think different. Or' – he swished at the long grass with his foot – 'even if they didn't agree, perhaps she'd wait and marry me anyway, when she was old enough.' His laughing mood was gone, and he was deadly sober now. 'It would be hard for her, to defy her parents like that, but she might do it all the same – what do you say, Sprat? Do you think she might?' He seized her hand again.

For a moment Sprat found it difficult to say anything at all. One half of her mind was alight with joy, the other was dismayed. She had never really asked herself what would happen if she was forced to choose between defying Ma and losing Denzil. Both situations seemed equally impossible. If she was a character in one of Gypsy's tales, she thought bitterly, or the heroine of one of Mrs Meacham's books, she would have chosen Denzil instantly – and of course everything would have come out all right in the end. This, however, was real life, and she tried to imagine life without Ma and Pa, or a life in which they refused ever to speak to her again. It wasn't easy.

At last she managed to say, rather hesitantly, 'I think she might, Denzil, in the end. But not yet. Not straight away.'

Denzil looked a little hurt for a moment, but then he smiled. 'Of course not yet,' he said, lightly. 'Got to make my fortune first, haven't I? Anyway, I haven't exactly asked her yet. You won't see me with my dull little darling for a very long time.'

He was laughing as he spoke, but he took his hand away and, although he walked with her all the way to the road, he didn't offer to touch her again.

Sprat went back to Fairviews with a vague feeling of loss.

James Raeburn was dressing for dinner. It was an idiotic convention – in an out-of-the-way place like this. If you could call it 'dining'. No 'going in to dinner' like civilised beings. Violet had to be half carried to the table, where she sat triumphantly, overflowing her chair like a human dumpling, and her guests simply joined her there. And now she was planning a special 'Coronation supper' next week, with a roast goose and five courses, just for the three of them. Secretly he was irked by the whole charade.

Still, Violet seemed to set a lot of store by it, and James had never been one to disappoint a lady – not even a grotesque old lady in a heliotrope parody of an evening gown. Aunt Jane seemed to enjoy it, too, and it was important to keep her happy.

He sighed. Fitch had set things out as he liked them – the windows slightly open to 'air' the room, the fire stoked and his clothes laid ready for him on the bed. Black socks and sock suspenders; dinner suit, carefully cut to disguise his creeping waistline; braces; and a white dress shirt with tucks across the chest, handmade for him, as always, by a little man he knew in London. A new stiff collar awaiting him in the collar box, with the studs laid ready and his favourite pearl cufflinks set out beside them. In spite of himself, he smiled slightly. There was always a kind of pleasure in wearing fine things, though it was an expensive pleasure. Aunt Jane would be appalled if she knew what this little ensemble had cost him. He shuddered to think what he owed at his tailor's. But one couldn't wear off-the-peg: at his club a decent turn-out was the expected thing.

He stripped to his drawers and put on his dressing robe – best Afghan, bought at great expense – then sent Fitch down to the kitchens for hot water. If he was going to dress for dinner, he would do it properly – including a wash and shave. His dressing set was nearby and he took out his tortoiseshell brush and began to tidy his hair, looking at his reflection in the mirror on the washstand. What was he doing, burying himself in this provincial grave?

Tomorrow, he said to himself firmly. Tomorrow I will tell Violet, and make arrangements to go back to London. Or, perhaps if not tomorrow, straight after the Coronation – it would never do to offend his hostess. He rubbed a little pomade into his hair and looked at himself critically. Certainly he was looking better. The sea air perhaps, as the doctor had recommended. And there were other compensations. The house was comfortable, the scenery was good, and life was cheap, if not exciting. Yes, he could wait another week or two. But end of the month, certainly, at the latest.

A timid tap at the door interrupted his deliberations.

'Come in, Fitch,' he said, without moving from the mirror. 'You can put the water in the basin.'

But it wasn't the water. It was the little servant girl again, Nicholls or whatever her name was, and she was looking at him scarlet-faced. 'Begging your pardon, sir . . .'

She was embarrassed, he realised with amusement, at finding him once again in a state of undress. Not accustomed, probably, to seeing gentlemen in their dressing robes. And he did look rather dashing in his, he was aware. He put down his brush, pulled his stomach in a little, and turned to face her, 'Well, my girl, what is it?' He smiled at her indulgently.

She was gazing at him like a frightened puppy. 'Begging your pardon, sir,' she said again. 'But Miss Raeburn says, do you have some liver salts? She is feeling a little dyspeptic and she knows you generally keep them.'

James glowered. Drat the aunt. Here he was trying to cut his customary dash, if it was only to a serving maid, and there was Aunt Jane wanting to borrow his Enos. True, he did occasionally suffer with his stomach, but there was no need to advertise this to the world and make him seem middle-aged and foolish. He said, with bad grace, 'I believe there is a packet somewhere.' He waved a hand vaguely. 'On my dressing stand, perhaps.' It was there, of course, and the girl went to retrieve it. That neat little bottom again. He watched her, appreciatively, his ill humour forgotten.

'Thank you, sir. Miss Raeburn will be pleased.' She gave an awkward little bob and moved toward the door.

He said, more to keep her there than anything else, 'Good. Though deuced if I know how Aunt Jane contrives to have indigestion *before* dinner.'

Nicholls (was it?) smiled. 'Oh, she always has a sandwich brought up before dinner, sir. Says the sea air gives her an appetite and it wouldn't be ladylike to eat too much.'

She said it with such earnest simplicity that James threw back his head and laughed. 'Does she, by George? How like Aunt Jane. Perhaps I should write to Mr Asquith and tell him to send some of those damned suffragettes down here – see if a little sea air would help their appetites at all!'

To his surprise, the girl stiffened. 'The hunger strikers, you mean, sir?'

'The news has reached you down here, has it? Wretched women had London abuzz with their nonsense when I left. Scuffles in the streets, disrupted meetings, women chaining themselves to buildings and throwing vegetables at public figures. Damned if I know what the world's coming to.'

'Yes, I know, sir. Denzil told me,' the girl said, as if that explained everything. 'He saw it in the papers.'

James frowned. Of course, the London news columns were full of it. Yet somehow he hadn't expected the servants here to know about it. It was rather disappointing. He had dimly hoped to dazzle her with his metropolitan gossip. 'And who,' he enquired archly, 'might Denzil be?'

'Oh, just a young man I know, up to Penvarris. Some clever, he is. Works in Penzance, reads the papers and knows all sorts.'

She had a sweetheart, then. In that case, James mused privately, she was probably not half as innocent as she pretended. He filed that heartening information away, and said in a teasing tone, 'And what is his opinion of the suffragists, this rural paragon of yours? Denzil or whatever his name is?'

She turned still pinker but said, 'I aren't rightly sure, sir. Thinks they're daft to do these things, but they have a point, he says.'

'A point? Votes for women? What on earth would women know about voting? The silly things would just vote the way their menfolk told them to.' He looked at her with mock severity. 'Well, wouldn't you vote the way your Dennis – or whatever he's called – expected?'

She looked flustered by the question. 'I . . . I don't know, sir.'

He raised an eyebrow at her. He had expected instant capitulation, but she hadn't given it. A girl of spirit. He rather liked that. 'Well, I do. It would be a fiasco. The system is a fiasco already. When I was a young man, voting was a privilege. And now look, with these reformers and anarchists – they've given the vote to every man jack of a tradesman. Even, God save us, agricultural workers. Country's going to the dogs.'

She said nothing. She was looking uncomfortable, as if she was waiting to get away. Well, he hadn't finished. It pleased him to keep her there – she was more of a pleasure to look at than most things in this place. He said, 'I suppose you think it would be a fine thing to vote?'

'I think it would be grand,' she said. 'Lord Falmouth or someone, I'd pick. Or Mr Tavy, the solicitor.'

Her naivety amused him. 'You can't pick just anyone you like, even if you do have the vote.' He laughed. 'You have to vote for a candidate chosen by the party. And anyway you

96

couldn't vote for Falmouth, he'd be in the House of Lords.
They aren't elected at all.' He had made her feel foolish, and she
was looking downcast. He favoured her with a benevolent
smile. 'You see, I'm quite right. You know nothing about
voting at all. So don't go worrying your pretty little head about
things that don't concern you.' He chucked her playfully under
the chin.

She looked at him, blushing but defiant. Deuced attractive, in
its way. 'It might concern me, sir, one day – if these hunger
strikers get their way.'

He laughed, in what he hoped was a suitably masculine
manner. 'Oh, hunger striking! That will all be over in a week
or two: mark my words. Just a fad. All started by that dreadful
Miss Wallace Dunlop – appalling girl. She tried the same trick
on her parents when they threatened to stop her music studies.
Refused to eat and the foolish pair capitulated. Then the
Pankhursts got into the act, and next thing you know they
are all at it, one after another like a herd of silly sheep.'

'You know them?'

He didn't, of course, not personally, but the girl was looking
suitably impressed and he did have one trump card. He ignored
the question. 'Even Kitty Marion has joined in – got herself
arrested and won't eat . . . Kitty used to be such a dear jolly
little red-headed trouper in the music hall when I knew her.'

That had done it. Nicholls was gazing at him wonderingly.
Impressed by his superior knowledge of the world, clearly. He
took a step towards her.

'Nicholls!' Aunt Jane's voice in the distance. 'Drat the girl,
where has she got to?' The words were accompanied by an
impatient tap of her stick.

Nicholls gave him an apologetic smile. 'The Enos, sir.'

'Of course.' He patted her arm encouragingly. 'We must talk
again.'

She did not recoil this time. On the contrary, she smiled
gravely. 'Yes, sir. Imagine you actually knowing one of the
hunger strikers. Wait till I tell Denzil.' And she scurried off.

A moment later, he heard Aunt Jane, scolding.

He turned back to the glass, wryly. So it wasn't his dashing looks which charmed her, or his being on first name terms with stars of the musical stage. It was the fact that he knew a woman who was in prison. How are the mighty fallen.

When Fitch returned with the water a moment later, James vented his annoyance by complaining – with some justice – that it wasn't hot enough.

Four

Denzil was still cursing himself for a fool. What did he want to do that for? Opening his big mouth. He'd got carried away talking to Sprat and now he'd frightened her off. That sudden look of panic on her face. What was it she had said? She might, Denzil, in the end. But not yet. Not straight-away. And a minute earlier she had been looking thrilled to bits.

What had he hoped? That she would say, 'Of course, Denzil, anything for you?' He didn't know. He only wished he hadn't forced her to say anything at all. Well, it was no good standing here all night like a granite post. He slashed at the grasses morosely with a stick and stumped off up the lane home.

He stopped at the gate. Something was wrong, he could sense it. No smoke at the chimney. The door was not open as it usually was on fine days, with Mother watching out for him and pretending not to – busying herself with a broom in the hall, or occupied in the garden with the beans – while the smell of new baking wafted on the air. Tonight the door was firmly closed, the curtains tightly drawn, and there was a pair of unfamiliar boots on the front step.

Denzil felt a shudder go through him. If anything had happened to Mother! He'd never forgive himself, then, for loitering in the lane. He rushed to the door and lifted the latch but, to his amazement, it was bolted from inside.

He hammered on the door. 'Mother? Are you all right? Mother?'

Blessedly, his mother's voice came from within. 'All right, Denzil, I'm coming.' Relief turned him weak at the knees.

99

It seemed a long time before the door was opened, but she was there, looking flushed and strained and twisting a duster between her hands. 'It's all right, my lover. I'm some sorry to have locked you out. Only, Denzil, you'll never guess what's happened . . .' She looked at him and her eyes were full of tears.

Something *was* up. He'd known it the minute she called him 'lover'. Mother wasn't one for endearments, as a rule.

He stepped into the house. 'What is it, Mother? What?' He stopped. A figure was coming down from upstairs. A heavy, swarthy figure, bearded and balding, was swaggering down the staircase, buttoning his shirt.

'Stand out the way, Mary, and let the lad see for himself.' The man came on down the stairs, grinning. 'Let's look at you.' His eyes skimmed Denzil from head to foot. 'So you're Denzil. Just as I expected. Fancy suit, soft hands. Proper little gentleman, aren't we? Still, I aren't complaining. Your mother's done you proud.' He extended a strong, calloused hand, seized Denzil's own and wrung it vigorously. Denzil winced, fearing for his fingers. The man leaned forward, still smiling, and brought his face close to Denzil's. 'Well, young fellow, say something. I daresay we've both changed a deal since we last met. But I'd know you anywhere, for all you've grown like a tree. You know who I am, Denzil? You recognise me?'

Denzil swallowed. He would not, in a hundred years, have recognised the face. Nor the voice – the man had a strange, foreign twang to his speech. But as the man leaned nearer Denzil smelt the breath, and with a dreadful sickening of the stomach, suddenly he knew. He seemed to have lost all power of speech. He nodded, withdrawing his hand sharply.

'Well?' The man rocked back on his heels and hooked his thumbs belligerently behind his braces. He was much shorter than Denzil remembered, a good inch shorter than Denzil himself, but he was powerful and stocky. Somehow he still managed to fill the room. 'What do you think of this, then?'

'He fell out with Bill,' mother put in, helplessly. 'I never expected this. He just—'

'Shut up, woman,' the man said, without glancing towards her. 'I'm talking to the boy. I want to hear what he has to say for himself.'

Denzil looked at his mother. She was leaning back against the wall, still twisting the duster. Even her voice had become pale and worn, as if she had aged ten years. Denzil thought of the locked door, the drawn curtains, the unbuttoned shirt, his mother's red-rimmed eyes. Comprehension dawned and an unreasoning anger rose in him.

For a moment he clenched his fists, seized by a wild desire to knock the man to the floor and wallop the daylights out of him, but he controlled himself fiercely. After all, absence or no absence, beer or no beer, the man presumably had rights. It was none of Denzil's business if he chose to exercise them.

'Well,' the man said, smiling his beery self-satisfied smile again. 'I'm waiting. What's the matter with you, are you simple or something? Haven't you got anything at all to say to me?'

Denzil mastered himself with difficulty. Father had always been too free with his fists, he told himself firmly. He would not allow himself to go down the same road. He glanced at his mother again. She was shredding the duster, looking at him, silently pleading 'Don't make trouble, Denzil' with her eyes.

Denzil found his tongue. He took a step forward. There was a silence. The very house seemed to be waiting. Then he said, in a voice that was deliberately cool and clipped. 'Of course, I have something to say to you. Hello, Father. Welcome home.'

Sprat was still glowing with amazement. Imagine that! Mr Raeburn actually knowing one of the hunger strikers. Knowing her as a real-life person, not just a name in the papers.

She tried to imagine willingly going without food for days, and failed. She could remember one winter, when the weather was fierce and times were especially hard in the cove: the whole Nicholls family had 'made do' with bread and dripping for a week. Sprat recalled what hunger pangs were like. Those women up London were some brave to put up with that on purpose.

'Are you listening to a word I'm saying?' Miss Raeburn said.

Sprat came back to the present with a jolt. She didn't want to irritate Miss Raeburn. The old lady was a dear, but she could deliver a surprisingly sharp rebuke when she'd a mind to.

Sprat liked her, all the same – there was a quiet determination under those old-fashioned grey and lilac dresses, that permanent faint scent of lavender, those little lace caps and neat Victorian button boots. Sprat had come to hate those boots – they seemed to take hours to do up with the little ivory buttonhook. Apologetically, she said, 'Yes, Miss Raeburn.'

The thin face softened. 'Then, if you were listening, perhaps you can explain why you are standing there doing nothing, instead of making up my salts as I asked you to do?'

'I'm doing it, Miss Raeburn,' Sprat said, suiting the action to the word, and hurrying so much in the process that she almost upset the bedside jug as she poured the water into the glass. She stirred in the Enos and the old lady sipped the mixture doubtfully, as if the bubbles might make her sneeze.

'There. I should have brought my own Epsom salts, but I do believe that is a little better already,' Miss Raeburn said, handing the glass back to Sprat, 'though I shall certainly have to send into town for some before the Coronation. Violet is talking of having goose, and that always upsets my digestion. Now, I am unconscionably late getting ready for dinner. You can take down my combs.' She seated herself at the dressing table and waited for Sprat to begin before she added, 'What took you so long?'

'Mr Raeburn was talking to me, Ma'am.' Sprat muttered, apologetically.

In the heavy gilt-edged mirror, the thin eyebrows arched. 'Indeed? James is not known for his conversation. It must have bored you exceedingly.'

It was obvious what Miss Raeburn was thinking – that Mr James had been flirting with her – and she hastened to correct the impression. 'Oh, no, Ma'am. He was talking to me about the suffragists up London. Says he even knows one of the hunger strikers.' She took out the last of the combs and let the silver hair spill down over the bony shoulders.

No reply. Sprat applied herself silently to the task of brushing.

'So,' Miss Raeburn said unexpectedly, a little later, when the mauve dress was safely buttoned and the hair refastened into place. 'James has been dazzling you with his accounts of his suffragist friends? Well, don't you let him fool you, my dear. James has very clear ideas of what women are good for, and voting for parliament isn't one of them.'

Sprat hardly knew how to reply, so she said 'No, Ma'am,' meekly.

But Miss Raeburn hadn't finished. 'James is like his father. All the men in our family were the same. It wouldn't occur to any of them that a woman could actually think, or do anything particular except marry and have babies. And if she didn't do that, as I didn't, she was a disappointment, to be tolerated only as a convenient chaperone and a possible source of inheritance when she dies. Oh, don't shake your head, I know exactly what my nephew thinks of me.'

Sprat was shaking her head in surprise at this unexpected outburst, not because she was denying anything. 'No, Ma'am,' she said again.

'No doubt you think much the same yourself, Nicholls? A poor old lady, to be brought out of mothballs once a day and taken down to dinner?'

Sprat said, 'No, Ma'am,' for the third time, although of course, it was exactly what she had thought, sometimes. But Miss Raeburn wasn't listening.

'Well, I'm an old lady now and it's far too late, but if I were a little younger, I tell you, for two pins I'd be out there on the streets of London waving a banner with them.' The eyes met Sprat's startled gaze in the mirror. 'Does that surprise you?'

It astonished her, but it wasn't Sprat's place to say so. She said, 'Yes, Ma'am. I mean, no Ma'am. You wouldn't want to be arrested, Ma'am.'

Miss Raeburn smiled. 'No, though it would be almost worth it, to see James' face. In fact, sometimes I'm tempted to bequeath my money to the Women's Movement, instead of leaving it to James to squander away. So next time he wants to talk to you about suffragists you can tell him that!'

'Yes, Ma'am.'

' "Yes, Ma'am",' the old lady mocked. ' "Yes, Ma'am", though of course you wouldn't dream of doing anything of the kind.' She gave a dry little laugh. 'Any more than I would ever do what I threaten, I suppose. All dreams and no action, most of us, that's why we'll never make suffragettes.' She got stiffly to her feet. 'Now then, where's my stick? You can help me downstairs. Those salts have done the trick nicely. I have developed quite an appetite for dinner. Violet was suggesting a small sherry with the soup.'

Mrs Mason's arrival had put Ma in a taking. Of course, now that Sprat was staying up at Fairviews, the sleeping arrangements were easier. Mrs Mason and her daughter had the big bed in the front bedroom, while Ma and Pa squashed up together in Sprat's little bed in the back. It was a bit of a squeeze, but it was a darn sight more comfortable than trying to sleep in the armchairs downstairs like they used to do before when the Masons came.

Comforting, too. Ma had never been a great one for touching, and even now she usually slept well away from Pa in the bed, in case she rubbed up against him and he started wanting what he called 'his rights'. Now, though, Pa had to put his arms around her to keep them both in the bed, and since there was no room for hanky-panky, she found it unexpectedly agreeable.

But having the Masons meant a great deal more to do. Extra meals to cook, fires to lay and sheets to wash, water to heat and slops to clear – for naturally, Mrs Mason and her daughter, being paying guests, wanted a hot wash and couldn't be expected to empty for themselves. Extra cleaning, too. Ma was being particularly careful about that. During the year or two that Ma couldn't have her to stay, Mrs Mason had lodged somewhere else, and she had mentioned – more than once – lying in bed there and seeing cobwebs in a corner. Ma wasn't going to have the same said of her, no-how, and she went right through the house every day, cleaning everything like a spring tide.

Worst of all, there was no Sprat to lend a hand, and sometimes Ma had really felt the want of her. This morning, for instance. Ma was up early but when she went to the zinc safe to fetch the milk she found it had turned, and was only fit for baking. She should have thought of that: Mrs Mason's daughter – Elsie her name was, but Ma could never think of her as having a name of her own – had been feeling peaky last night and wanted cocoa. That had used the last of the fresh. Of course it was Ma's own fault – it was she who suggested the cocoa – but knowing that didn't help matters. If Sprat were here it would be easy: she would simply have sent her over to Crowdie's farm with a milk jug and basket, and there would have been fresh milk, cream and butter on the table before Mrs Mason and her daughter were even up.

As it was, Ma would have to make the journey herself. It was enough to vex an archangel, but there was no help for it. She struggled to her feet – she had been fetching the new bread from the bread kettle where it had been baking overnight in the embers – stoked the fire, set out the plates and a fresh pot of her own blackberry jam and, sighing deeply, tied a good shawl over her shoulders and a clean pinny around her waist. She always did that, going out, in case she got 'run over by a runaway horse' as people said. You had to make yourself look a bit decent, even at this time of day in the drizzling rain.

Pa was already out at the yard, under the lean-to, laying down the 'stocks' for Zackary's boat. He had already made the half-model, sanding down the layers of fine yellow pine until he got exactly the shape he wanted, and now he was out setting the supports on which the keel would be laid, soon as ever the wood arrived. He looked up and waved good-naturedly as she went past. He was cheerful then, despite having had no breakfast yet. Perversely, that made her more irritated than ever. Pa was good, of course he was – never complained like some men would, even when she had to leave him to get the limpets and bait his own pots of a morning – but you never saw a man having to go traipsing about the countryside shopping. 'Course, he had his own concerns, what with this boat building to see to. All the same it was aggravating, hearing him whistling so cheerfully over his work, when she was faced with this vexing walk, a mile or more uphill in the wet.

It *was* wet, too. Not so much the summer drizzle as the morning sea mist wisping dankly up the valley: it crept remorselessly under the shawl with her, as if determined to make her hair lank and her shoulders damp. The grasses and wild flowers beside the path were heavy with moisture, too, and they seemed to rub themselves deliberately against her ankles until her boots and skirt hems were clammy and sodden. Altogether, by the time she reached the farm lane, Ma's mood was no more sunny than the morning.

Five

M a found her way to the byre, where Crowdie's son was finishing the milking, but even Crowdie's cheerful 'Morning, Myrtle!' and the friendly warmth of the beasts did nothing to restore her good humour, though she did manage a tight smile when he measured out the milk, creamy, fresh and frothing from the pail to her jug.

'Drop of butter, I'll take, while I'm here,' she said, and he went off to fetch it from the cool of the 'dairy room' next to the house. She didn't go with him, as she might have done, but stood unhelpfully in the cowshed, as if she was fascinated by watching the boy emptying his bucket into the churns ready to take out and sell, and setting aside some of the cream to scald.

Crowdie was soon back with a good-sized pat nestling in a piece of waxed paper: a peculiarly strong yellow butter, churned and shaped by his wife with her own butter pats, and stamped with his own particular thistle design. Ma didn't particularly care for it – it was too strong for her and she preferred the paler 'shop' variety – but Pa liked it and the Masons seemed to feel that tasting real farm butter was an important part of coming to the Cove at all.

She gave Crowdie his fourpence ha'penny and turned to go. The jug was even more difficult to carry, now it was full to the brim, and if she was not careful she would be late with the Masons' breakfast. She snorted slightly with annoyance. Crowdie must have heard her.

'I should go back the top way, if I were you, over the stile,' he said heartily. 'Ground's some slippery, this weather, and that milk'll be the very dickens to get home, without you go on the road. Long way round, but I daresay it's worth it. Miss your footing easy as winking, in this mist, and then you'd be down in the Cove a sight faster than you bargained for.'

Ma felt like snorting again. There is nothing so vexing as someone who says something obviously right which you hadn't thought of yourself. However, Crowdie wasn't family, he was a neighbour and you couldn't go venting your annoyance on him, so contenting herself with a short, 'Well, can't stand here gossiping,' she seized her jug and took herself off.

She did, though, turn in the direction of the road rather than the cliff path – although she took care to do it out of sight of the cowshed. As she clambered over the top stile, setting her jug and butter carefully on the granite step as she did so, she saw a figure in the lane, coming towards her through the mist, and suddenly she very much regretted coming that way at all.

It was a man – a stocky, bushy-haired man – and by the look of it he was already the worse for drink; though where he had managed to lay hands on it at that hour was more than she could think. He was walking unsteadily, with that careful attention which only the slightly drunk achieve and he was talking to himself under his breath. That alone would have been enough to make Ma turn tail, but as he drew closer she recognised who it was. For a moment she stood transfixed, refusing to believe her eyes, and by the time she had recollected herself it was too late. He had recognised her.

'Well,' he said, lurching up belligerently. 'If it isn't Myrtle Jenkins.'

She contemplated scampering back the way she had come, but he had positioned himself deliberately between herself and the stile, where her purchases were still on the top step. She raised her chin defiantly. 'It isn't Myrtle Jenkins at all! Myrtle Nicholls, I am now and have been for years, so mind who you go talking to in that tone of voice – though I see you're still the same Stan Vargo as ever was. 'Tisn't above seven o'clock and already you're staggering.' She made a lunge for the jug, but he blocked her way.

He just stood there, his good jacket too tight and too short around him, swaying slightly and saying nothing.

She muttered resentfully, 'What are you doing here anyroad? Thought you were gone to Canada.' She didn't say 'and good riddance' but she hardly needed to. Stan Vargo knew well enough what Ma thought of him.

He leered, thrusting his beery face towards her so that she flinched. 'Well, so I was, but I'm back, so don't you forget it.'

'Aren't like to, am I?' she retorted, with more courage than she felt. 'When you come staggering up here and stand in my way and won't let me pick up the things I've bought – me with paying guests waiting at home. I've a good mind to shout for Crowdie. He'd be up here with his pitchfork, and we'd soon see who was swaggering then.'

In fact, it was a question whether Crowdie would have heard her, what with the mist, but the threat had an unexpected effect. Stan Vargo lost his bluster, and flapped his arms helplessly, for all the world like Pa's fishing boat when something took the wind from its sails. 'Here,' he said, in a voice that had become a wheedle, 'what you want to be doing that for? I'm just going down to see Crowdie. Man's got a right to walk along a lane, I should hope, without you threatening to shout the place down. I haven't hurt'ee, have I?'

She took advantage of the moment to seize her goods, and – more confident now – demanded, 'What you want Crowdie for, at this hour?' For a moment she wondered if he had come for milk, and somehow spent the money on ale on the way, but then the truth dawned. 'Come looking for a job, have you? Well, in that case, you should have more sense than to turn up smelling of drink. Who'd take you on, in that state? And why didn't you try down the mine, first off? You know something about mining, at least.'

She saw his face and realised that he had, indeed 'tried down the mine' and been turned away. Explained why he'd been drinking, most like. Of course, he'd knocked down a mine captain, or something, years ago. In spite of herself she felt an unexpected surge of sympathy. 'Folks round here've got long memories,' she said gruffly.

He rounded on her. 'Me for one. I know more about that girl of yours than you think. So don't you go telling everyone what doesn't concern you, or I shall tell them a thing or two myself. You understand me, Myrtle Jenkins?'

'It's Nicholls!' she said, but her heart was thumping. What did the man want, money? But it seemed not, already he was lurching off again – the way he'd come – taking her advice perhaps, and sobering up before he went to see for work. Drat Crowdie – if he hadn't suggested it she would never have come this way. Wild horses would not have dragged her down that lane, now, and she turned back over the stile and made her way, with difficulty, down the steep path to the Cove. Spilt some of the milk, doing it, and the Masons were up and waiting by the time she got home.

Denzil was settling into the new job readily. There was more to do, of course – especially with these dock strikes causing delays – but it was a sight easier to do it without Tom Courtney sending you out for coals, or wanting you to sharpen pencils every five minutes. In fact, there were so many letters to send that Mr Bullivant was talking about having to invest in a telephone, one of these days. In the meantime, he brought in someone pro tem to do the menial chores, so Denzil could devote all his time to what he was trained for.

The new office boy was Claude Emms, the younger son of one of their customers, an insignificant youth, with hands and feet too big for himself, and a good head for figures, although he was not – as Denzil discovered – overendowed with other kinds of intelligence. Mr Bullivant had agreed to 'give him a chance' – to please his father as much as anything – and the poor lad was clearly terrified. Denzil spoke kindly to him and showed him how to mix the ink and insert the pink blotting paper in the holders without tearing it. Claude repaid him by trying diligently, if inexpertly, and becoming his devoted slave. The inner office was noticeably warmer, even though the days were cool.

Tom Courtney didn't like it, naturally, but he was so busy dealing with enquiries in the outer office that he had no time to intervene, and Denzil found that very soon, between them, he and Claude were getting as much done as ever, although Claude was not a type-writer at all.

The problem was the briefcase. The extra walk to Bullivant's, and the necessity to be there at eight thirty sharp meant that he had to start off very early, so he couldn't catch the horse-bus, even if it was raining. And that, of course, caused problems of its own. He couldn't afford to have his clothes ruined. He took to leaving his good things in the office and going in to change before walking to Bullivant's – he still had the key from going to lay the fires in the winter. It added at least an hour to his day, morning and evening, and if it rained his walking clothes got drenched. Once or twice lately they'd still been damp when he put them on again at night. He couldn't have that. Catch a chill now and he risked losing his position altogether.

So Denzil was the possessor of a brand new coat, vulcanised to keep out the wet. He was proud of it – he had never owned a new coat before – but he was aware how the extra weekly payments would eat uncomfortably into his rise, when he got it. Until then, there was no help for it; the money would have to come out of what he took home. And, of course, when the weather turned bad, it would be Claude's job to set the fires, so he would have to relinquish the key. At that point, he would have to move to Penzance.

In the meantime, the early start relieved him of the necessity of seeing much of his father, who was now always down at the public house by the time Denzil got home. He would come in, shouting or singing, when everyone else was in bed, and was still sleeping it off when Denzil left in the morning. In some ways that was a relief, but it was all very hard on Mother.

Perhaps his father would get down to the mine and ask for a job. He had been talking about it for days but, of course, he had done nothing about it while he still had money from Canada in his pocket. Too frightened to go, Denzil suspected, in case they turned him away. They didn't forgive you easily for knocking down a mine captain. Though Father had managed to bring home a recommendation from Canada, so perhaps that would help. It was to be hoped that it did. It was Father's money that paid the rent. And if Denzil himself was taking home a bit less, Mother was going to find it hard to make ends meet, especially with an extra mouth to feed.

Well, it was no good sitting here fretting – there was work to do. Denzil turned back to his entries, but a moment later he had stopped again, staring. Not that there was anything the matter with the invoice. It was a routine matter – a small quantity of wood being shipped as incidental cargo from Plymouth on a coastal steamer. Most of it had arrived and been passed to the waggoner for delivery. But – like so much else these days – part of the consignment had been delayed by the strikes and was being sent on by rail. Nothing surprising there. It was the name of the consignee which made Denzil stop and stare.

Albert Nicholls, 12 The Row, Penvarris Cove. To be notified on arrival.

And who, Denzil thought, would be coming to the office to sign for that? It wouldn't be Sprat: Ma would walk to Penzance from her deathbed rather than let Sprat come anywhere near Bullivant's. All the same Denzil wrote the name in his ledger with particular care.

Saturday afternoon was Sprat's half-day. It was her last chance to go home before the Coronation, and she was anxious to get there. The men would start building the bonfire tonight, before the Sabbath, and Pa had promised she could help. She could vaguely remember the last Coronation, the whole Cove out building the 'beacon' on the beach, and crowding into Ma's

112

kitchen afterwards for saffron cake and tea. More fun than the day itself.

There'd been a chain of beacons then, too: the Covers were to wait until they saw the glow from Land's End and then light their own. Trouble was, Norah swore it was Penvarris beacon they could see, and people refused to take their lead from 'up-overers'. There was a lot of wrangling before anything was done. Sprat was only little then and had to go to bed, but she remembered sitting in her nightshirt, listening. She'd heard them laughing, dancing and singing for what seemed to be hours, until the men had to go and take out the boats before they lost the tide.

Of course, that was years ago. Perhaps this time she could watch the bonfire from Fairviews. It promised to be big enough – the men had cleared a huge patch for tonight's fire, and the pyre would be added to, bit by bit, for days.

So no sooner had lunch been cleared away than she was off, skipping down the path to the Cove like a child. It was a fine, clear afternoon, with a skittish wind frisking little crests on the waves, and the light sparkling on the water. For all her hurry, Sprat stopped a moment on the curve of the hill to watch: men busy with their boats, Mrs Polmean out scrubbing her step, two women sitting at their doors gossiping and knitting in the sun, Norah Roberts down at the harbour wall in a plaid shawl, pinny and battered hat, helping Half-a-leg to spread the nets. No sign of Ma.

Busy with the Masons, no doubt. Sprat felt unreasonably irked. She hadn't been home for days, and she would have liked Ma to make a bit of a fuss of her – sit down with a cup of tea and tell her all the news – but with the Masons there she wouldn't have the time. Sprat hadn't seen Denzil either – not since that awful day by the stile. If only she had managed to say 'yes' instead of blurting out her doubts like that. She'd found an excuse to wait on the road, quite late, several times but she hadn't seen hair nor hide of him. It was probably only his new job, keeping him late. She was almost certain it was. Unless she'd hurt his feelings so much that he was avoiding her.

If only she could be sure.

Well, it was no good standing here on the cliffs like a day-mark. She set off down the path towards the busy scene below. Norah was still at the nets. No chance of slipping past her today.

Sure enough, as soon as she saw Sprat, Norah abandoned the nets and came hurrying across to meet her, the ridiculous imitation flower on the old hat bobbing on its stalk as she came.

'Well now,' she said placing herself squarely in Sprat's path. 'Here's a turn up for the books and no mistake.'

Sprat looked at her doubtfully. 'What is?'

A smile of triumph crossed Norah's face. 'Haven't you heard? Half the Cove's talking about it. Stan Vargo, that's what. Back from Canada, propping up the bar every night in the Cornish Arms as if he'd never been away.'

'Stan Vargo?' For a moment the name meant nothing to her.

'Father of that Denzil of yours.'

'He's not "of mine" at all,' Sprat said automatically.

Norah gave a righteous sniff. 'You keep it that way. Your Ma and Pa might be as weak as water, but Stan Vargo isn't a man to tangle with. Handy with his fists, always was. Put a stop to that sort of nonsense, quick sharp.'

Sprat said, 'Oh?' but her mind wasn't on it. Denzil's father! Was that why Denzil hadn't come? She didn't know whether to be more hopeful or less.

Norah had all the prompting she needed. 'And . . .' she began, tightening her shawl around her, but an outraged roar from the harbour interrupted her.

'Norah! Norah! Dammit woman, where've 'ee gone? Are you giving me a hand here, or have I to come and get 'ee?'

Norah hollered back, defiantly, 'All right! Keep your whiskers on!' But she nodded a hasty farewell to Sprat and hurried back to her task. Norah wore the pants in that house, Pa always said, until Half-a-leg wanted them.

Sprat watched her go, and then made her way to the house. Ma was in the kitchen, with the fire stoked high, trying to dry

114

out Pa's working clothes while Mrs Mason was out. His old trousers and collarless twill shirt were draped over the settle while his matted woollen jumper and socks steamed on a string hung from the mantelpiece.

'Got 'imself soaked, he did,' Ma said, without further greeting. 'Working in the rain. Cripple himself with rheumatics if he goes on. First of that timber came yesterday, and nothing will do but he must lay down the keel straightaway, out there wetting and clamping it all hours. To overcome the twist of the grain, he says. And then he comes in dripping wet and expects me to dry his things while he takes the Masons for a row round the harbour. I'll give him "overcome the twist". And me with guests to see to.' She slapped a loaf of homemade bread on the table. 'Here, give me a hand with this, will you, now you're here? Half-a-leg brought me in a bit of fresh fish. Do nice for their tea but I'll have to clean it first – can't have the bread tasting of mackerel.'

Sprat set the kettle on the fire and squeezed up on the settle, avoiding the damp clothes. She knew Ma, all this grumbling was a kind of welcome. 'Round the harbour, eh? Nice day for it.' She began buttering and slicing the bread as she spoke. 'Do that girl a bit of good, too, spot of fresh air.'

Ma put down her gutting knife. 'Well, something needs to.' Her voice was troubled. 'I aren't happy about that girl, Sprat, and that's a fact. Seemed to be doing handsome, first off, but these last few days she's looking pastier than ever. Caught a chill, I expect, out walking in the rain. Don't know what Pincher's thinking of, taking her out in the boat.'

'Thinking of you, I expect,' Sprat said, brushing the breadcrumbs into her hand and going over to put them in the fire. 'Knew you'd want five minutes with me to hear what Mrs Meacham's planning for Thursday. Feed a regiment, it would. I'll bring you a bit home next time I come. Now, are you wanting a cup of tea?'

And they chatted happily about provisions until Pa and the Masons came in and it was time to help with the beacon.

115

Six

I t was Tuesday afternoon and in Bullivant's front office Tom Courtney was enjoying himself.

'I'm sorry Mr White, we're doing our very best, but I'm afraid there's nothing we can do at present. The dock strikes, you understand.'

He loved saying 'we' in that way. It suggested that he was part of the company. And he was. Much better out here in the front office dealing with customers, not stuck away in that pokey back room with only Denzil Vargo for company. People must have seen him with Bullivant at Taylor's funeral, too, up there at the front, black armbands and all.

'Well,' White was saying meekly, clutching his bowler hat to his ample waistcoat in an apologetic fashion. 'I'll call later in the week.'

Tom condescended a smile. 'Office is closed Thursday of course, for the Coronation. I'm sure you saw our flags out, and the notice in the window?' Tom himself had spent most of his lunchtime putting them there, and he was very proud of the effect. The black silhouette portraits of King George and Queen Mary particularly. He'd found them in a magazine – 'Make your own Coronation display' – and he'd cut them out and pinned them against the flag. Suitably respectful to a dead employee but in keeping with the celebration. Bullivant had been delighted. It was only a pity, Tom thought, that he hadn't cut them a bit better. Queen Mary was a little pointed around the nose.

'Very nice, I'm sure,' White said. 'Open Friday as usual, I suppose? I'll call in then, Mr Courtney.'

Tom beamed. Regular customers were already calling him by name. And Bullivant had singled him out for attention, even invited him to spend the Coronation holiday with the family.

It had happened last Sunday, when Tom had gone to the house again, for tea.

'We're going to St Ives on Thursday, to watch the gig-boat regatta. My wife's cousin rows in the Penzance boat, and a little party of us has hired a charabanc. Don't suppose you'd care to join us, since the office is closed? Daresay you'll find us a lot of old fuddy-duddies, but there'll be a picnic, and I'm sure Olivia would enjoy some young company, wouldn't you, my dear?'

Olivia blushed to her rabbit's ears. Tom was concentrating on balancing his teacup and wrestling with a piece of particularly dry and tasteless seed-cake at the same time (he had made the mistake, once, of saying something flattering about it, and now it was produced for him at every opportunity) but he had enough presence of mind to recognise the compliment and accept at once.

'I should be delighted, Sir,' he said, with real enthusiasm, and had spent every waking hour since planning for the occasion. Not, of course, that Tom knew anything about boat racing. But Bullivant had singled him out, that was the important thing. Singled him out to escort Olivia, besides, and that set him dreaming. It was as good as an invitation to court her. Even if the prospect was less than riveting, it was devoutly to be desired. The man who married Olivia could be sure of a handsome dowry in compensation.

The front bell rang as somebody came in, waking Tom from his reverie. It was Mr Tavy, the tall thin stick of a solicitor, calling on official business – probably one of the customers who hadn't paid his bills. Tom leapt from his post with alacrity and immediately showed him in to Mr Bullivant.

He would have left at once, but Mr Bullivant made a point of introducing him, 'This is Mr Courtney, we have hopes of him. Bright boy, just taken over the front office, and doing very well, very well.'

Tavy said nothing, but Tom went back to his desk feeling ten feet tall. The feeling was still with him at closing time.

The sight of Denzil, humbly waiting to escort the briefcase, when he himself had only to put on his hat and go home, improved his mood still further. He swung out into the street, and seeing the skinny girl from the milliner's shop out putting up the shutters, he gave her such a warm smile that for days afterwards he found her lying in wait and simpering pinkly as he passed. Tom was not displeased. Two young ladies setting their cap at him. It made a fellow feel 'quite the thing'.

Denzil missed the horse bus that night and arrived home late – later than ever because of the extra work in the office – to be greeted by the delicious smell of cooking meat as soon as he opened the door. He paused in amazement. The Vargo household had hot cooked meat once a week, if they were lucky, and that was likely to be a bit of boiled bacon or tongue.

He stood there savouring the smell. Father had done it, then. Got himself taken on at the mine. That was something. At last he'd be bringing a bit in, regular – always supposing that he didn't spend it all on drink before Mother saw a penny of it. Of course he wouldn't have wages yet. This, whatever it was, must have been bought with the remains of the Canada money. Trust father to go spending on some daft luxury, instead of worrying about the rent. Denzil shook his head sorrowfully.

'Mother?' He went through into the kitchen.

Mother wasn't there, but his father was – standing in his shirtsleeves with a carving knife in his hand, looking pleased with himself and fleshier than ever. In front of him, on the table, was a huge piece of pork. He looked up when he saw Denzil, and waved the knife in welcome. He was obviously in an expansive mood. 'Well, come in, Denzil, come in. See what your father has brought you home. Haven't seen anything like this too often, I dare swear.'

Denzil looked at the meat. It was a wonderful sight. Mother had baked it in a pan under the embers, for the skin was crisp

118

and brown and the flesh succulent. It made his mouth water to
look at it. Though, of course, they couldn't afford it – and there
was Mother wanting new boots.

But he was being churlish. That pork looked delicious – and
there was a dish of potato and turnip on the table. Often that
would have made a meal on its own. 'They took you on then,'
he said, aware that he sounded grudging.

His father scowled, and for a second Denzil expected an
outburst, but at that moment Mother came bustling in from the
outhouse with a bottle of preserves in her hand. She smiled
when she saw him – he hadn't seen her smile for days – and said
with determined cheerfulness, 'Smells grand, doesn't it Denzil?
Your father's been doing a bit down Crowdie's farm this
afternoon, and Crowdie gave him this in return. Eat like kings
tonight, shan't we?'

Denzil's answering smile froze on his face. 'What good is
that, when it comes to the rent? I thought you were going down
to the mine looking?' The words were out before he could stop
them. Of course, it was obvious. The mine wouldn't have him,
and he'd gone begging to the neighbours. Crowdie had found
some menial task for him, and given him a bit of pig out of
charity.

Father's face had turned an angry red, and he brandished the
knife menacingly. 'You mind your tongue, young fellow, or
you'll wish different. You aren't too old to feel the end of my
belt. This is my house, and don't forget it.'

'He did try down the mine,' Mother said, placatingly. 'Only
they aren't needing men, this minute. They'll let him know, of
course. Meantime, he wasn't idle. He went to Crowdie's and
lent a hand shifting stones for the wall.'

'Nothing to touch a miner when it comes to shifting stone,'
Father said, proudly. 'Crowdie said so himself. Find me more
work, too, come harvest and he's wanting to rebuild the pig-
house before winter. This wet weather's ruined the maize, he
says and he can't pay me cash, but he'll let me have some milk
and eggs and a piece of meat now and again when he has an

animal slaughtered, so sit down and we'll have a bit less of your lip.'

Ruined crops, indeed. Consideration for Mother more like, Denzil thought. If Crowdie paid Father money he knew what he'd do with it.

'It'll be grand, Denzil,' Mother said. 'I'll go back scrubbing to Mrs Eyles, and I'm sure the vicar'll have me. That'll pay the rent, more or less, and with your money and Father bringing in food, we'll manage handsome.'

Handsome, Denzil thought, as long as Crowdie had stones to shift. But there was no point saying so. Mother had enough problems as it was. They didn't often all eat together – he mustn't ruin it. He sat down, opposite his father, and held his tongue for the remainder of the meal. The pork was delicious, especially with Mother's apple preserve, but it left a bitter taste.

After dinner, Mother took the plates into the scullery. Father turned to Denzil, grinning. 'Now, wasn't that a bit handsome?'

Denzil nodded. 'Yes.' Was Father trying to make the peace? 'Yes,' he said again. 'Delicious.'

Father leaned across the table, smiling conspiratorially. 'Thing is, Denzil, I wanted a word with you. If I'm getting paid in food, I'm not going to have money, am I? And you can see how that will be awkward.'

So Father had seen the difficulties. Perhaps Denzil had misjudged him. 'It's all right,' Denzil said. 'Like Mother says, we'll manage between us.'

''Course you will.' Father's voice was dismissive. 'Only, how am I to manage, that's the thing? Man needs a bit of money in his pocket. You now, you wouldn't be without a penny or two.' He gave a wheedling smile, 'And you're getting paid again Friday.'

Denzil felt himself pale. 'I haven't got money.'

Father's face darkened and he slammed his fist on the table. 'You're a liar. You got money, I heard it in your pocket.' His voice shook with rage.

Denzil said patiently, 'I've got money, but it isn't mine to spend. I owe it to the tallyman.'

Father got to his feet and pushed the table roughly aside. It bounced against the wall, scattering the remaining forks and sending the preserve jar smashing to the floor. 'Ungrateful little wretch.' He was unbuckling his belt, 'Eats my food and refuses to give me a penny for it.'

The belt was in his hand now, buckle side out, and he advanced threateningly. Denzil looked around wildly. He snatched up the carving knife and held it before him. The other man hesitated, breathing dangerously.

There was a terrible pause as the two men eyed each other. 'Denzil!' Mother came in from the scullery, her voice high with anguish.

'He wants money,' Denzil said, holding the knifepoint steady and not moving his eyes from the belt. 'Money I owe for my clothes.'

'Give it to him. For God's sake Denzil, give it to him. He'll half kill you if you don't.' She moved to her husband and seized his arm. 'Leave the boy, Stan. Leave him alone. He'll give it to you, won't you, Denzil?'

The man flung her aside, against the wall. She slumped there, nursing her arm, saying pitifully, 'Denzil, for God's sake. You see what he's like.'

Denzil did see. Slowly, one hand still holding the knife, he withdrew a shilling from his pocket and put it on the table. His eyes never left the man. 'For your sake, Mother, not for his.'

The man relaxed, arrogant in victory, and began threading his belt back into his trousers. 'There now, I knew you'd see sense. No need for violence.' He reached out a lazy hand for the coin.

Denzil brought the knife down savagely between the out-stretched fingers. 'Oh, no you don't. Not a penny until you apologise to my mother.'

She said 'Denzil!' pleadingly, but he ignored her.

'Go on,' he said, 'say it. Tell her you are sorry for pushing her

about. It's not going to kill you, is it? Do you want that money
or don't you?'

For a moment Denzil wondered whether the man was going
to pick up a chair and kill him with it but, after a short, snorting
pause his father mumbled, 'Well, I never meant to shove her.
You, I was mad with. Ungrateful little cub, refusing to give
your old father a few pence.' He was resentful, his eyes fixed on
the shilling as he spoke.

Denzil withdrew the knife, and used the blade to flick the
coin contemptuously towards the man, then watched him
pocket it greedily.

He had lost the battle of wills. Father had the money and
would spend it all on drink. Denzil had nothing for the tallyman now. There would be interest on interest, and there was
every likelihood the same thing would happen again. If he was
not careful he would never get out of debt. Why then, watching
his father put on his scarf and hat, and swagger out towards the
Cornish Arms, did Denzil feel that somehow he had won?

Life at Fairviews had never been busier. Mrs Meacham was
taking the Coronation seriously, and threw herself into planning the day as if the King himself were coming. The best white
table linen had to be starched and ironed and mended, all the
silver polished with red lead, the crystal and glassware washed
till it sparkled, and great bowls of rose petals set in the dining-
room for days to perfume the air.

Florrie and Mrs Pritchard almost came to blows over the
cleaning – Florrie polished everything with beeswax and lavender, and then Cook followed her round sweeping the floor
with a brush. That raised dust, in more senses than one, and
Sprat had to polish everything all over again. Armfuls of red,
white and blue flowers were cut from the garden, and more
delivered to the door, all of which had to be arranged in great
brass vases under Florrie's eagle eye.

The house, though, was looking lovely and Mrs Meacham
was clearly enjoying herself. She had come – positively – to life,

and spent hours now 'sitting out', directing operations from her chair. Fitch was sent to raid the wine cellar, and Mr Raeburn was entrusted with the loyal toast. Mrs Meacham had wanted to sing again – 'God Save the King' perhaps – at the end of the great occasion but the doctor advised her against it. Too much for her system, he said, so she contented herself with cutting out little paper gondolas for Sprat to fill with sugared dragées and put on the 'banquet table'.

It was a banquet, too. Mrs Pritchard had spent days baking and boiling, and the kitchen already bulged with delectable dishes – galantines, jellies, ginger fingers, chocolate cake, chicken pie and flans. And the chief dishes had not yet been cooked. It would have fed the Cove in comfort, Sprat felt, and all this for three elderly people, though Mrs Meacham had promised all the staff a taste and a 'Coronation Basket' to take home afterwards.

So Sprat was busier than ever, what with washing Miss Raeburn's hair (a special shampoo made of rosewater and egg yolks) and helping prepare her beaded dress. The wretched thing had been hung in mothballs and had to be aired, as well as freshened under the arms, and sponged round the hems.

'Amazing,' she said to Miss Raeburn on Coronation Eve, as she helped her into nightgown and cap, 'this is just one house. Think of what it must be like, all round the country. Thousands and thousands of banquets.'

Miss Raeburn looked at her wryly, 'Even more amazing,' she said, 'to think that the Coronation would happen perfectly well without any of it. I'm not so sure it is a good thing. Violet and I are not accustomed to excitement and, as for James, no doubt he'll eat and drink too much and suffer for it afterwards. He shouldn't do it. His doctor warned him, but he takes no notice.'

Sprat gazed at her in amazement. Miss Raeburn could startle you sometimes. But there was no time to think about that. There was too much to do. Florrie was downstairs wanting help with supper trays, and candlesticks.

No time, either, to think about home, or wonder what Denzil

was doing. She did, however, make herself one promise. Come tomorrow, she would make time to look down at the beacon. It was a sort of link. Ma and Pa would be there, and there was always the chance that Denzil could see it, too.

PART THREE
Late June 1911

One

T he Coronation bonfire was a great success. Not a large
    crowd, when you thought how many people had been to
the last one, but most pits and factories had declared a whole
holiday, so sons and daughters came home for the day, and
brought their own families with them. There were more young
people in the Cove that day than there had been for years.

There were games in the afternoon. Ma and the Masons took
down a chair to watch, while Pa and Half-a-leg dragged two of
the visitors off their feet at the end of a tug rope, and the visitors
beat them hollow at running. Peter Polmean, a willing, moon-
faced boy – a bit 'wanting' but able to be trusted with a simple
message – had been sent up to Penvarris beforehand for a bag
of 'soft toffees', and the children ran races to win them. It was
hardly fair, Ma thought, no two children were the same age, but
it didn't matter – there was a toffee for them all. Peter Polmean
ran in every race, from the babies upwards, and came to share
his trophies with Ma, who was his 'friend' because she sometimes gave him a penny for running errands.

The toffees were horrid, so soft they clung to the teeth, but
afterwards there was saffron cake, splits, cream, and hot sweet
tea. Everyone toasted the new King – the Churchgoers in
blackberry wine and the Methodists in cordial. As the long
evening drew in, there were murmurs from those who 'had to go
home', so Half-a-leg went into his kitchen for a brand, and
thrust it into the beacon.

'Here!' Norah said, 'Don't do that. Wait till you see the other
fires.'

Half-a-leg laughed. 'Wait all night for them, you will. The others can follow us, for once. Anyhow, too late now. Where're those fish to?'

It *was* too late. The furze was already crackling merrily, and pretty soon everyone gave up grumbling and gathered around the fire to hold small fish on sticks of wood to the flames. The blackberry wine went round again, Half-a-leg got out his squeeze-box, and soon everyone was singing. Hymns, mostly, with the men doing the bass parts and the women holding the treble. Even the Masons joined in. Sitting there, with the last light fading, the smell of fresh-cooked fish mingling with the smell of bonfire, and the singing voices echoing over the rippling water, Ma felt an unexpected pang.

Perfect, it would have been, if only Sprat was there.

Tom had a discomfiting afternoon. It was his own fault, of course, accepting Bullivant's invitation with such alacrity. But here he was, out on the harbour, freezing to death, bored to tears and sticking out like a sore thumb.

It wasn't at all as he'd imagined. He'd had some image of boat races from a woodcut he had seen in a journal – university men in boaters and blazers, and bottles of champagne in the sunshine. Nothing could have been further from the present outing. It was every bit as dull as Mr Bullivant had promised: the men all stout and middle-aged, the women either stout – with formidable buttocks and faces to match – or thin, frail and apologetic. Olivia, although she showed more animation than usual, had eyes only for the sweating fools in the rowing boats, labouring miles out against the tide, and – after what seemed like an endless wait – labouring back in again.

'Pilot gigs,' Bullivant said to him heartily. 'Used to race each other once, to see who could get out to the ship first and guide her in. Six oars each – and they'd go out hell or high water if there was a boat to bring home. You still see it, sometimes, though it's mostly contract work now. But they do this every year, all round the coast. My wife loves to see it. Some of them race right out to the Scillies.'

Tom felt that he didn't care if they raced clear round to Australia, as long as he didn't have to stand in the cold and watch them, but he nodded with gritted teeth.

There were a good many locals about, cheering and clapping, dressed in whatever they stood up in. Some of them were waving flags, or sported ribbons in their buttonholes, but every man in Bullivant's party – barring himself – had come wrapped in greatcoats, over working suits and waistcoats. His own rakish boater, hastily bought for the occasion, looked embarrassingly out of place, and the smart striped blazer he had found in the pawnbrokers merely earned him a mocking catcall from an urchin boy, and raised eyebrows from at least one of the party. 'Didn't know you were a varsity man?' Tom, who hadn't known that it was a varsity blazer, began to wish devoutly that he were somewhere – anywhere – else.

Besides, in spite of the fine weather, it was damnably draughty. There was a sharp little wind from the sea which seemed bent on whisking his hat off, and cut through his ridiculous clothes like a cleaver. There were booths set up selling whelks and pies, but these delights were denied to him, like the wicker chairs which the booths offered to their patrons.

The party had brought rugs, but these had been commandeered by the ladies, and had either been spread on the wall to sit on, or wrapped demurely around bony ankles. Tom consoled himself with thoughts of tea, but the picnic, when it was produced with a flourish from the wicker hamper, proved to be limp tongue and potted shrimp sandwiches, which had to be washed down with warm lemonade. When Mrs Bullivant said brightly, 'Where's Tom? We've brought some of his favourite seed-cake,' his misery was complete.

Then, of all things, they wanted to go down and look at the boats. There was nothing to see, they were just boats, but the way the party went exclaiming over them you'd think they were blue pennant Cunarders at least. Of course, Olivia wanted to 'sit in' the one rowed by her relative, which was tied up beside the steps. Tom tried to help her down into it by stepping down into the boat, and almost managed to crown the afternoon by tipping them both into the water. Olivia jumped back just in time, leaving him stranded in the wretched thing. It rocked horribly, lurching treacherously under his feet. He just managed to regain his balance by grabbing wildly at a rope, and everyone laughed as though it were the greatest joke.

'Mind your step, young Courtney,' Bullivant hollered heartily, as Tom clambered gratefully back to the safety of the step. 'Not as stable as it looks.'

Stupid device, Tom thought mutinously. Almost had him overset and spoiled his clothes in the water. And he would have had to be ignominiously rescued, since he couldn't swim.

He was cold, hungry, humiliated and bored. Even when the wind finally lifted his boater and carried it merrily out to sea, he was too fed up to care. Only one thing rescued the afternoon. He managed to squeeze Olivia's hand as he helped her back into the charabanc. She didn't seem to mind.

Father went out early, Coronation morning, while Denzil was helping his mother in the garden, and didn't come home all day. Not dinnertime, which didn't surprise anyone, but when he didn't arrive for supper Mother was beginning to fret.

'Where's he to? He hasn't had a morsel all day.'

Denzil pushed back his plate – Mother had stretched the pork to make one last meal. 'Down the Cornish Arms, I should think, drinking the King's health at someone else's expense.'

Mother gave a wistful smile. 'It'll have to be. He won't have a penny of his own by this time.'

'He's not the only one,' Denzil said. 'I've had a job this week, and no mistake, with him taking that money. At my wits' end worrying how to pay the tallyman.'

Mother looked at him, concerned. 'You aren't in trouble, are you, Denzil? Don't you go borrowing money to pay your debts, my handsome, or you'll never get out of it.'

Denzil smiled. 'Can't afford to start paying compound interest. No, in the end, I pawned my pocket watch, the one your father left me. Hated to part with it but I had to do something. Goodness knows how I'll ever redeem it.'

Mother sighed. 'I'd help you if I could, you know that. Maybe I could find you something you could pawn. That silver teapot, for instance.' She went to the mantelpiece and took it down. 'Here, you take it. He'd never notice it was gone.' She was shaking out needles and thread on the table as she spoke.

Denzil got up and went round to join her. 'No, Mother, no. You'll need it yourself one of these days, to keep up the rent.'

She looked at him, hopelessly. 'We're never going to keep up the rent, Denzil. This month, perhaps, and next, but one of these days he'll drink it all, and the both of us'll end up in the workhouse.' Her voice was shaking.

'Mother!' He had never heard her talk like this. 'You shan't end up in the workhouse, I'll send money home, you'll see.'

'And what do you think will happen if you do? You've seen what he's like. I can't stand up to him no more than you can. No, you see to yourself. You've got your own way to make.' She looked at him. 'I'd be better off in the workhouse, sometimes. Out the way of his temper, at least.'

Denzil shook his head fiercely. 'I'll pay the rent direct.'

She had emptied the teapot now and was thrusting it towards him. 'You take this anyhow. Get grandfather's pocket watch out of hock. Your father need never know.'

'*Know what?*' Father! They had been so engrossed that they had not noticed him come in. He was standing in the doorway, drunk and menacing, his face twisted with rage. 'Well, woman? Spit it out. What needn't I know?'

She went towards him, 'Nothing. I was talking to Denzil.'

He pushed her aside. 'Stealing my silver, is that it?'

'He didn't steal it, Stan.' She was talking fast. 'I gave it to him to pay his debts. 'Tisn't the boy's fault, Stan, you leave him be.'

He whirled round, striking her fiercely across the face, 'Shut your noise woman, and fetch me my supper. This is between me and my son. My son!' His voice was sneering. 'A great, wet streak of candle grease with a stuck-up voice, who never did an honest hand's turn in his life. Thinks himself too good for the likes of me – and then steals my silver. Well,' he took a step forward, his hand unfastening the belt again, 'we'll see about that.'

Denzil stood his ground. He said deliberately, 'Don't hit my mother.'

'Or?' It was contemptuous.

Denzil felt his heart pounding and his mouth was dry, but he said firmly, 'If I ever see you lift a finger to her again, I'll hit *you.*'

There was no backing down this time. His father let out a bellow of incoherent rage and, whirling round, seized the rickety chair in the corner, and brought it down with a crash in the direction of Denzil.

Denzil saw it coming, and had time to side-step. The chair crashed against the wall, so forcefully that it splintered into pieces. The jagged leg made a formidable weapon and his father was advancing on him again.

Denzil raised his fists.

'Stan!' His mother seized her husband's arm, pleadingly, 'Denzil! Don't! He'll kill us both.'

It was possible, Denzil realised. The man was maddened with drink and anger. But there was no time to think. His mother was already sprawling on the floor and Father was advancing on him, wielding the broken chair.

Denzil had learned to box at school, and he attempted a punch, but the man brushed it aside as though it were a cobweb, and brought the chair leg down on Denzil in a slashing blow. Denzil raised his arms to protect his face, and the wood caught him savagely just below the shoulder, making him flinch with pain. A moment later, a glancing blow hit his face. He could feel his eye closing and the swelling of the hot weal where the wood had struck him on the cheek. The man, breathing heavily, raised his arm again.

This was no time for gentlemanly fists. Denzil, driven by some primitive impulse, lowered his head and butted the man, with all his force, full in the stomach, and then – without pausing – kneed him viciously in the groin.

His father, with a look of amazement – let out a howl and doubled up in pain. Before he could straighten up, Denzil seized the heavy iron skillet from the hook on the wall and brought it down with all his weight on the back of his father's head. The man gave a little moan and slumped to the floor.

'Denzil,' his mother, bleeding from a cut on her cheek, shouted out. 'Denzil, what have you done?'

'He's breathing,' Denzil said, breathing heavily himself. 'Stunned him, that's all. God knows what will happen when he comes to. He'll kill us.'

She shook her head. 'I'll be all right. It's you I'm afraid for. You make him worse, somehow. Go. Go now, before he wakes up.'

He hesitated, 'I can't leave you. The man's an animal.' Like father, like son, he thought, sick to the stomach with the realisation of what he'd done.

'You must.' She was weeping, but her voice was firm. 'I'll write. The vicar down St Evan will help me. Where'll you go?'

He hadn't had time to think of that. 'Can't go anywhere today, got no money.' A thought came to him. 'Got the key to the office, though. I could go there, tonight. I'll find somewhere tomorrow. I'll let you know where: send a message to St Evan.' Supposing any landlady would have him, he thought. A proper sight he'd look, with a bruised arm and swollen face. But he didn't say that to his mother. She was looking panic-stricken as the man on the floor stirred. 'Yes, all right. I'll go. And mind what I said, I'll see the rent is paid. I promise you that. I won't have you in the workhouse.'

He didn't stop to take his belongings – he had none to speak of anyway – and he left the teapot on the table. He held his mother briefly in his arms, then, pulling on his vulcanised coat and his hat, he set off into the night. In the distance, he could see the beacons burning.

Two

Mrs Meacham was better than her word. Sprat could hardly wait to get home the day after the Coronation, with her basket of treats: a great slice of cold beef, some chicken jelly, half a fruit cake and little mushroom things which Cook called 'volley-vons'. Make a feast for the Masons, that would.

She had hardly reached the front door, however, before Ma was there to greet her. 'Sprat, my handsome, I'm some glad you've come. I'm sorry to send you off again, minute you arrive, but I want you to run up to St Just – quick as you can.' She didn't even glance at the basket.

'St Just?'

Ma nodded. 'See you can get the doctor to come here, as soon as may be. Elsie Mason's been took bad in the night. Running a terrible fever, she is, tossing and turning, and doesn't know anybody. Now she can't seem to move her legs. And if doctor's worried about money, tell him Mrs Mason'll write off to her bank, soon as she gets the bill.'

A doctor! Sprat looked at Ma, open mouthed. People in the Cove didn't have doctors – not unless they were dying, and sometimes not even then. But the Mason's were London folk. Perhaps it was different there.

'Well, go on then,' Ma said urgently. She looked pale and worn, as if she had been up most of the night. 'Don't just stand there. I promised Mrs Mason I'd send you, soon as you came.'

Sprat nodded, and set off up the path. The men were on the tide-line raking over the remains of the beacon, but she hardly heard their greeting. Doctors were for the gentry – unless there

135

was a desperate birth, or someone half cut his arm off on a piece of rigging. It was two miles or more to St Just, and she hurried all the way. What if the doctor wouldn't come? Or suppose he was out? Everyone knew he covered half the parish on that chestnut mare of his, or drove about in his little shay. He could be gone hours.

She was lucky. The doctor was saddling up as she turned in through the gate and, as soon as he saw her, he stopped. 'Hello there!' he said, with a smile. 'What's happened to Mrs Meacham? Not fallen and broken anything, I hope?'

He recognised her, then, from his visits to Fairviews. Absurdly, that made her feel better. 'No sir, 'tisn't Mrs Meacham this time, it's someone from up London. Boarding with my Ma, and been taken sick down the Cove.' She blurted out the whole story.

He didn't interrupt. When she had finished, he looked grave. 'I'll be there in an hour. Perhaps less. I promised to look in on the vicar's child who has taken a chill. I'll do that first – mustn't take infection there. I'll come as soon as I can. I know the house – I think I attended an old lady there, once.'

She nodded. 'Ma's mother. She died after.' That sounded awful and she added quickly, 'Ma's used to fever. She had my Aunt home ill for months. She'll know what to do till you get there. Thank you, sir, I'll tell her you're on your way.'

'No, wait!' his voice called her back. 'Better you don't go back to the house. If this is that fever from London it could be highly infectious. It's been in all the journals. Spreading like wildfire and people are dying from it. Can't have you taking it up to Fairviews. I'm sorry, my dear, I'll explain to your family. But while there's this fever in the house, you'd better not go home.'

He swung into the saddle and was gone, leaving Sprat gazing after him. Not knowing what else to do, she went and sat on the top stile and looked at the sea, watching the men on Crowdie's farm shifting barrows of stones to the yard.

She waited a long time, but there was no sign of Denzil.

*   *   *

Denzil woke early, stiff and sore from a cold, uncomfortable night on the tiled floor. He had managed to let himself in, in the dark, but – having neither lamp nor candles – had not dared go further than the lobby. Not that he'd have lit a lamp if he had found one, the light might have attracted the attention of a passing policeman. He had only narrowly dodged them and their bull's-eye lanterns as it was.

He scrambled painfully to his feet. His arm throbbed and his left eye refused to open properly. When he touched it, his whole cheek was puffy and swollen, and his head swam. He lurched out into the yard and splashed his face in the horse trough, but it didn't help. He had no clean shirt, which was an oversight, but he did struggle into his office clothes, which were still where he had left them. He could hardly raise his arm to put on his coat. There was no mirror in the building but he tidied himself as best he could.

There was nothing to eat, but he cupped his hands and scooped up some water to moisten his tongue. The clock in Bullivant's office said six fifteen, too early to do anything but wait. He did, though, let himself into the back office, where he could at least sit on his stool. There was kindling and coal, and he lit a small fire. He would have to account for that, to Bullivant, but the warmth made him feel a little better.

When the clock had edged around to eight, he let himself out and set off to pick up the briefcase as usual. One or two passers-by gave him a startled look, and he realised that his bruises were attracting attention. He would have to say something to Bullivant. He was still rehearsing ways of confessing everything when he arrived at the house and knocked the door.

The housemaid who answered it took one look at Denzil, screamed, 'Oh, my dear Heaven,' and went running back into the hall. A door opened inside the house, and Mrs Bullivant came bustling out, followed by a plain girl with loopy hair whom Denzil instantly recognised as the famous Olivia. At the same moment, Bullivant himself appeared at the foot of the stairs.

137

There was a moment's silence and then everyone spoke at once.

'Vargo? What is the meaning of this . . .'

'What has happened? You poor boy!'

'Father, who is it?'

Denzil said, through a mouth that almost refused to answer his bidding, 'I'm sorry Mr Bullivant. A bit of an accident.' He looked at their shocked faces and his courage failed him. 'A runaway horse.' He was a poor liar and he felt himself flush as he said it.

Mrs Bullivant clasped her hands together, and looked at her husband triumphantly. 'You said as much, didn't you, Charles? Those Coronation fire-crackers would upset the horses. Poor lad. Look at his face. It reared up at you, I suppose?'

Denzil nodded dumbly. He didn't trust himself to voice another lie.

Bullivant was looking at him benevolently. 'Should have sent in word, young Vargo. We'd have managed without you for a bit. You can't be seen in the office with a face like that. You get off home, come back in a day or two.'

Denzil felt a prickle of horror across his scalp, and he almost swayed. 'I can't afford to do that, Mr Bullivant. Need the money. No one'll see me. I'll keep out the back.'

Bullivant shook his head, 'All the same . . .'

There was nothing for it. Denzil took a deep breath. 'Truth is, Mr Bullivant, I can't go home. Matter of fact, I even slept in the office last night – I still got that key you gave me, and with one thing and another—'

'In the office!' Bullivant interrupted.

'I'm sorry, Mr Bullivant.' Denzil said abjectly. 'Didn't know what else to do. Couldn't go home, and I'd have been on the street all night else.'

'Well . . .!' Bullivant began, but his daughter interrupted him.

Her sallow face flushed as she said, urgently, 'Of course he couldn't walk home, Papa. With his poor face so damaged it is a

138

wonder he can stand.' She turned to Denzil, and gave him a timid smile. 'You should have come here, Mr Vargo. I'm sure Papa would have arranged a cab for you. Perhaps he could do so now.'

Bullivant coughed and looked embarrassed. He would do no such thing, Denzil knew.

Denzil covered the moment, 'You are very kind, Miss Bullivant, but he could hardly do that. It is no casual distance to Penvarris. It takes me over an hour to walk.'

'Penvarris!' Now Mrs Bullivant was joining in. 'You walk there and back every day? Why ever don't you take a room in town?'

Denzil's arm throbbed and his head was spinning, or he might not have said, bluntly, 'It is not as easy as that, Madam. A landlady would want payment in advance. If I could find the money, I was hoping to do it today, in fact, but who is going to take me anyway, with my face in this state?'

There was a silence. Mrs Bullivant looked at her husband, but neither of them spoke. It was Olivia who burst out, 'Why, he could take a room here, couldn't he? There is that nursemaid's room in the attic which is standing empty. I have heard you talk of letting it, before. And Papa could simply deduct the rent from his wages, couldn't you, Papa?'

Papa looked as if he wished Olivia struck dumb. 'I hardly feel, my dear . . .'

But Mrs Bullivant said sharply, 'Charles, that boy is going to make a spectacle of us all by collapsing on our doorstep if you are not careful. If he slept in the office, I daresay he hasn't eaten, and he must be perished with cold. No wonder he is faint. Bring him inside, for pity's sake, and let us at least finish this conversation away from prying ears.' She took Denzil firmly by the arm, but it was the damaged one, and he flinched at her touch.

She looked at him sharply. 'Your arm, too? Come in and let me see.' She led the way into the drawing-room. Denzil obediently rolled up his sleeve, noticing – through a mist of pain –

that the room was rather less grand than Tom had described it. Bullivant stood by, helplessly, and watched. In the company of his wife, he didn't seem at all the fearsome and decisive figure who dominated the office.

Mrs Bullivant looked at the arm. It was ugly, a swollen mass of greenish-purple and blue. She tutted. 'A horse, you say? Courageous of you. A wonder the animal didn't break your arm.' She turned to her husband. 'Now then, Charles, you'd best send Daisy out for a cab, and get yourself to the office. And when she's done that, Daisy can bring me my zinc ointment, some witch-hazel and a clean hot cloth wrung out in vinegar. We'd better do something about these bruises. It's obvious the boy can't work today.'

Olivia gave Denzil another smile. 'And he can stay here, can't he, Papa? Until he's a little better?'

To his amazement, Denzil heard Bullivant say, wearily, 'Very well, my dear. As you wish. For a day or two, perhaps.'

The doctor's visit was a trial to Ma, not just because of his errand. As she explained to Norah Roberts afterwards, on the doorstep, he was a kind of visitor. 'After all, it wasn't a Nicholls who was ill. I didn't know whether to offer him tea and splits. Besides, Sprat never came to say he was coming, and I hadn't dusted the window sills. He must have noticed.'

Norah, who had called by on the excuse of borrowing a bit of sugar, nodded sympathetically. 'I'm surprised at Sprat. She might have come back and let you know.'

Ma had been feeling irritated about that herself, but she wasn't going to stand here and listen to anyone else say so. She said stoutly, 'Doctor told her not to, he says, and she did what she was told, like a sensible girl. Dangerous thing, this fever. Catch it easier than winking. Doctor is going to send the fever cart, soon as he can arrange it, and move Elsie to the isolation hospital. Some trick that'll be, down this hill.'

It was intended as a hint, but Norah didn't move. Everyone knew what the fever cart meant. The very sight of the high, dark-varnished wagon, with its slatted sides like a wooden window blind, its canvas stretchers and lugubrious horse, was enough to send a shiver down anyone's spine. Few people who were taken away in that waggon ever came home again, except – like Gypsy – in time to die. Mount Misery was well named.

'Never had time to do the sills,' Ma said again. 'Not by the time I'd set up sheets soaked in disinfectant across the bedroom door and got another bath of it on the doorstep. Mind, the doctor was impressed with that. Just as well I had the stuff to hand, out in the wash-house since Gypsy died.'

Norah was suitably awed. 'What's all that for?'

'Keep the germs off,' Ma said. 'Can't be too careful, with fever in the house. Mrs Mason wants to get a room nearer the hospital, but we'll have to be careful for a week or two, see we don't catch it or pass it on. All right in the open air, the doctor says, but we shouldn't get too close to people.'

Norah's eyes widened. 'Suppose I shouldn't stand here, then. Keeping you gossiping, when you've got work to do.' She edged away.

Ma smiled to herself. Powerful things, those germs. Wasn't much else would keep Norah Roberts away if there was news to be had.

''Course,' Norah called, from the safety of the road, 'if there's anything we can do, Half-a-leg and me . . .'

'There might be, at that,' Ma said, struck by a sudden thought. 'Pa's got some grown frames ordered for this boat. Got held up by these strikes. All paid for and that, but now they've come and they've got to be signed for.'

'Groan frames?' Norah said. 'What they groaning for?'

'Grown,' Ma explained, exasperated. 'Grown on purpose like, to make the right shape. Lot of folk steam the frames these days, but you can still get grown ones if you know where to look. Old ways are best, Pa says. The stuff can come out with Crowdie's timber for the barn, and he'll get it down to us, but someone'll have to go down Bullivant's and tell them. Can't go ourselves with this fever in the house.'

'Well,' Norah said, ' 'Fraid I aren't able to help you there. Only went to Penzance market Thursday so I shan't be going again for a week or two. If I hear of anyone who is going, I'll let you know. Though Mrs Meacham must send someone into town. No end of stuff wanted, in a house like that. They could drop that note in for you, no trouble. I'm sure Mrs Meacham wouldn't mind, things being as they are. Why don't you get Sprat to ask about it?'

'See what would happen there, can't you? Wheedle Mrs Meacham and go to Bullivant's herself.' Ma was startled into indiscretion.

Norah smiled grimly. 'Wouldn't hurt if she did. She wouldn't see that Vargo boy anyway. Seems Mr Bullivant has left him scribbling out in the back office, got in a lad to run errands and promoted another boy to the front counter.'

'How d'you know that?'

Norah smirked. 'Half-a-leg's cousin rows in the gig races, and Bullivant was there yesterday, with this boy, making a fuss of him. Talk of Penzance, it is. Not that I'm surprised about Vargo. Never amount to anything, those 'up-overers', for all they give themselves airs. Anyhow, I'll have to go. Half-a-leg'll be wanting his tea. Ta very much for the sugar.' And wrapping her shawl around her, Norah toddled away.

Ma watched her go, thoughtfully. If Norah Roberts was right – and she usually was – she might send a message to Fairviews after all. Someone from up there was sure to go into town soon, and it was unlikely to be Sprat. And even if it was, it seemed she wouldn't see Denzil. Pa needed the wood, and no one else could go. Yes, best thing all round. When Mrs Polmean's Peter came past later with his winkle-pickings Ma gave him a penny to take the consignment note up there with a message for Sprat.

It gave her one less thing to worry about.

Three

S prat was astonished to have a caller – and even more astonished to find that it was Peter Polmean. He was a big boy, but what Norah Roberts called 'Not-azackly', so Sprat asked him to repeat the message three times to make sure.

Even then, she didn't believe it. 'You sure, Peter? Ma wants me to take this in to Bullivant's for her?'

Peter grinned his big 'not-azackly' grin. 'Oh, 'ess! I heard 'un, clear as a bell. Ask'er, when they goes in town for summat, can she fetch this to Mr Bullivant's same time. Right in me ear-'ole, make sure I had it right.'

'I see.' Sprat did see. The message wasn't for her, personally, to go to Bullivant's. Florrie went generally, once a week, and obviously Ma meant for Sprat to ask her. But Ma couldn't write to speak of, and Peter's spoken version gave Sprat an idea. She looked around, and her eye lighted on the tea tray, still waiting to be cleared.

'You like cake, Peter?'

The moon face lighted up with childish pleasure. 'Oh, Miss Sprat, I do love a bit a cake. Only me mother won't let me have 'un if there's jam in 'un. Says I plaster myself in it.'

'Well, you're quite safe, Peter, this is sultana cake.' She put a slice of it into his grimy hand, and saw his grin widen. 'Thank you for bringing this.'

'You want a winkle?' he said, offering the smelly bucket.

She shook her head, smiling, and closed the door. Through the window she could see him, wandering happily off down the cliff path, stuffing the sultana cake into his mouth with his wrinkly hand. Halfway down, he stopped and put the rest of the slice carefully into the bucket, obviously intending to share it with his mother. Peter might be 'not-azackly', but his heart was good.

Sprat felt full of scheming by comparison. Somehow, before Monday, she had to find some reason for being sent to Penzance. It wasn't easy. Most things were delivered weekly to the house and the things that weren't – bluing, for instance, or wicks for the lamps – were purchased by Florrie when she went into town with the order.

It was Miss Raeburn who presented the opportunity, as Sprat was helping her to prepare for bed on Sunday night.

'It's no good, Nicholls,' the old lady said, tucking her thin hair into the starched night cap and waving away the glass of hot milk which Sprat had brought up for her, 'I simply cannot manage that tonight. It is as well we do not have a Coronation every month. All this rich food is too much for my stomach. I do wish I had brought my Epsom salts. Remind me to ask Florrie to fetch some when she goes to town on Wednesday. And I want some lavender water and scented soap from the chemist. I don't want to offend Violet, but I do prefer my own brand. Till then I suppose I'll have to suffer.'

Sprat took a deep breath. 'If you could spare me,' she said humbly, 'I could go and get them for you tomorrow. I know what soap you like.'

She half expected a rebuke, but Miss Raeburn smiled. 'And how long would that take you? You will be wanted to serve at dinner.'

'Wouldn't take above an hour or two,' Sprat said, rather inaccurately. 'I'd be back in plenty of time, especially if I came home on the horse bus.' Wasn't her fault, she told herself, if it was the same one Denzil caught.

Miss Raeburn was nodding thoughtfully. 'Yes, it might be a good idea. There are a number of small errands you could run for me at the same time. My black shoes need heeling, and you can take my fob watch to be cleaned. I notice it is losing slightly.' The shrewd eyes twinkled. 'And whatever it is that you want to do in town, Nicholls, I'm sure you can manage to do it at the same time. No, don't protest! No one ever volunteered to walk from here to Penzance unless they wanted to go in the first place.'

Sprat was blushing to the tips of her ears. 'I do have an errand to run for my Pa, if I can.'

The old lady smiled.' Of course you may do that. As well as your own errand, if necessary.' She gave Sprat such a knowing look that Sprat blushed the more. 'Only be sure you don't miss the bus. I don't wish to incommode Violet.'

'Yes, Miss Raeburn. Thank you, Miss Raeburn.'

But the next day, laden with her shopping – Miss Raeburn had added all kinds of things to her list, from sal volatile to sealing wax – she found that she could hardly pluck up the courage to go into Bullivant's at all. It seemed so brazen somehow, accosting Denzil at his work. Half a dozen times she walked past the doorway without daring to go in.

There was no help for it. If she did not deliver that note soon the office would be closing. She swallowed hard, took a deep breath and marched resolutely up the steps, through the entrance hall and into the front office.

Denzil wasn't there.

She had a confused impression of book-lined shelves, glass partitions, wooden counters and mahogany doors. A smart young man with pomaded hair and a brilliantine smile came out into the office and asked what she wanted, so she explained her business and handed over the note.

The youth looked pained. 'Split consignment,' he said. 'Might be an extra half a crown for cartage.'

'Don't know anything about that,' Sprat said. Where was Denzil?

The youth sighed. 'Need a special chit for this.' He started scrabbling through a sheaf of papers.

Sprat said, placatingly. 'Wonder you keep track, sometimes. All those papers to see to.' The extra fee wouldn't be a problem.

Mr Zackary's son kept a shop in town. She'd pop over and let him know. Her eyes, however, kept searching the inner recesses. The door to the back office was wide open, but she couldn't see Denzil anywhere.

The young man produced a slip of paper triumphantly. 'I've got that in hand then,' he smiled. 'You leave it to me. Was there anything else, Miss?'

She found herself saying, 'Mr Vargo . . .?'

His face darkened. 'Mr Vargo isn't here, I'm sorry. Hasn't been in for days. Is there anything I can do?'

She shook her head, hastily, and hurried out. All the cheerful goods displayed at the shopfronts and spilling into the street – enamel saucepans, apples, handbags – seemed suddenly dreary. Even the mechanical pig with the cleaver and striped apron in the butcher's window had a melancholy air.

Denzil wasn't there. Why? Was he ill, perhaps? Her heart seemed to sink to her boots. Well, there was nothing she could do. She left the message at Zackary's and that left only one job to do. Miss Raeburn's watch.

She took it in, as instructed, to the jeweller's at the bottom of Causewayhead, but as she set off again the heavens opened. In seconds, it was raining stair-rods. That was all she needed – to get her good coat and her uniform sodden! She dashed back to the shelter of the doorway.

All at once the door of the jeweller's opened again, and a young woman came out. Sprat knew her slightly, she had been at school in Penvarris years ago. She was clearly in service, too, though her uniform extended to a neat waterproof cape. She looked at Sprat dispiritedly.

'Some weather, innit?'

Sprat nodded. 'Pass off in a minute, I expect.' She nodded towards the small brown-paper packet in the girl's hand. 'Buying something?'

The girl grinned at the pleasantry. 'For me? Not likely. I've come down for Mrs Trevarnon – brought a ring in last week, and wanted it altered. Never gave it a thought till today, when she decided to wear her burgundy costume, then, suddenly, nothing will do and I must come and fetch this to go with it. And now look at the rain. I shall get soaked. All for a bit of a ring. Pretty thing, though.' She opened the envelope and drew out the box. 'Want to see?'

Sprat grinned. 'But . . . Mrs Trevarnon?'

'What she doesn't know won't hurt her.' The girl lifted the little lid. 'Pretty, innit?'

It was pretty. A red stone set around with little diamond things. Surely, Sprat thought, she had seen something like it before? 'Lovely.'

'Should be lovely, too,' the girls said. 'Cost a guinea, just to have it altered. And she paid no end for it in the first place. Thirty guineas, I heard her say.' She laughed. 'I wish someone would give me thirty guineas. I wish someone would give me thirty pennies! I need a new blouse, and that two and six would do me nicely. Anyway, rain's stopping.' She put the box carefully away. 'Can't stand here gassing all day, she'll have me for tripes.' She pulled up the hood of her cape and set off into the downpour.

Sprat loitered a little longer. That ring. What did it remind her of? Of course! That ring of Gypsy's that Ma sold. Couldn't be the same one, could it? 'Course not. This one was worth twice as much. Probably lots of rings looked just the same – like wedding rings. She'd heard Gypsy say her wedding ring was made of special gold – something to do with carrots – and cost ten times as much as Ma's, though it looked exactly like it.

Well, no time to stand here dreaming. Time to make a dash for the horse bus.

It was still raining, and she was dripping wet by the time she caught it. She was hoping against hope, but there was no sign of Denzil.

After the girl had left, Tom stood for a moment staring after her. Didn't often get girls coming into the office, especially not pretty girls like that one. Well, he had impressed her, though he hadn't been able to find the chit he was looking for. The docket he had in his hand wasn't the right one at all. He'd have to enter it all up, though since it was going out on an existing load, there would be no extra fee. He'd only said that to look important.

The girl was right, it was no wonder things got confused sometimes. It was always these extra bits and bobs that caused the problems – like that extra consignment which had nearly got him into difficulties after the flood. Hadn't remembered to enter it up, but he'd managed to talk himself out of trouble. Though Vargo had known, he was sure of it.

Denzil Vargo. The very name was enough to make Tom grit his teeth. The blighter had been nothing but a thorn in the flesh ever since he arrived. When Denzil had failed to appear for work the day after the Coronation, Tom had been secretly elated. There had been no message, and Bullivant would not put up with unannounced absence for long.

His glee was short-lived. Far from being in disgrace, it turned out that Denzil had contrived to wangle his way into Bullivant's own house, with Mrs Bullivant running round after him like Florence Nightingale. Some nonsense about being kicked in the face by a horse. Worst of all Tom's own Sunday visit had been discreetly postponed. Tom felt a certain sympathy with the horse.

Trust Vargo to have that smashing-looking girl come chasing after him. Very beguiling: with her sparkling blue eyes and fair hair. Trim little figure, too. The mousy girl in the milliner's shop seemed very drab in comparison. And as for Olivia! Tom cursed inwardly at the unkind hand of fate and went back bad-temperedly to searching for his chit. Mr Taylor'd had a 'system' for papers, but Tom had put his stamp on things by reorganising the drawers and now he couldn't find these slips for the life of him.

He was interrupted in his search by the arrival of Mr White, the owner of White's Emporium. He was an important customer, and couldn't be kept waiting. Tom slid the paper into his coat pocket and stepped forward to deal smilingly with him. He was good at talking to customers – so good, that when Mr Bullivant came in a little later, with Olivia on his arm, Mr White said, loud enough for Tom to hear, 'Pleasure to come in here, these days, Bullivant.'

Bullivant smiled, and Tom preened, stealing a look at Olivia. Rabbit's face she might be, but she had money coming to her. More than could be said of Denzil's girl.

Mr White was still talking. 'I'd be glad of some advice, too, if you've got a moment. These dock strikes are affecting us badly – I'm thinking of switching to rail. Won't delay you long.'

Bullivant looked reluctant, but said heartily enough. 'Of course. Come into my office for a moment. Olivia, my dear, excuse me a moment. Tom will get you a chair, I'll be as quick as I can.' He turned to the customer, 'Don't know that it will help to change to the railways. The trouble is spreading to them, too, from what I hear.'

Mr White scowled. 'Everyone after shorter hours and more pay – I don't know! And the government encourages them! Talking of a sixty-hour week and a fortnight's paid holiday. For shop workers, if you please!' He jerked his head at Tom, 'Mind you don't start getting ideas, young fellow!' He followed Bullivant into the inner office.

Tom fetched the required chair and Olivia sat down in it. He had never been alone with her before. There was a silence. Tom didn't know what to say, and Olivia didn't help. She sat composedly with her hands in her lap.

He thought of something. 'Hear what he said, did you? Pleasure to come in here these days.' He smiled at her encouragingly.

'That's nice.' She didn't sound thrilled.

'Bet your father's pleased, having me in the front office. First impressions count. And it's not just meeting people, there's a lot of paperwork and things.'

'I'm sure there is. Please, don't let me interrupt your work.'

'Talking to visitors *is* my work,' he said, but she refused to be charmed. He said, rather sourly, 'Of course, we're doubly busy today, being short-handed.'

This time she did smile. She lifted her head and the little rabbit's eyes were positively animated. 'Oh, yes. Poor Denzil. You must miss him sorely.'

For a moment, Tom was flattered, then realisation dawned. The animation was not for him, it was for that damned Denzil. 'He only works in the back office,' Tom began scathingly, but he was interrupted by the reappearance of Mr Bullivant and the customer. Olivia was commandeered by her father, and Tom had the front office to himself again.

There was a bubbling hatred in his heart. Damn Denzil Vargo, and his young woman, too. Devil take the both of them. The wretched chit could wait.

And then, of all confounded luck, a drenched messenger boy arrived on a bicycle and produced a damp envelope containing 2/6d. 'From Mr Zackary. To pay the extra cartage on that consignment. Wants a receipt, mind.'

Tom hesitated. Look a proper chump now, explaining this away. He hadn't found that paper either. Well, he'd see to it afterwards. He took the consignment note from his pocket, stuck on a postage stamp from the sheet in the book, and scribbled – *Payment in full. Received with thanks.* – across the bottom. He put it in an envelope and handed it to the boy.

'New system,' he said, feeling the need to excuse himself. 'Excess cartage fee. Have to do something to speed things up, what with all these dock strikes and split consignments.'

The boy nodded. 'Causing problems everywhere,' he said. 'There'll be shortages of coal, soon. Stop the pumping engines down Penvarris, that would, and then where will they be? Down the poorhouse, that's where.' He tucked the envelope into a leather pouch at his belt. 'That's where I'll be, too, if I don't get on. Pouring torrents it is out there, and I've got to cycle to St Evan with this.'

Tom nodded vaguely. The half-crown was still on the counter where he had checked the contents of the envelope. It looked comfortingly solid. Tom shut his eyes. Who was ever going to know? Everything balanced. Mr Crowdie's bill had already been paid, the rest of this consignment was neatly entered into the books. Who was going to notice this extra bit of cartage? Certainly not the girl. She knew nothing about it, she had said so herself. Serve her right, anyway, and Denzil, too. And the Bullivants, for that matter. That trip to the gig boats had ruined his best boots.

Tom stretched out his hand and put the money in his pocket. Oddly, it made him feel a little better. He was positively cheerful by closing time.

Denzil was rather enjoying his unexpected stay with the Bullivants. The nursemaid's bedroom, which Mrs Bullivant had been rather apologetic about, was considerably more comfortable than his room at home. There was a rag mat on the floor, a good iron bedstead with a soft mattress and patchwork blankets – even a small fireplace and a little bucket of coals. There was a curtained corner partition with a rail for hanging clothes – supposing that you had any – and a marble washstand with a washbasin set into it, a white jug and a tiled surround with a soap dish and a little mirror behind. Denzil had never had such luxury in his life.

Mrs Bullivant, to his surprise, seemed to treat him as if he were a sort of family invalid instead of a perfectly healthy young man who happened to have an injured face, and a mere employee at that. True, what he saw in the mirror had rather alarmed him, but Mrs Bullivant insisted that he went to bed, and sent Daisy up with scrambled eggs and repeated cups of beef tea. Denzil, who had eaten nothing since the night before, devoured it gratefully. If this was comfortable living, he thought, he could readily adapt to it.

Daisy, the maid-of-all-work, seemed to regard him as a curiosity. She must have been rushed off her feet, with the house to see to, but every time he looked up she seemed to be hovering outside his door, which was just ajar, pretending to be busy with a dustpan and brush.

At last he said, 'Making extra work for you, all this.'

She had been waiting for him to speak because she put down her tools at once and came to lean against the door frame.

'Feeling a bit better, are you? We're all right to chat for a minute,' she said. 'Mrs B's gone off to one of her charity meetings, and Mr B's taken Miss Olivia down town. See how that Mr Courtney's doing without him.' She was a big, florid dark-haired girl, with a voice as generous as her bottom.

Denzil gazed at her from his wounded eye. 'You know Mr Courtney?' It was a silly question. Of course she did, from serving him tea every Sunday.

Daisy grimaced. 'Been here a few times. Friend of yours, is he?'

Denzil said carefully, 'We worked together for a time.'

She smiled knowingly. 'I don't believe you like him any more'n I do. Too big for his boots, if you ask me. But Mr Bullivant seems to think the sun shines out of him. Mrs B, too. Mind, she would. Heart as big as Bodmin Moor.'

'And Miss Bullivant?' Denzil found himself asking.

'Oh, Mr B's got it in mind to marry them off, that's clear. Friend of the family and all that. Lord knows what Miss Olivia thinks about it. Aren't so many young men been allowed within smiling distance, so it's at least a novelty, though I wouldn't care for it myself.'

'But surely,' Denzil said, 'Mr Bullivant wouldn't . . . I mean, it was Miss Bullivant who suggested that I could stay here. Her father only agreed for her sake. If he thought she didn't want to—'

'Oh yes,' Daisy said. 'Do anything for her. But it wouldn't occur to him that Miss Olivia might have opinions about it. Treat her like a child they do – see how they've got her dressed – and she doesn't know any different. Glad to be settled and provided for, I daresay – and it takes care of the business, besides. Glad I haven't got money to worry about, sometimes.'

She wouldn't say that, Denzil thought bitterly, if she had as little as he did. He was about to ask her about her own life, when there was a noise in the street below. Daisy hurriedly peeped through the landing window.

'It's Mrs B come home,' she said, collecting her brushes hastily. 'And me here gossiping with half the chores undone. Here, give me that tray and I'll take it down with me, make myself look a bit busy. Anything else you're needing? I'll bring you up a bit of tea later on.'

But if she did, Denzil did not see it. She hadn't been gone five minutes before he was fast asleep.

Four

O n Tuesday morning, the fever cart came. The doctor had been quick about it, but it couldn't be soon enough for Ma. The last few days had been a nightmare. Everything boilable had to be boiled, from teacups to hairnets, and every-thing else – including her hands – plunged into baths of neat disinfectant before and after every visit to the sickroom. Every day had become wash-day, which meant the house and garden were full of damp washing. And special food had to be prepared – isinglass jelly and arrowroot gruel – until the girl was too sick even to sip at that. Mrs Mason had offered to help, but Ma wouldn't have her in the kitchen, and since she wasn't allowed in the sickroom either, she skulked unhappily around the house, making twice the washing-up, needing to be fed and comforted and offered endless cups of tea. No, the fever cart hadn't come a moment too soon.

It clattered, skittering down the hill, its high wooden sides swaying dangerously, and the horse half on its haunches to brace the weight. Half the Cove came out to watch as it came to a standstill at the end of the Row; the other half, as Pa said later, stayed inside and watched behind the curtains.

Ma was already at the door as the driver and attendant opened the long back doors of the cart and took out the rolled canvas stretcher, and she showed them silently where the patient was. It was a wriggle to get it from the narrow hall into the best room, and even more of a squeeze to open it out when they got there, but they managed it finally.

Ma watched from the doorway as they scooped Elsie Mason

up in a clean blanket and strapped her securely to the stretcher. She was moaning deliriously but she didn't stir, and they hoisted her between them and took her out to the cart as if she weighed no more than a feather.

'Make sure you air the room, mind,' the attendant said, when the stretcher was safely slotted into place. 'Boil everything, in a mild poison solution for preference, and you'd better keep yourselves to yourselves for a week or two. Doctor thinks it's infantile paralysis, so it's unlikely you'll catch it, but you can carry germs, so keep away from others, young people specially.'

'Infantile paralysis!' Mrs Mason, who had been hovering nearby, got out her handkerchief and began to cry. Ma, thinking about all that bedding to boil, felt like sobbing with her. Thank goodness she had kept that rubber sheet after Gypsy died, so at least the mattress wasn't infectious.

'Mind,' the attendant said, swinging up the wrought-iron step at the back of the cart. 'Might be brain fever yet. So you take care of yourselves. First sign of a cold, even, you make sure you call the doctor and hang the expense. He's very good, more concerned to stop the fever than to see his money, so send for him if you need him and he'll sort the fee out after.'

He probably meant that to be comforting, but somehow it wasn't. Ma nodded. She could see the assembled Covers at the other end of the Row: Norah Roberts standing on a brick to see better; Half-a-leg looking grave; and Mrs Polmean keeping a discreet distance. Only Peter Polmean was expressing what everybody thought, watching with eyes as big as saucers while he held his nose firmly to keep himself from breathing in germs.

The driver got up in front and the cart lurched away. Poor girl, Ma thought, fevered and sick and being bounced about in that wooden cart like a penny in a collecting box. Good thing she was strapped in, or she'd slip off the bed again, going up that hill. And then to be in Mount Misery, separated from her family. How would she feel, herself, if it had been Sprat? She turned to Mrs Mason, gruffly, 'Well, no good us standing here snivelling. Let's go and have a cup of tea, and I can make a start

155

on that room. Week or so, you'll be able to take those lodgings up Mount Misery and be a bit near her.'

Mrs Mason gave her a wan smile and Ma went round to light the copper before she put the kettle on the fire. She'd do the sheets today and Pa would have to give her a hand with the blankets tomorrow. She sighed. It wasn't so hard on Pa, he had that boat to see to. Happier than a sandboy, he was, now those frames had come, though everything was taking an age because he was working alone. Half-a-leg came down to the yard whenever Norah wasn't looking, and gave a hand with the heavy work, but Peter Polmean, who would have loved to have helped (nothing skilled, of course, but he could fetch and carry and so save Pa hours of climbing about) might have caught the fever and had to be kept away.

So Pa was almost as busy as she was. Just as well, perhaps – it would have driven her mad having him under her feet all day, as well as Mrs Mason. Ma prodded at the coals vexedly and the kindling went out.

'Drat!' She got down on her knees and lit it again, blowing on the fire until it drew. She took the bucket, full from the rainwater butt, and began to pour it into the copper.

'Mrs Nicholls?' It was Mrs Mason behind her, making her jump. 'There's the post boy just come with a letter. He's brought my bank draught too.'

Drat, Ma thought again, as she went around to the front. Must be Mr Tavy again. What did he want this time? She rubbed her hands on her apron, took the envelope and tore it open.

But the letter wasn't from Tavy. It wasn't even to her. it was written in indelible pencil, of all things, and very short, but it was in a good neat hand, and it began, as near as she could figure it, 'My dearest Sprat.'

Ma felt the colour rise to her cheeks. She glanced at the envelope again. Yes, it did say 'Miss W Nicholls' – clear as day. She hadn't meant to open it, only she'd never expected it was for Sprat. Who could be writing to her? The writing on the envelope was in a different hand, in ink.

She glanced around the kitchen as if Norah Roberts might be watching, but there was no one there. Mrs Mason was still outside, telling her woes to the post boy. Ma squinted at the signature. 'D . . . something . . . z . . .il.' She jerked upright. Denzil. She looked again. Yes, it had to be. There was a V, too, and a 'go' at the end. Denzil Vargo! She felt a kind of triumph at having deciphered it, but a moment later it faded. Denzil Vargo writing to 'my dearest Sprat'? Was that really what it said? She was sure it was. She struggled with the message for a few moments, but she couldn't work it out. She was still puzzling over it when Mrs Mason came in.

She put the letter in her pocket and set the kettle on the hob.

'Not more bad news, I hope,' Mrs Mason said, dolefully. 'You look whiter than one of your own sheets.'

'No,' Ma said briskly. 'Just a note about my sister's affairs. Still upsets me, that does. Now, I'll just go and see to that copper while the kettle boils. You can set out the cups if you've a mind to.' And leaving Mrs Mason astonished at this unexpected privilege she went back to the wash-house.

But even there she had no more luck with the letter. It wasn't about Pa's wood, the message was all 'I, I, I'. The only thing she could work out was the address – written from Penzance. Typical Vargo, that would be, pushing off without warning and only writing to say he'd gone.

Well, she wasn't having him send letters here. Less still was she going to pass them on. Anyway, Sprat wouldn't be coming here, not for days, so what she didn't know wouldn't hurt her.

Ma opened the door of the copper fire and pushed the letter in.

Denzil was back at work within a week. He had to put up quite a fight to do it, the Bullivant's didn't seem to understand that if a man had no money he couldn't afford to sit idle.

He wouldn't have minded staying home. Life was very comfortable in his little room. Daisy brought him three meals a day, and he had been provided with a table, chair and writing materials. His arm still felt as if an elephant had rolled on it, and half his face – when he saw it in the mirror – was a swollen, blackening mass, exactly as if he *had* been kicked by a runaway horse. He was rather ashamed of that falsehood, but it was far too late now. In fact, when Mrs Bullivant had pressed him for details, his reticence had been interpreted as modesty and the story seemed to have grown.

But he already owed for his keep – he dreaded to think how much – and he would never find permanent lodgings without a deposit. To say nothing of the tallyman and keeping his promise to Mother. He simply had to get back to work as soon as possible. He told Mr Bullivant so, one evening, when he had been 'invited down' to the drawing-room of which Tom thought so highly.

He was wearing his suit, though he could not face the additional agony of raising his arm to put on the waistcoat, and had done his best to look tidy. Without Mother to do his washing, his good shirt was beginning to get grubby around the edges. Bullivant, though, looked at him kindly enough.

'My dear fellow, your face! You can't be seen in the office like that.'

'I could stay out the back,' Denzil said. 'No one would see me there. Perhaps I could even sleep there, have a mattress under the counter like they used to do, years ago. Claude could carry your briefcase for a few days, and send out for a bit of food for me occasionally. It's summertime, and I'll be right as rain in a trice. Find myself a room nearby and pay you what I owe. Need to be back working to do it, that's the thing.'

Mr Bullivant looked hearteningly as if he was going to agree to this, but his wife interrupted, 'You wouldn't be interested in keeping on your room here, Mr Vargo? We'd been thinking of letting it sometime, and you seem a pleasant young man. Better someone you know, than strangers in the house.'

Denzil shook his head, carefully. It ached appallingly when he moved. 'I could never afford it, Mrs Bullivant. I owe money as it is, for my office clothes, and I have to send money home, pay the rent for my mother.'

Mrs Bullivant glowed. 'What a fine son you are. But surely . . .?'

Denzil swallowed, 'That's just it, Mrs Bullivant. I haven't a penny to my name. Gave them the last of it at home, before I came away.' He didn't mention his father directly. 'Pawned my pocket watch last week to try and make ends meet. One and six a week, that's all I could afford and then there'd be food and fuel to find.'

'It seems to me,' Mrs Bullivant said, 'you'd do better to stay here. Four shillings a week, all found, including laundry. Mr Bullivant can stop it out of your wages.'

Denzil hesitated. It was tempting. Nothing in advance, no bills and no horse bus. Plenty of food and warmth besides. With his new pay rise he might manage, just. But at that rate he already owed the Bullivants four shillings, let alone Mother's rent and the three bob he was behind with the tallyman. He sighed. 'I don't think—'

'And as for these last few days,' Mrs Bullivant went on, 'you forget about that. Do the same for anyone in trouble, I should hope, let alone a clerk at the company. So would any Christian soul. You can pay us back, if you're here in the winter, giving Daisy a hand with the coals. Save a lot of traipsing around in the mornings, besides, having you here in the house.'

Denzil found himself smiling, 'In that case,' he glanced at Mr Bullivant, 'if I've merited that rise . . .?'

His employer said gruffly, ''Course you have. Matter of fact, I meant to mention it. We're getting behind with everything, with you not there.'

'In that case,' Denzil said happily, 'I'd be delighted. Thank you.' A great weight of worry seemed to roll away from him as he spoke. Money would be very tight indeed, but he would manage somehow.

'All very well,' Bullivant said, 'but the lad can't be seen out like that, I said so before. Perhaps he could sleep under the counter, as he suggested, until that face is something like, at least.'

159

'I'll send down a mattress,' Mrs Bullivant said. She seemed as delighted as Denzil. 'And a blanket.'

'And a pillow,' Miss Bullivant put in, 'and a wash jug and bowl, and he'll need a towel too. And we could send down food every day . . .'

'All right, all right,' Bullivant bellowed. 'By the time we've done all that it would be easier to have him stay here and come and go in a hansom. Just make sure he keeps out of sight at the office. Now, if that's settled to everyone's satisfaction, I'd like to read my newspaper. I'll see you eight o'clock as usual, young Vargo, and we'll go down by cab. Just see to it I never regret the decision.'

But he was smiling as opened his paper, and Miss Bullivant, clutching her mother's arm in triumph, was looking pleased as punch.

Sprat was beginning to worry. She hadn't seen Denzil since that meeting at the stile, though she'd haunted the horse-bus – volunteering to take the late post up so often that Miss Raeburn had commented on it.

But there was no Denzil. Was it because of what she had said? Was he working late, perhaps – he had warned her about that. But when she went into town he wasn't at the office. Perhaps he *was* ill. That fever of Elsie Mason's was fearfully catching – had she managed to pass it on, without knowing? Up at Fairviews, she didn't hear the village gossip. Denzil could be lying there sick and she would know nothing about it. Not even Norah seemed to have any news.

If she had been an up-overer herself the solution would have been easy – just ask the neighbours or, if necessary, knock at the Vargos' door and pretend she needed to borrow something. But being from the Cove, she couldn't very well do that.

She could, perhaps, find an excuse to visit Bullivant's again, when she went in to collect Miss Raeburn's watch and shoes. The old lady had already suggested another trip to town: 'There are one or two things I need – tooth powder and vanishing cream. You did a good job last time.'

But that was not until next week, and here it was Saturday afternoon. It was her half-day, but she couldn't go home as she usually did, because of the fever, and for an hour or so she hung about Fairviews aimlessly. She even talked to Mr Raeburn's manservant while he ate his soup. She had hardly spoken to him before, he slept in the annex next to Mr Raeburn's room, and didn't mix with the female staff. He was usually aloof, but today he kept her fascinated by talking about London: the theatre shows, the gaslights, the fashions and the underground trains. She was almost sorry when he had to go back to his duties.

In the end, she did go up to Penvarris. Of course, she told herself she was going to the shops at St Just, to get a piece of cambric for Ma's birthday handkerchief, but since she chose the route which took her past Denzil's door, it came to the same thing.

There was nobody about, beyond a bunch of village urchins playing stumbly-jacks in the dust and teasing the chickens which had strayed into the lane. No one in the garden of the Vargos' cottage. That surprised her. Generally, Denzil's mother was in her garden, any summer afternoon, darning clothes in the sunshine if she wasn't tending her plants. But there was no one, and all the upstairs curtains were drawn. Perhaps Denzil was ill. Sprat loitered uncertainly at the gate.

A man came around the corner of the house, hitching up his braces. But it wasn't Denzil. This man was bearded and dishevelled, with his collarless shirt unbuttoned to the waist. Sprat stared at him.

'Well,' the man said, nastily. 'Seen what you wanted, have you? Haven't worn your eyes out looking?'

Sprat felt herself colour. 'It's just . . . I wondered . . .' she muttered, and then, finding her courage, 'I heard there might be illness in the house.'

He turned an ugly brick colour himself. 'Dunno who told you that. Fell over and banged her head, she did, that's all. Gave herself a bit of a bang, but she'll be right as a trivet in a day or two.' It was a strange voice, Cornish beyond a doubt, but there was something else in it, a sort of foreign twang.

For a moment, Sprat was baffled. She didn't know who he was, or what he was talking about. And then light dawned. 'Mrs Vargo, you mean,' Sprat said. 'And you must be Mr Vargo. Denzil's dad.'

The heavy face darkened dangerously. 'What if I am?' he said, viciously. 'Who might you be, when you're home? Not from round here, are you? No,' his mouth twisted into an ugly grin. 'Don't tell me – I believe I know. You're that Jenkins child, I can see it a mile off.'

'My name's Nicholls,' Sprat explained, with as much bravado as she could muster. 'My Ma was a Jenkins but Albert Nicholls is my Pa.'

'That what they told you, was it? Well, you listen to me, you little brat. You keep away from here, you understand? Go on, get off with you.'

'I was only . . .' She was about to say that she was going to St Just.

'Looking for Denzil, were you? Oh, don't look like that, I've got ears. I know what's been going on. Well,' Stan Vargo pushed his face towards her and the stench of stale ale washed over her like breakers in the Cove. 'Well, he isn't here, and he isn't going to be here. He's gone, disappeared, vamooshed. Too mighty for the likes of us. And a bloody good riddance, too.'

Sprat was close to tears. 'Where is he?' she said, desperately. She was used to Pa and his mild ways – she wasn't prepared for his reaction.

The man lifted his arm in fury and she thought he was going to hit her. At the last moment he seemed to change his mind and instead he brought his hand down against the gate rail with such force that he splintered it. Up the lane, the boys had stopped their games to watch.

'Dammit, woman, can't you take no for an answer? I don't know and I don't care, and I wouldn't tell *you* if I did. If I ever lay hands on him, I'll break his face in – and yours, too, if I ever find you here again. Now clear off where you belong, before I come out and make you.'

Sprat found herself edging uncomfortably along the wall, back in the direction of Fairviews. But the man hadn't finished. He was still shouting after her. 'And stay away. I'll have no damned Jenkins hanging round my door. Mind what I said. Catch you here again and you'll soon wish different.'

She scrambled over the stile somehow and half ran, half fell down the path that led to Fairviews and to home. Everything that was once comfortable and familiar now seemed different. Denzil was gone and that horrible man had threatened her. She longed to go back to the Row and have Ma comfort her, but even from the path she could see Mrs Mason standing at the door. She turned away, up to Mrs Meacham's, scrambled into her little bedroom and bolted the door.

Then she lay on the bed and sobbed. She hardly slept or ate that night, and she had barely recovered next morning in time to appear, white-faced and shaken, and serve Miss Raeburn's breakfast.

Five

'Very well, Fitch,' James Raeburn said heartily a day or two later. The cliff walk had tired him a little and he was breathing heavily. 'This will do very nicely.' He indicated the spot with his stick, a grass bank sprinkled with wild flowers, overlooking the sea.

Fitch, who had been bringing up the rear with baskets and hampers, struggled past him on the path, and began laying the rug out without a word. The man seemed, James noted with satisfaction, just as breathless as he was. This daily 'constitutional', suggested by Violet's doctor, seemed to be doing him good.

'This will bring roses to the cheeks, eh Fitch? Spot of fresh air and sunshine?' He lowered himself carefully on to the cushion which Fitch had laid for him. 'Wind in the hair, that sort of thing?'

Fitch, laying out sandwiches and cake from the hamper, smiled faintly but said nothing, but James was determined to share his enthusiasm.

'Isn't this better than London in the smog?'

Fitch gave him a look which seemed to suggest that at least, in London, a man could serve refreshment without having to lug it up a cliff face first, but all he said was, 'Very fine in London at the moment, sir.'

He was right, of course. James had seen it in the papers himself. But this afternoon not even being contradicted could ruffle his cheerfulness. He looked around, at the perfect blue sea shimmering out to the horizon, where a half-dozen fishing boats drooped their red-brown sails in the lack of breeze while a cloud of sea gulls whooped over them – mere pale specks at this distance – in the clear sky. 'Too many damned people in London,' he said, stretching out a hand for the tea which Fitch had just poured him. It was lukewarm, despite the towels around the flask, but it was wet, sweet and refreshing. 'Though I suppose we shall have to go back soon.' He picked up an egg sandwich and motioned to Fitch, 'Have something yourself.'

Fitch perched himself on a boulder, poured some tea in an enamel cup and drank it thirstily. It seemed to cheer him up. That was good. James did not like to see Fitch out of sorts – it disturbed his own good humour.

'Trouble with London,' he said expansively, leaning back on his cushion and feeling the warm sun through the tweed of his coat. 'Too much damn politics. All these protests, people demanding "rights" – it isn't English, somehow. The place'll be like Russia in a year or two, if this goes on: workers marching on Buckingham Palace and trying to overthrow the King.' He prided himself on having these 'man to man' conversations with Fitch occasionally. It made him feel up to the minute, a bit of a liberal like those philosophical johnnies, with his finger on the popular pulse.

Fitch, who had been permitted a leftover sandwich and a piece of cake, was busy eating them, and couldn't have offered an opinion if he'd been expected to.

James threw him a sideways glance. 'Think it will come to it, do you, Fitch? Government by the common man? Votes for women, all that nonsense? Think the government will capitulate and we shall all be ruled by servants and women one of these days?' He lay back and watched a single lazy cloud form and reform over the sea.

'There's many a man ruled by women already, sir,' Fitch said, adroitly avoiding the question. 'That's why I've always remained a bachelor.'

James chuckled. 'I hear they're going to introduce an in-

surance stamp for domestic staff, next. As if you didn't cost me
enough. Still, can't all be like my aunt, and keep an attendant at
someone else's expense, eh? What do you think of her, then?
Nicholls or whatever her name is?'

'I have hardly seen the young lady, sir,' Fitch said. 'Only
talked to her once – she seemed bright enough then. She keeps
herself to herself.'

'She does,' James had made several attempts to engage the
girl in conversation himself, but she had been as listless as a
dead fish. 'I hope my aunt is not working her too hard. Good
servants are hard to get, eh Fitch?' He smiled. 'So don't you
worry about the stamp.'

'I won't, sir,' Fitch replied.

There seemed to be nothing else to say. 'Well,' he got to his
feet. 'Time to go back. Might take another stroll out here
tomorrow. I'll see you at the house.' He picked up his stick and
strode off, leaving Fitch to pack the remains of the picnic and
follow him slowly back to Fairviews.

Turning the corner, he allowed himself a long swig from his
hip flask. He deserved it after all that fresh air and exercise,
whatever the doctor said, but he preferred to enjoy it without
Fitch watching. The man would only frown in that disapproving manner. Not that he would say anything directly, of
course.

Treating Fitch as a conversational equal was one thing, but
when it came to practical matters they knew exactly where they
stood.

Sprat did go into Penzance again for Miss Raeburn. There was
no excitement this time, only a great anxiety, and she could
hardly wait to finish her errands and get to Bullivant's. There,
at least, she might find news of Denzil.

But when she got there and peeped inside, there were queues
of customers waiting. Furious, some of them looked, muttering
about consignments that were late arriving. She couldn't go in
there with all that, so she slipped outside again. She hadn't any

proper business in the office. Closing time pretty soon, perhaps she would see him then.

She hung around the office for ages, but there was no sign of Denzil. In the end, she accosted the little errand boy on his way back with string and stamps. 'Mr Vargo in, is he?'

The boy shifted uncomfortably. 'Might be. Why's that then?'

'Wanted to see him.'

The boy shook his head. 'Won't do that, then. Mr Denzil's here, but he isn't seeing anybody.'

That was a relief. Denzil was there. 'He'd see me,' Sprat said.

'He won't see anyone. Not even family. Told me so himself. Anyway, I'm not to let anyone in. Mr Bullivant's orders.'

Sprat paled. 'Not in any trouble is he? I wouldn't interrupt his work for the world . . .'

'No,' the boy said, 'nothing like that. Mr Bullivant's got him staying at his house for a few days – or rather his daughter has – and he's taking him to and from in a hansom cab.'

Denzil? It was unbelievable. Sprat was still trying to imagine it, when something in that last remark struck her. 'What do you mean, "his daughter has"?' Suddenly things were taking an unwelcome turn. 'Is she friendly with Mr Vargo?'

The boy grinned. 'Not half,' he said, cheerfully. 'Supposed to be walking out with Mr Courtney from the front office, but she'd sooner have Mr Vargo any day. Any fool could see that.'

Sprat almost dropped Miss Raeburn's packages. 'I see.' She forced herself to say, 'Is she nice, this Miss Bullivant?'

The boy grinned broader. 'Very nice, by all accounts, if you aren't particular about looks. Good-hearted, Mr Vargo says. Mind, she'll be worth a penny or two one of these days, too, else Mr Courtney wouldn't be so keen.'

The pavement was sinking under Sprat's feet. 'Dark-haired, I suppose?' The conversation at the stile was coming back to her. What had he said, 'dull and dark-haired and uninteresting, nothing at all like you. But her parents aren't too keen.' And Sprat had thought that he was teasing her.

'Oh yes,' boy said. 'Dark-haired and a bit plump. You all right, Miss?'

Sprat nodded dumbly. No wonder there had been no Denzil on the horse-bus. He was living here in Penzance, as he said he might. Biding his chance with Miss Bullivant no doubt. Well, he had warned her.

'Well, they'll be waiting for this string. Sorry I couldn't help you with Mr Vargo. Shall I give him a message, tell him you were looking for him?'

For a moment, she was tempted, and then she shook her head. 'No,' she said. 'No. Just an old friend. Doesn't matter. Doesn't matter at all.'

Tom came down the office steps briskly. It was a minute or two before closing time, but he'd worked through his lunchtime trying to placate all those irritated customers, and in the end Mr Bullivant had taken them into the inner office to see them in person, and let him go early.

It should have afforded him satisfaction to be walking off, knowing that Denzil Vargo was compelled to stay there working until Bullivant had finished, and that might be another hour yet. But when Vargo did go home, it would be to Bullivant's house, in Bullivant's cab, to eat Bullivant's food and smile at Bullivant's daughter. Tom tried not to think about that.

Of course, now that Denzil was back at work, the Sunday invitation had been renewed, so Tom had revisited the house himself – not as a mere lodger but a proper invited guest. Nevertheless, it was not the same, knowing that Vargo was snugly upstairs in a little room making himself at home, while Olivia insisted on prattling about him all the afternoon.

Vargo! He could scarcely form the word without spitting. He rammed on his hat and started off along the street. The milliner's girl would have cheered him with her blushes and smiles, but she was not there.

There was someone, however. A girl huddled in a shopfront, holding her hand to her eyes. She seemed to be crying. Tom assumed his most courtly expression. Might have a chance here, if he played his cards right.

As he drew nearer, he realised that he knew her. That girl who had come into the office last week, asking for Denzil. He was sure it was. Almost sure anyway, though she looked a bit of a sight now, with her face all puffed with weeping.

Tom took off his hat. 'Miss . . .?' He searched for a name but couldn't find it, so he said again, 'Miss? It's me, Tom Courtney from Bullivant's. You all right?'

She looked up at his words. 'Oh,' she sniffed and took a deep breath. 'Oh, it's you. Yes, yes. I'm quite all right. Bit of bad news, that's all. Don't know what came over me, making a spectacle of myself in the street.' But her voice trembled as she spoke.

'That's too bad,' Tom said, awkwardly. A thought occurred to him and he proffered his clean handkerchief. 'Here, this is bigger than yours. Wipe your eyes.'

She hesitated, but she took it and gave him a watery smile. 'I need a counterpane not a handkerchief, the way I'm carrying on. I'm some sorry. Kind of you to stop. There, that's better.' She stopped dabbing her face and looked at him with sudden interest. 'Mr Courtney, is it? I didn't realise, though I've heard Denzil talk about you often enough.'

Tom grimaced. 'Nothing to my credit, I'll be bound. Doesn't care for me, doesn't Vargo, though I'm damned if I know why – saving your presence, Miss. Don't you believe everything you hear, I'm not as black as I'm painted, as you see.' He indicated the handkerchief with a smile.

She smiled wanly. 'No. You have been very kind. And thank you for the handkerchief. I have to go, catch my bus home. I'll be grand now, really.'

'Nonsense,' he said. 'You'll let me walk you to the bus stop at least. Can't leave you to go alone in that state. Let me carry those parcels for you.' That sounded decently chivalrous, he thought. He was enjoying this, and not just because he was scoring over Denzil Vargo.

She hesitated again. 'I can manage . . .'

He laughed. 'What kind of escort lets a lady carry her own parcels? Come on, hand them over.'

She did so, with a doubtful smile.

'Now then,' he said, as he swung into stride beside her, 'What's this all about? Can't have you walking about flooding Penzance.'

She shook her head. 'It's nothing, really. Just – a horrible man threatened me the other day. And then I wanted to see Denzil, and I couldn't. Got a bit mad with him, that's all.'

Tom nodded in what he hoped was a judicious manner. 'Yes, he's . . . uh . . . shut himself away.' So, she didn't know about the horse. Well, he wasn't about to oblige Denzil Vargo by telling her. 'Living at the Bullivants' now, you heard that?'

She nodded. 'Yes. Got friendly with Miss Bullivant, I hear.' Her voice was bitter.

So that was it. Well, dammit, the girl had reason enough to be upset. He had reason enough to be upset himself. He gave her a confiding smile. 'I'm afraid so,' he said. 'Not quite the thing – for either of us. Olivia's supposed to be walking out with me, you know. Quite an established thing between us, though there's no formal engagement. But there you are, Bullivant can't see what's in front of his face, and Denzil knows how to be charming.' He couldn't resist the opportunity to add, 'Probably why he never cared for me. Not that one can blame him. She'll inherit everything, by and by.'

Drat. He had said too much now. He could tell by her face.

'Never mind,' he said. 'Daresay it'll blow over. Cheer up, let me buy you a penny cornet. There's the "Stop me and Buy One" man. No, don't argue. It's jolly hot today, and we've got something in common, you and I.'

She smiled uncertainly.' Thank you. Yes, I believe I will. I'm Sprat Nicholls by the way.' She paused. 'Serve Denzil jolly well right. Anyway, what's it got to do with him?'

'Nothing at all.' Tom put his hand in his pocket and drew out the coin. The last of that extra cartage money he hadn't entered up. Well, it was going to a good cause. And with all these 'exceptional consignments' there might be another opportunity.

She didn't have ice-cream often, he could tell that by her smile.

Six

Taking the letters to the post was not the pleasure that it used to be. Every time she did it now, Sprat was reminded of the times she had sped to up the road on eager feet, hoping to meet Denzil. But there was no Denzil now. Not even any hope of Denzil. He was in Penzance, and making himself charming to that Bullivant creature. And never a word from him.

That Tom Courtney seemed a decent type, too. She hadn't realised who he was at first. Denzil had always made him out to be a sullen, sneering bully, but this boy seemed genuinely pleasant and eager to help. Perhaps it was true what Ma said. You couldn't trust a Vargo. Certainly that father of his was a nasty piece of work. Sprat was still half afraid to go up past the gate, and she had brought her piece of cambric in Penzance.

She nodded hello to Crowdie over the hedge, and hurried on up the path. If only she could go home and talk to Ma, or Pa for that matter. But the doctor had been to Fairviews to see Mrs Meacham, and confirmed that Elsie Mason had paralytic fever. Older people could carry it, he said, but young people caught it, and germs could last a fortnight, so the Row was in quarantine for another week.

But in the meantime, there were these letters to post. She was in a hurry, because she had delayed coming out and if she wasn't quick about it, she would be too late. The woman who kept the post office generally stayed open a bit, for people coming off the bus, but even so it was going to be a rush tonight.

She was almost at the road now, and beginning to believe

172

she'd do it, but at that instant a man came down the path. She saw, with a sharp intake of breath, that it was Stan Vargo.

He was drunk, too, anyone could see that. He was leaning with one hand against the wall, and muttering to himself under his breath. She was unwilling to pass him, but there was no help for it, she'd have to go by or she would miss the post.

She tried not to look at him and simply hurry by, but the path was too narrow for that. He stepped towards her.

'Here, you!' He made a grab for her apron.

She twisted away and pretended to ignore him, her heart thumping. She was dry-mouthed with fear of him, but he was blocking her way.

'I'm talking to you,' he said. His voice was slurred, she noticed with rising panic.

She tried to keep her voice steady, but it wavered treacherously. 'What do you want?'

He smiled drunkenly. 'That's better – a civil tongue. Always want a civil tongue for your elders.' He lurched towards her. 'Bit of money, that's what I want. Spare a few pennies for a poor old man?'

'Haven't got any,' Sprat said. This was terrible. 'Only the money for the post and that's not mine.'

He looked at her again. His eyes were bloodshot and unfocussed but he seemed to register something. 'It's that Jenkins brat again.' He spat, suddenly, at her feet. 'That's what I think of Jenkinses. Wasn't for the bloody Jenkinses I wouldn't be here now.'

Sprat didn't know what to say or do. She stood like a trapped rabbit, watching his every move.

He seemed to have pulled himself together, but the effect was more terrifying than ever. He jabbed a finger at her, with horrid emphasis. 'You and your bloody family, I reckon you owe me. Striding round like royalty, Miss High and Bloody Mighty. Well, I know different. My boy's a sorry apology for a son, but at least he was born in wedlock.'

Sprat stood stock-still, too terrified to move.

173

'But you, you little cow! Nicholls, you call yourself. You aren't a Nicholls and never have been. You're a Jenkins – a snivelling, worthless little bastard – and you'll give me that sixpence or I'll make sure the whole world knows it. Understand?'

She could not have answered if she had wanted to. The words danced around her, making no sense. She knew what a bastard was, there had been one at Penvarris school: a thin little urchin, mocked, reviled and shunned. Respectable children threw stones at him and called after him in the street. She shook her head. 'I don't believe it.'

He sneered. 'You don't? Well ask that so-called Pa of yours. Ask him who was offered money to marry your mother and save her reputation.'

Sprat couldn't take it in. Pa . . . offered money to marry Ma? She shook her head.

'Wouldn't want that round the Cove, would he? Myrtle precious Nicholls and her mighty ways. Reckon your family owes me, for keeping quiet. So let's have what's in your pockets.' He lunged towards her. 'Now.'

She screamed as he pulled him to her.

He seized the letters from her and threw them, crumpled on the ground. 'Shut up you little cow.' He had forced her back against the hedge and she closed her eyes. She could smell his heavy breath and feel his hands grabbing at her, searching her pockets, tearing her apron.

This time when she screamed for help she kept on screaming. He didn't let her go. Instead, he took her by the shoulders and began to shake her savagely. 'Where's the money, you snivelling little brat. I know you've got it. Give it me or I'll shake it out of you.'

Voices. God be praised. It was Crowdie. 'Leave that girl alone, Vargo, or I'll set the dogs on you.'

The man loosened his grip and stepped away. Sprat opened her eyes. There was Crowdie striding towards them, the terrier at his heels, the bigger dog straining at the collar that Crowdie was holding. And behind him, brandishing his stick, James Raeburn came panting up the path, his face scarlet with effort and anger. 'What the devil's all this?'

Stan Vargo muttered something belligerent, then he glanced from one man to the other and his bravado seemed to crumble. 'Nothing,' he mumbled. 'Girl owes me money, that's all, and wouldn't give it me.'

'That's a damn lie, Vargo. I was in the field and I heard every word.' Crowdie turned to Sprat, 'Go on, my dear, get off with you. I'll deal with this.'

Sprat wanted to thank him, but no words came. Instead, she shook her head helplessly and, abandoning her letters where they lay, ran off down the path. She sped blindly past the men and dogs, tears coursing down her face. She didn't stop until she came, fever or no fever, to the Row.

James Raeburn watched her go. He was still panting heavily from the exertion, and he leaned against the field's stone wall to collect himself.

He nodded at Crowdie, almost unable to speak. 'Good . . . man . . .!' he managed, puffing. 'Heard . . . shouting . . .'

Crowdie nodded. 'Just as well we were here, you and I.' He was still holding the dog, which was now straining and snarling at the drunken lout backed up against the wall. 'As for you, Stan Vargo!'

The man whimpered. 'I never hurt her. Wouldn't have touched her. Bit of money, that's all I wanted.'

The farmer seemed tempted to let the dog have him. 'You're a disgrace, Stan Vargo. What d'you think you're about, attacking a respectable girl like that? Bad enough for your wife, poor woman, but you aren't in your own house now.'

James found enough breath to gasp out, 'There are laws . . . about things like this . . . demanding . . . money with menaces . . .' He could say no more, but he had the satisfaction of seeing the Vargo fellow pale.

The brute was nasty with drink, but not too fuddled to say,

175

'She innut so respectable as all that. 'F you knew what I know . . .'

Crowdie let the dog an inch nearer. 'I know what you said. I told you, I heard every word and I don't believe a word of it, any more than I believe that when I came you were asking her politely for sixpence. You're a liar, Stan Vargo, and a bullying one at that – and this gentleman's here to prove it. Now, get off home, before I let this dog at you, and if I hear so much as a whisper of this anywhere in the village, you'll never work here again, for me or anyone else.' He pulled the dog back and the man skulked away up the lane. The farmer turned to James, 'Thank you, sir, glad you were here.'

James was still leaning against the wall. 'Out walking on the cliffs . . . came as soon as I could . . . not as young as I was . . .' He smiled, though his heart was still knocking against his ribs. 'Poor Nicholls . . . terrified . . .' He was going to say 'I'd like to give you something for your troubles', but the words did not come.

There was a sudden terrible pain in his arm and he doubled over, as some unseen force clamped an inexorable band tighter and tighter around his chest and the world turned red.

Ma was scrubbing the kitchen floor, up to her elbows in soap and soda crystals. She couldn't believe her eyes when Sprat rushed in.

'Here,' she said, kneeling upright on the piece of old shirt she used to save her knees. 'You aren't supposed to be here. And mind out for my clean floor.'

But Sprat ignored her. Straight in she came, leaving a trail of footprints, and plonked herself defiantly on the settle. Ma was about to protest, but then she saw Sprat's face.

'My dear life, Sprat, whatever is it? Something wrong at Fairviews?' And then as a terrible thought struck, 'Not feeling poorly, are you?'

Sprat shook her head. She was crying, Ma realised, little wordless sobs that did not show as tears. 'It's . . . it's . . .

Oh, it's not true. Say it's not true. I wasn't born out of wedlock.'

Ma got to her feet slowly. Sixteen years of careful conceal-ment crumbled round her feet. She reached out for the kettle. A cup of tea was the Cove's automatic response to trouble. 'Who told you that nonsense?'

'Stan Vargo,' Sprat said, at last, all in a rush as though a dam had burst. 'Stopped me on the lane and threatened me. Said the family owed him, for keeping his mouth shut. Ask Crowdie – he was there.' She stopped and gazed at Ma, suddenly. 'Oh, my God. It's true, isn't it? I can see it in your face. You've gone all pink and peculiar. He was right. I aren't a Nicholls at all. Somebody offered Pa money to give me a name.'

Ma put down the kettle abruptly. 'Don't be so wet. 'Course they didn't. It was Pa wanted to take you. Minute he saw you he wanted you for his own.' She hid her trembling hands in her pinny. 'Well, since it's all over the village, I suppose you'd better know. I thought you'd never have to, but better to hear it from me than Norah Roberts. Oh, I wish your Pa was here.'

Sprat was staring at her coldly. 'Isn't my Pa, is he?'

'Don't be like that, Sprat, Pincher's been good to you.' She sighed. 'It was that Billy Vargo who was offered money. But he wasn't having it. Said the child wasn't his – tried to blame his brother.'

'Stan Vargo! My father?'

'That's what Billy tried to claim – wasn't true, of course, but how do you prove it? Billy disappeared next day and pushed off to Canada. Never said a word to anyone. I didn't think any-body knew, but I suppose Stan Vargo found out, in the end, while he was over there.'

Sprat was still staring, her breath coming heavily. 'You mean – you and Bill Vargo!' Her voice was aghast.

For a moment Ma was bewildered, then she said. 'Oh my dear Sprat, you still haven't understood, have you? It wasn't me who upset everything by walking out with Bill Vargo and defying the Cove. I was married to Pincher and living up

Plymouth years before. 'Course we had her up there, soon as we heard she was in trouble, and I raised you as my own. Came away from there to escape the gossip, and nobody here knew different.'

Comprehension was dawning on Sprat's face. 'So . . .?'

'That's right,' Ma said wretchedly. 'I aren't really your mother, Sprat. Gypsy was. But . . .' She wanted to add something, something about loving her, but she'd never have done it and the words were awkward. In the end, she abandoned the idea. She blew her nose in her pinny end and said gruffly, 'So there you are. It's out now and so much the worse.'

Sprat had got to her feet and was standing there, shaking. She looked as if her world had shattered into sand. 'All these years,' she whispered, 'And you never said.'

Ma pulled herself together with an effort. 'Never meant for you to know. Blasted Stan Vargo. I wonder who else heard.'

'I don't know,' Sprat said, in a peculiar high-pitched voice. 'But you needn't concern yourself. They won't hear it from me. And I shan't embarrass you any more. I'm going,' her voice broke and the tears began at last, 'and I won't be coming back.'

'Sprat! Listen!!' But before Ma could stop her, she had bolted through the door.

PART FOUR
July 1911

One

'Sprat wait!'

But Sprat didn't wait. Ma hurried after her, but her knees were stiff from scrubbing, and by the time she got to the door Sprat was already out of sight. Gone back to Fairviews no doubt, where she couldn't be reached.

Ma went back to the kitchen and sat down heavily on the settle. A thousand times over the years she had lived this scene in her imagination, but now that it had happened it was even worse than she'd dreamed. She had imagined Tavy letting the cat out of the bag, or Sprat herself putting two and two together – goodness knows the child was the very image of Gypsy. She had even feared that Billy Vargo might come home one day, guilt-stricken and looking for his own. Those things would have been bad enough, especially for Sprat, but essentially private. Never in her wildest dreams had she guessed that blessed Stan Vargo would turn up drunk, shouting it from the house-tops.

And now what? Pa would have be told, first thing, before Norah got hold of the story and the whole family became outcasts. They'd have to move on again, probably, if only for Sprat's sake. Ma was a stalwart churchgoer but she said the words aloud. 'Damn you, Stan Vargo. I hope you roast in hell.'

Angry tears were threatening to disgrace her. Ma gave a deep sniff, set her chin and almost mechanically began changing her pinny. This was no time for weakness. She'd go down and find Pincher, that's what. He didn't like to be interrupted, when he was busy with his boat-building, particularly when he was

181

doing a tricky job like putting in the king plank, but he'd have to put up with it for once. She blew her nose fiercely and picked up her shawl.

There was a noise at the door. Sprat! She had come back! Ma went weak at the knees with relief. 'My love!'

But the cry died on her lips. It was not Sprat, it was Mrs Mason, come back from posting a letter to her bank. Ma had almost forgotten her existence.

She looked at Ma in dismay. 'Is something the matter, Mrs Nicholls? There isn't bad news, is there? Nothing's happened to Elsie?'

For a moment Ma fought down a wild desire to tell Mrs Mason exactly what she thought of Elsie, but a paying guest was a paying guest. She even managed a thin smile. 'No, nothing like that, Mrs Mason. Nothing to concern you.' She hoped that her words would dispose of the matter, but Mrs Mason was looking at her anxiously without taking off her bonnet, and after a moment Ma felt compelled to add, 'Just our Sprat, that's all. Got herself accosted in the lane by a drunk, and frightened herself silly. I thought you were her come back.'

'Awful,' Mrs Mason said mechanically, staring at the shawl round Ma's shoulders.

Ma took it off. 'I was going down to tell Pincher,' she said. 'But I won't do, seeing you're here. Want a cup of tea, do 'ee? Kettle's just on.'

'I think,' Mrs Mason said, 'that you'd better sit down a minute. You've gone the colour of cobwash. I've run you off your feet, these last weeks. Fortunately, I've found a room now, right close to the hospital. I'll be out of your way in no time.' She took off her bonnet. 'Your daughter all right?'

She isn't my daughter, Ma thought. And now she knows it. But she is. She is! Only daughter I ever had. And Gypsy never wanted her – more interested in finding herself a husband. Glad enough to hide away with us till the child was born, then hand it over to us. Just as well. James Jamieson would never have married her if he knew, and our mother wouldn't have had her home if she heard. Ended in the workhouse, most like, if it hadn't been for me and Pincher.

'Mrs Nicholls?' Mrs Mason was saying anxiously.

Ma pulled herself together. 'Yes, yes. Fine now. Thanks.' She picked up the cup of tea, and then realised with a start that she'd left Mrs Mason to make it. Furthermore the floor was only half scrubbed and there was a pail of dirty water left about. 'Give me a turn, it did. Thank you for the tea.' She got up at once and busied herself with her tasks.

Even when Pincher came in, she couldn't very well say anything with Mrs Mason there. But that night in bed, when their guest was safely asleep, she poured it all out to him. He was upset, as she knew he would be, and when he drew her gently to him, despite the narrowness of the mattress she didn't even protest. In fact, it was quite comforting, for once.

Sprat's first impulse was to bolt back to Fairviews, but when she reached the fork in the path, she realised that she could not bear to do that after all. James Raeburn must have heard it all, her humiliation and disgrace, and for now she could not face him. She hesitated for a moment, and then ran on blindly all the way to St Evan. She found herself heading, without conscious intention, to the churchyard.

Gypsy's grave. There it was, same as ever, with Ma's Sunday bunch of wild flowers still withering on it. Sprat stared at it a long time. If she had any idea of flinging herself down upon the gravestone and sobbing 'Mother', the sight of that sober granite made it ridiculous.

Mother. Even now it didn't seem possible. Gypsy – with her respectable marriage, her fashionable clothes and stylish ways – no better than she should be, almost disgracing the family with a bastard child.

But so many things, at last, made sense. That legacy, for example. Ma's exasperation when Gypsy used to come whirling in, after a long absence, asking, 'And how's my little darling?'

Those visits had always seemed charmed and magical. Looking back, Sprat also realised how very rare they'd been.

Above all, it explained Ma's attitude to Denzil. It had always seemed unlike her, to take against him so much just because he was an up-overer, though heaven knows for most of the Cove that would have been enough. But he wasn't just an up-overer. Sprat felt a horrid little prickle at her scalp. If all this was true, Denzil was her own blood relation. At best a cousin, at worst . . . more. In any case the son of the family who had disgraced her own.

Sprat sat down sharply on a nearby headstone. It was hopeless then. Strangely, she didn't for a minute really believe that story about Stan Vargo, and it was clear Ma didn't either. There was her own name, for one thing – Wilhemina. It was as clear as the nose on your face. But, like Ma said, how could you prove it? And it was no good waiting, and hoping disapproval would go away. With that story about Stan Vargo anyone could deny the banns, and that would be the end of that. She wouldn't put it past Ma herself, where the Vargos were concerned. Even without that problem, who would marry them? The church didn't exactly forbid you to marry your cousin, but she'd heard the vicar preach against it – supposed to make your children turn out peculiar, so *he* wouldn't do it, supposing you asked him. No wonder Stan Vargo had shouted at her and seen her off, that day at the gate. She wasn't merely a cousin and a Cover, but a bastard cousin at that.

Bastard. The shame of it! She took a long, shuddering breath. Was this what had driven Denzil to run away to Penzance without a word?

Once you thought about it, it all made sense. Naturally, his father would have told him. That was why Denzil had gone, why Stan Vargo had hollered at her so. Of course it was! Suddenly her anger against Stan Vargo evaporated. After all, it wasn't his fault. This was all Gypsy's doing, and Ma's for not telling her the truth years ago. If she and Denzil had known, of course they'd never have got themselves into this.

Oddly, she found her own resentment was mostly for Ma – or Aunt Myrtle, as she really ought to be called. Intended it for the best, perhaps, keeping quiet to save Sprat from shame. But deep down Sprat didn't believe that. It wasn't Sprat that Ma was trying to protect, it was Gypsy, and the family's reputation. Ma's own good name, in fact.

Well, she had lost it now. Crowdie had heard already, and Stan Vargo would be telling everyone. Supposing Norah Roberts found out? Sprat shut her eyes. The true horror was still to come, she realised suddenly: all the strangers name-calling and whispering in the street, and people you'd been friendly with for years suddenly pretending they didn't know you.

It wasn't even like the girl in Gypsy's fairy stories. Gypsy had been fond of a story about a poor girl whose father was really a wealthy man and claimed her in the end. There was no chance of dreaming like that. Her father had been brother to that horrible Vargo, and wouldn't even own her when he was bribed.

At least there was a single grain of comfort. Denzil had not deserted her lightly. In her heart, she had never really believed that. But this, she could understand. Trying to save her from finding out the awful truth. It even made sense of Miss Bullivant. Trying to forget, most likely. Just because he couldn't marry *her*, it didn't mean he would never marry anyone. But it wasn't so simple for Sprat – once this got out no decent man would ever look at her again. In the end, she'd have to get away, as far from the Cove as possible.

So what was she to do now? Go back to Fairviews, that was the first thing. That wouldn't be easy – Mr Raeburn would have told them all about it. She might even lose her position. They might not want to be attended by a bastard, some people cared about things like that, and Mrs Meacham would be furious anyway. Sprat had been away far too long, and even now the letters hadn't been sent. She'd left them lying, torn and crumpled, on the path.

Well, the problems had to be faced sometime. It was no good

sitting here. She got up heavily from 'Prudence Williams, aged twenty-three, and her infant sons' and began the long walk back to the house.

He wasn't dead, rather to his surprise. There had been moments there, when the agony was at its worst, when he rather wished that he had been, but the worst of the pain had ebbed at last and he found himself sitting rather ignominiously in the middle of a public path, with the farmer chappie bending solicitously over him.

'Now look here, Sir, don't you try to move' – this because James was indeed making ineffectual moves in that direction and discovering that the effort was beyond him – 'I'll go and find someone. I'll be back d'rectly.'

James nodded. He would have liked to make some manly declaration that he could manage splendidly unaided, but since it was abundantly clear that he could do nothing of the kind, he submitted to being left ingloriously on the dusty path, like a parcel waiting for collection. There was still a horrible tightness in his chest, and he was feeling sick and wretched.

Help seemed to be a long time coming. James had time to recall, with sharp regret, a number of times he had ignored (not to say actively disobeyed) his doctor's advice, but at last Crowdie reappeared with a couple of strong men and a stout ladder. Once they were there, they wasted no time. Coats were buttoned up and slipped over the rungs and James hoisted upon them.

James was no sylph, and the ladder was narrow. Also, the rungs could be felt perfectly clearly through the coats, so the makeshift stretcher was both precarious and uncomfortable and the journey back to Fairviews seemed to take an agonising eternity. Nevertheless, he was grateful. Left to himself, he doubted he could ever have managed it.

His arrival caused instant consternation. The farmer himself had gone on ahead to alert the household, and by the time the ladder bearers were lurching down the path with their uncomfortable burden, there was already a little reception committee waiting: Aunt Jane was standing at the front door with Fitch, Florrie, and Cook.

'Are you all right, James?' she asked, rather unnecessarily. Obviously, if he was 'all right' he wouldn't be lying on a wretched ladder, being delivered to the door like a grocery order. But her concern was touching.

He attempted to raise his head. 'Fitch—' he began, but his aunt was too quick for him.

'You lie where you are. Fitch is going for a doctor.'

'I'll take him up there in the cart,' Crowdie said. 'Long walk to St Just, this time of night. I'd offer him the cob, but he says he can't ride.'

'I would send Nicholls,' Aunt Jane sounded annoyed, 'but she isn't here. I don't know what has come over the tiresome girl. She only went out to the post, and she has been gone almost an hour.'

James tried to struggle upright and almost overset the ladder, but Crowdie was already explaining. 'Might be a minute or two yet, Ma'am. Set on, she was, attacked in the lane. That's how this gennulman had a turn – heard her screaming and ran up to help.'

Even to James' blurred eyes, Aunt Jane looked seriously impressed. If he survived this, he thought, the incident might do him no harm at all in her eyes. 'Attacked? By whom? We'll see about that!' She was ready to call for a policeman, clearly.

Crowdie shook his head. 'Fellow looking for money. Shaking her, he was, till we came along. Far too much to drink by the look of him, and talking drivel, like they do. Frightened the poor girl rigid. Good thing we came along when we did, though this poor gennulman's suffered for it.'

'Poor James,' Aunt Jane said, tenderly. The news seemed to have changed her attitude completely. 'You are quite a hero, it seems. And I thought you'd just been overdoing the whisky as usual. Well, we must get you into bed at once.' She turned to the stretcher bearers. 'Florrie will show you the way. As for you,

Mr Crowdie, I shall see you have something for your trouble. Now about this cart . . .'

He heard no more. The farmhands clattered him upstairs, and with Florrie's help, bundled him unceremoniously to bed in his drawers. It was not at all what he was used to, but he was ashamed to find how pathetically glad he was to be there.

Two

S prat was expecting trouble. Expecting it in a dull, wooden sort of way – after the events of the afternoon it seemed that nothing else mattered – but expecting it all the same. And even now she hadn't posted the letters!

She went back the way she'd come, down the path, her heart thudding so hard that she was sure the cows over the hedge could hear it, but there was no Stan Vargo, only the crumpled envelopes scattered in the grasses. She collected them up and smoothed them as best she could, but they were dirty and torn. And she had missed the post. Whatever would the ladies say? She put the letters mournfully in her pocket and hurried on to the house.

Crowdie was there. That was his cart tied up beside the gate. She stopped at the sight of it. He must have come to tell them what he knew – what Stan Vargo had said about her birth. It shook her, she hadn't expected that from Crowdie, but what other explanation was there? She had not expected to come home to this, with everyone gossiping about her shame already.

She was ready to turn tail again – where to, she had not stopped to think – but at that instant the front door opened, and Crowdie came hurrying out of it with Fitch, Mr Raeburn's man. That was another shock – Crowdie using the *front* door like that – and it was a moment before she noticed Miss Raeburn, who seemed (odder and odder!) to be seeing them out.

Miss Raeburn, however, had noticed her. 'Nicholls! There you are at last. Thank heaven for that. Now you can go with Mr

189

Crowdie, and Fitch can stay with his master. I'm sure my poor
nephew would prefer that.'

Sprat found herself staring like an idiot.

'Well, girl, don't stand there like a gatepost. Get into the cart.
There isn't a moment to lose. You know where the doctor
lives?'

'St Just?' What had happened now, Sprat wondered. It
couldn't be Ma, Sprat was with her only half an hour ago.
Surely Elsie Mason hadn't died of the fever? She ventured a
question. 'What . . .?'

But Crowdie was already down the path and helping her up
on to the cart. 'Of course, you didn't know, did you? Happened
after you'd gone. It's Mr Raeburn, put a strain on hisself
hurrying up the hill to help you, and now he's had a heart
failure. Proper hero he was, wasn't he?' He squeezed her arm
sharply as he spoke, and she realised that this was a kind of
warning.

She glanced at him and saw the message in his eyes. 'He was
wonderful,' she said. Crowdie nodded. She turned to Miss
Raeburn. 'Wonderful,' she said again. 'I can't thank him
enough.'

The old lady flushed with pleasure. 'It just shows, Nicholls.
One shouldn't be quick to judge. Well, I am glad you're safe.
Hurry along now and fetch that doctor quickly. That's the best
thanks you can give my nephew.'

Crowdie had already unhitched the reins and they were off.
After they had turned the corner, Sprat said slowly, 'What was
all that about? It was you stepped in and saved me.'

Crowdie winked. 'Best thing, I reckon. The old lady's so
proud of her nephew, she hasn't stopped to ask questions. Was
wonderful, too, when you stop to think, a gentleman like him
coming running just for the likes of us.'

'Yes.' Sprat felt herself colour. 'Though I suppose . . . when
he's better . . . He must have heard.' She was humiliatingly
close to tears again.

Crowdie shook his head. 'Never heard a word, I shouldn't

think. Too busy being took bad.' He looked at her sideways, 'Anyway, who's going to pay any attention to Stan Vargo? Drunk as a stoat, and violent with it. Wouldn't trust a word he said, meself.'

Sprat looked at him doubtfully.

'I mean it. If Stan Vargo told me that cows had four legs, I'd want to count them, personal, afore I believed it.'

There were tears in her eyes now. 'So you won't . . .'

'Go spreading that nonsense around the Cove and the village? My dear Sprat, I got enough muck-spreading to do on the farm, without setting out to do it anywhere else. No. I shan't say a thing, and neither will you if you're wise. And nor will Vargo, if I can help it. Here.' He stretched out his free arm and pulled her to him. His jacket was hairy and he smelt of cows, but she leaned against him gratefully for a moment. 'Better?'

She nodded tearfully, and sat up very straight, comforted and embarrassed by the hug. It was odd, though. She had come back to Fairviews expecting to find her life in ruins, and it was rather uneasy-making to find that everything – apart from poor Mr Raeburn of course – seemed to be very much as usual. 'I only wish Ma and Pa had told me,' she began fretfully, a few minutes later.

'Told you what?' Crowdie said. 'Dunno what you're blathering about, I'm sure.'

'But Mr Vargo said . . .'

'I dunno what you're talking about!' Crowdie said, firmly. 'So let it be.'

There was nothing to be said to that, and they drove a while in silence, until Crowdie began to tell her all about Mr Raeburn and the makeshift stretcher. 'Turned blue round the gills, he did. Even his ears were grey. I better tell you all about it. Doctor'll need to know.'

Sprat, almost unable to believe her good fortune, gave him a grateful smile.

Crowdie gave her a careful account of the accident, and by

the time they got to St Just Sprat had quite a lot to tell the doctor. Just as well, he wanted every detail. He listened gravely, but what he heard must have alarmed him, because when she had finished he sent for his horse and set off with such despatch that he reached Fairviews long before them. By the time Sprat got back, Mr Raeburn had already been re-arranged so that he was half sitting up in bed, and the doctor was downstairs again giving the strictest instructions.

'A nourishing diet – light foods at first, calves-foot jelly and panada – but good nourishing dairy food as soon as he is able. Lots of cheese, butter and eggs. I'll give you a receipt for a digestive porridge, too, magnesia and bicarbonate of potash, and perhaps a little sago gruel made up with wine. He will need a nurse – I can recommend an excellent girl – and, of course, rest. Plenty of rest. I understand Mr Raeburn is from London. He won't be fit to travel for a long time, I fear. Twelve weeks complete bed rest at a minimum, and he won't be able to undertake such a gruelling journey for at least three months afterwards. In the meantime, as he is more comfortable now, perhaps a milk and soda water? I'll look in again tomorrow.'

Miss Raeburn was listening to this and looking grave, but Fitch, standing behind her, was looking graver still. Anxiety for his master, Sprat thought sympathetically, but when he came past her – going into the kitchen for a tray – she distinctly heard him mutter, 'Six more months. Six whole more dratted months. I'll be consigned to Bedlam by that time, even if he isn't.'

Denzil was recovering slowly. The bruising on his face had faded to a dull brown, though it had been interestingly multi-coloured on the way, and his arm no longer made him wince every time he moved it. Another week or so, he thought, and he'd be back to normal, or at least fit to be seen in the town carrying the briefcase. In the meantime, he was sufficiently recovered to begin to appreciate his unexpected good fortune.

He could so easily have found himself, by this time, out on

the streets with no home, no money, and no job – and worse yet, still owing pounds to the tallyman. And that (supposing that he didn't die of cold and hunger) could only have led, in the end, to prison or the workhouse. And here he was, instead, enjoying more luxury than he had ever known in his life.

He didn't see the Bullivants much, of course. He was expected – he expected himself – to mind his own business and stay in his room. In fact, it was an active pleasure. Daisy had found some books in the box room 'from when Miss Olivia was young', and though they were of a determinedly improving nature Denzil devoured them eagerly: young women who stole and came to awful ends, virtuous paupers, missionary tales, it was all a joy to him. He had never had the leisure to read books simply for enjoyment and he felt slightly ashamed, as if the pleasure were sinful. Just as well it was summertime, or he might have drawn attention to himself by using up all his candles.

And then there was Miss Bullivant, of course. She had been very kind to him, in her candid way, and she took an interest in him even now. Once or twice she had come out of the drawing-room when he was on his way upstairs, on purpose to speak to him. She was always pleasant and obliging, and so solicitous about his welfare, it sometimes made him go quite pink about the ears. A good woman. Too good for Tom Courtney, anyway. It was a pity her mother dressed her up like twelve-year-old: Denzil was no expert on female dress, but even he could see that childish fashions did nothing to flatter Miss Olivia's plain, amiable face, and dumpy figure.

Poor Olivia. Nature had not blessed her with beauty. None of that sparkle and vitality which so animated Sprat.

Sprat. There, he had allowed himself to think of her. He had been trying, for days, to banish her from his mind. He had expected some sort of reply, at least, to his letter – if only a message to ask after his health. But there had been nothing. He had faintly hoped that she might make an excuse to come into the office about that consignment of wood, but, no, that had all been delivered and paid for long ago. He had entered it up himself. Mr Zackary, paid in full.

He sighed. Frightened her off, that's what he'd done, talking about making choices between himself and her folks. What did he have to go and open his big mouth for? Perhaps she would come round to it 'one day', like she said. All he could do was wait and see.

Well, it was no good moping, he was back at his desk, and he must get on with his work. There was a great deal of type-writing to be done, mostly letters to carters and waggoners, trying to arrange transport for consignments. It was more and more difficult. The dock strikes were getting worse and there was talk that the railways would follow suit. Bullivant's would be in a pickle then. Staff might even be turned off. What then? He'd end up in the workhouse if he wasn't careful, and that would be the end of ever seeing Sprat.

It all made him so depressed that even Claude noticed.

'Anything the matter, Mr Vargo? You're looking some glum.'

Denzil smiled. 'Thinking about a girl, that's all. You wait, young Claude, it'll be your turn before you know it. Now, when you've filled up the inkwells, you can find me the sealing wax and we'll do up these envelopes.'

Claude hesitated, the stick of wax in his hand. 'If it was the same girl I saw, I can't say I blame you, Mr Vargo. She was a looker, that one, and no mistake.'

Denzil stared. 'You've seen her?'

Claude nodded. 'Yes, she came here looking for you – oh, over a week ago. 'Course, you weren't seeing anyone then, I had to send her away – Mr Bullivant's orders. Real upset, she looked.'

Denzil put down his pen. 'Why didn't you tell me? After-wards at least?'

Claude turned a dismal shade of pink. 'Well, I might have done, only . . . I thought perhaps you wouldn't want to know.'

'Wouldn't want to know? That she'd been here asking for me?'

Claude shook his head. 'No, no. Wasn't that. It was just –
what I saw afterwards. Thought it was better not to say anything at all, though perhaps I should have. After all, it didn't do
any harm, and she looked happy enough with it. Proper cheered
her up, it did.'

'What did?'

Claude looked at him helplessly. 'The ice-cream,' he said,
unhappily. 'I saw her at the bus stop, later on. Mr Courtney was
with her, carrying her parcels. Bought her a penny cone.
Seemed to cheer her up like anything.'

On Denzil, however, the news had quite the opposite effect.

Three

S prat first heard about Miss Raeburn's plans on Friday afternoon. It came as a complete surprise.

The doctor had just visited again (some people must be made of money, Sprat thought) and was sitting in the drawing-room sipping tea with Miss Raeburn and reporting on progress. Sprat, serving sandwiches and cake, loitered in the doorway to listen, while the nurse, recently engaged on the doctor's recommendation, stood beside Miss Raeburn's chair awaiting instructions. Miss Bloom was a big strapping woman with hefty arms. With her long, grey dress and white starched apron she looked like a benevolent heifer in uniform.

Sprat rather took to Nurse Bloom. She had swept into Fairviews like a young gale, and the quiet rhythm of the house had been instantly altered. Unused rooms were opened up, dust-sheets removed, grates swept and windows opened. 'Get a bit of air through the place and blow the germs away,' she boomed, and even Florrie reluctantly obeyed, throwing away the dusty pot-pourri and sending Sprat out with scissors for fresh blooms from the garden.

Nurse Bloom breezed through the kitchen, too, and took charge of Mr Raeburn's diet, banishing Mrs Pritchard's delicate broths and jellies as 'deficient in nourishment' and ordering – to the doctor's immense approval – beefsteak, cheese and eggs to build the patient up. Neither Cook nor Florrie would normally have stood for such interference, but at the first murmurings of discontent Miss Bloom simply folded her substantial arms and said it was all 'on medical grounds' and the grumblings subsided, at least until the next time. Cook and Florrie had formed an uneasy alliance, in the face of the common enemy, so a kind of peace reigned, even below stairs.

Nurse Bloom was here in the drawing-room now, listening attentively to the doctor.

'No salt or spices,' the doctor was saying. 'Bad for the blood. He's having beef and mutton, I presume?'

'Yes, doctor. And a little rabbit now and then. And we're restricting fluids to reduce the dropsy. No tea or coffee, and apart from the bedtime whisky, only a glass or two of blackcurrant or rosehip.'

'Hhmph. Well. Go on with the foxglove extract, and give Glauber's salts in the morning. Otherwise, I think we are doing all we can. But the immediate danger is over. It's a matter, now, of managing his convalescence. Complete bed rest of course, for another six weeks at least, and then we'll try getting him up on a chaise for ten minutes or so. Mustn't embarrass the heart too early.' He put down his teacup and turned to Miss Raeburn, speaking loudly and distinctly, 'Well, my dear lady, I'll look in again next week. Don't hesitate to call if you need me, of course, but otherwise I'll leave things in Miss Bloom's capable hands.'

Miss Raeburn put down her cup and saucer. 'He is out of danger?'

The doctor looked judicious. 'In my judgment, yes, although in these cases it is never simple. The heart, you see, becomes fatigued and any over-exertion—'

'Yes, yes,' Miss Raeburn interrupted impatiently. 'I understand that. It is only that I wanted to be sure that it was safe for me to go.'

The doctor looked reproving. 'You intend to return to London?'

Miss Raeburn looked reproving in her turn. 'Naturally not. But there is business to attend to. I have already been away longer than I expected. I should make arrangements about closing up my flat and putting things into storage – and James', too. Also, if I am to remain here much longer I shall require other clothing. I have hardly come prepared for winter, and I cannot afford to take chills at my age. It will take a week or two, at most and then I can return here to my nephew. I think poor Violet would wish it.'

Poor Violet, Sprat thought, would wish it very much indeed. Mrs Meacham had already been commenting that life at Fairviews would seem dreadfully dull again when the visitors had gone.

'My dear Miss Raeburn,' the doctor said, 'your sentiments do you credit, but I must counsel you to be careful. It is quite an undertaking for a lady of your . . . ah . . . mature years . . . to be embarking on such a long rail journey unattended. Are you sure these matters cannot be dealt with by post?'

The old lady got to her feet. 'Thank you for your concern, doctor, but I am not quite helpless yet. It would be difficult to organise my wardrobe by long-distance telegraph, as it were. Besides, I should not be travelling alone. If Violet agrees, I would like to take Nicholls with me. With Miss Bloom in the house, I think Violet can manage here.' She turned and looked at Sprat. 'You would be agreeable to that, Nicholls? I should pay your wages, of course. From what Violet tells me, it might amuse you to see London.'

Sprat was so astounded that she could only nod. London! It was like a dream. For days she had been expecting the world to crash around her, but there had been nothing, not a word – not even from the baker's boy, who was as bad as Norah Roberts for spreading gossip. And now this. A chance to get away, away from the Cove, away from betrayal, away from Denzil and her broken dreams. London. 'Love to,' she breathed at last.

'In that case,' Miss Raeburn was saying, 'perhaps you can take this tray away instead of hovering in the doorway. Miss Bloom and I will see the doctor out.'

'Yes, Miss Raeburn.' Sprat busied herself with the tea things, smiling to herself. The old lady had been a treat to watch, standing up to the doctor like that. You wouldn't think she had

198

it in her. She was still smiling when Miss Raeburn returned a few minutes later.

'I have spoken to Violet, Nicholls, and she is agreeable to my plan. Your parents will have no objection, I suppose?'

My parents, Sprat thought bitterly, are hardly in a position to object. My mother is dead and my father is in Canada and neither of them wanted to know me. But she couldn't say that to Miss Raeburn. 'They can't very well object, can they, Miss Raeburn?' she said, sweetly. 'If Mrs Meacham tells me to go, I go. It was Ma found me the job here.'

That, after all, was nothing but the truth. Anyway, Ma could object all she wanted, she wasn't Sprat's mother. Sprat was on her own. She had left the Cove, left for ever, and she didn't have to tell Ma Nicholls anything – any more than Ma had ever told *her* the things which were really important. If Ma could read, Sprat would have sent a little letter from London, but as it was she would send a message – via Cook and Mrs Polmean. That was dignified, it meant she had done her duty, and it saved her going back to the Row again. She did not feel that she could face that – not ever. And no one here would think it was odd: with the fever still in the house, she had every excuse to stay away. 'No, Ma'am,' she said again. 'It'll be just grand.'

Miss Raeburn twinkled over her starched lace collars. 'In that case, Nicholls, you can go to the station on Monday and make some reservations. And you can pop into the chemist while you're there, and get some Glauber's salts for James. The doctor thinks them more suitable than Enos.' And with a rap of her little stick, she was gone.

London, and a chance to get away. It should have been a dream come true. Who cared what Pa and Ma Nicholls thought? But the stars were fading in the sky before Sprat got to sleep that night.

'I want a reservation please: first-class to London on the luncheon and tea train, Thursday week. Two travelling. In the name of Raeburn.' Sprat tried to keep her face composed.

She could hardly believe the words that she was saying. A first-class ticket! She had expected, at best, to travel third-class and leave Miss Raeburn to her luxury. But the old lady had been adamant.

'Nonsense, girl. You are coming as my servant and companion. What good are you to me stuck away at the other end of the train? Naturally, you won't come to the dining car, you can take some cold cuts, but otherwise I shall want you by me.' The shrewd grey eyes twinkled wickedly. 'The doctor fears I may be over-exerted, Cook is convinced I shall be kidnapped by white slavers, and Violet thinks I shall be robbed where I sit if I close my eyes for a moment. You must be there to protect me from marauders.'

Sprat nodded doubtfully. 'Yes, Miss Raeburn.' She knew that the old lady was mocking, but Sprat was not sure that these were joking matters. One did hear of dreadful things happening, especially in London. Cook was full of it. There had been that dreadful Ripper person, and everyone knew the big city was full of shadowy figures, desperate and full of drink, who would cheerfully set upon an old woman and a girl to steal a halfpenny.

All the same, the present thudding of her heart came more from excitement than alarm. 'Raeburn. R-a-e-b-u-r-n,' she added, seeing the booking clerk spelling it with a 'y'.

He gave her a disdainful look. 'When, how didn't 'ee say so?' He crumpled up the form he had been filling and heaved a deep sigh. 'Now, start again shall we? Two first-class on the luncheon and tea train, Thursday? Supposing that it runs. Threatening a railway strike they are.' He didn't even look impressed as he made out the tickets. Sprat could have kicked him. Bet he'd never been first-class on a luncheon and tea train in all his life.

She put the tickets carefully away in her pocket, and hurried towards the station. She had already taken in Miss Raeburn's note and arranged the carriage – think of that, a cab all the way to Penzance! Now there was only the chemist to think of: the

200

Glauber's salts and some sal volatile for Miss Raeburn, who apparently liked to keep some handy when she was travelling.

Up Market Jew Street, into the warm dusty wind. It was a nice old town, Sprat thought. She would miss this, up London. Everyone in their summer best: children in sailor suits and ladies with muslin dresses, feathered hats and white-gloved hands. Bicycles and horse-and-carts, bustling housewives in coloured shawls, shopkeepers in aprons, and whistling bakers' boys with baskets on their heads. Even a motor car outside the bank: the street urchins had stripped off their tattered coats and caps and were clustering around it, goggling, shirt-sleeved in the sun.

She would not look at Bullivant's. Not even a glance. That whole sorry business was behind her. She fixed her eyes resolutely on the milliner's window opposite and mentally selected hats for Miss Raeburn until she was safely past the door – the little black bonnet with the sequins and cherry trim. She forced her mind to imagine it on, the ribbons tied just so, the little veil drawn over the forehead . . . There, she had hardly thought of Bullivant's at all.

'Sprat!'

She was imagining things. That wasn't Denzil's voice?

It was. She could hear him coming behind her, running, making the people stop and stare.

'Sprat! Wait!'

She turned. It *was* Denzil. He was looking pale and there was something the matter with his face, but his clothes were smart and there was a sleeker look about him, which she associated vaguely with townsfolk and having enough to eat. Her knees went weak at the sight of him.

'Sprat! Oh, thank heaven. I thought you hadn't heard me.'

He was walking beside her now, the same old Denzil. How could he be so cheerful, so unchanged?

She said nothing and, after a moment, he spoke again.

'You didn't answer my letter.'

She looked at him then. 'Never knew you sent one.'

He sighed. 'Sent it to the Cove. Didn't know what else to do.'

She shook her head. 'Well, that's it then. Haven't been home for weeks.'

'No, I heard.'

Her heart sank. The row with Ma, then, was all over Penvarris. Well, what did she expect? Norah Roberts must have seen her slam out, and that news would find its way around the village in no time, even if Crowdie was right – as he seemed to be – and the shameful truth of Sprat's parentage hadn't leaked out at the same time.

'Daresay you did.' It sounded sharper than she meant, and Denzil looked hurt. 'News travels quick, round our way. But don't worry, Denzil, I know what was in the letter. Why you left home and came to Penzance.'

He looked surprised. 'You know?'

She nodded. 'Your father told me. Grabbed hold of me in the lane when he'd had too much to drink and started shouting at me. Horrible it was, but he told me everything. Wonder it isn't all over Penvarris, but it doesn't seem to be. Not yet anyhow.'

She looked at Denzil, whose face was etched with horror. Suddenly she forgot her own upset, in sympathy for Denzil. It must have been awful for him too. She said, gently. 'It's all right, Denzil. You did what you had to do. We couldn't go on seeing each other, things being how they are, so it's better you've gone. I'm going away myself, next Thursday – up to London with Miss Raeburn.'

'Leaving? You are?' He seemed stunned. 'How long for?'

'Weeks,' she said. It wasn't quite a fair description, as Miss Raeburn expected to be home again in a fortnight, but it was kinder like this. She nodded, aware of the lump in her own throat. 'So, you be happy, Denzil. You hear? And . . . about Miss Bullivant—'

'What about Miss Bullivant?'

'You know perfectly well what about Miss Bullivant. I even thought for a minute it was her you were talking about, that day up at the stile.'

'Miss Bullivant?'

'Oh come on, Denzil, don't look like that. Of course she's sweet on you, and don't pretend she isn't. I heard it several places.'

'Tom Courtney!'

She managed a smile. 'Not just him. The office boy noticed it and all. But I don't mind, Denzil, really. You court her and be happy. You got a chance there, you take it. I understand how it is, since it's hopeless between us.' The words pained her, and she reached out and squeezed his arm. 'I'll always be fond of you . . . always. As a . . . as a . . .' she wanted to say 'cousin' but it was better to face the worst. 'Like a sister,' she finished, with a gulp.

The life seemed to drain from his face. 'Like a sister? That's all? That's really all?' His hand closed over hers. 'I don't know what they've told you, Sprat, but forget Miss Bullivant. She's nothing to me. Less than nothing. It's you I love. Always have.'

She snatched her hand away. This was hard enough without him making a spectacle in the street and people looking. 'I know that,' she said. 'But it's hopeless, isn't it? Don't go on so. Just get on with your life, and let me get on with mine.'

He stood looking hunched and helpless. 'You didn't used to feel like this.'

' 'Course I didn't. But I didn't know then, did I? I hadn't seen your father. That changes everything, doesn't it?'

'It does?' he said dazedly. 'I was afraid of this, but I hoped—'

Grief made her impatient. 'Oh don't be stupid, Denzil. I aren't living with that, even if you would.' Surely he hadn't really expected her to?

He shook his head. 'I see.' He sounded suddenly distant, as if he was the one who'd gone hundreds of miles away in a train. 'Well, I suppose in that case there is nothing more to be said.'

She reached out to squeeze his arm again, but this time it was he who withdrew his hand. She felt the tears behind her eyes. 'Oh Denzil,' she burst out, 'don't make this harder than it is.'

He flinched. 'No. Of course. I'm sorry, Miss Nicholls. I'll say

good afternoon. Don't miss your bus.' His raised his hat
politely and walked away. Sprat watched him till he was out
of sight, but he didn't look back.

Thursday. Denzil was at the station in time to watch the train
pull out. He waited till the last of the carriages had dwindled
down the track and then he turned away. So she had gone, and
not even a glance in his direction.

She had not known he was coming, that was true, but surely
she must have guessed that he would find an excuse to be here?
No, clearly, she had not even thought of him. He found himself
walking back up Market Jew Street in a kind of blur.

His feet were moving steadily, but his mind was in turmoil. He
had walked clean past Bullivant's, for one thing, and was going
the wrong way, but he couldn't just turn round – people would
think he was peculiar. He had made enough of a fool of himself
back there, gaping at the train like a two-year-old. And she had
not even looked for him. He should have known! Hadn't he
declared his love straight out the other day, and been rejected?

He still couldn't believe it. He had been so sure that Sprat
returned his feelings. But she had stood his world on its head.
She could not have been clearer. Fond of him, as a sister, that's
what she'd said. He should go away and live his own life,
because things were hopeless between them.

Why? He'd thought it over a hundred times and not made
sense of it. She'd heard about the fight with Father, she said so,
but surely she would have forgiven him for that in the end?
Father had told her off, too, apparently, out at the gate, so she
knew what he was like. No, it had to be something else. He was
so preoccupied with all this that he blundered into the road
without looking, and almost overset the cats' meat man, who
was standing by the kerbside with his handcart, haggling over
the price of tripe with Mrs Roberts.

'Oi!' the man shouted, steadying his flyblown wares with a
scrawny hand and glaring at Denzil furiously. 'Mind where
you're to!'

Denzil murmured something, but he hardly noticed. He was busy with his thoughts.

As he walked down the road, however, he was aware of Mrs Robert's voice following him. 'What do you expect? They are all the same, those Vargos. Just like his father. Hear what that man did to that Sprat Nicholls, the other day, did you? Set on her in the lane, by all accounts, and tried to steal sixpence. Attacked her. Shaking her and all sorts. Frightened her out of her wits. If 'twasn't for Crowdie and that gennulman from London, dear Heaven knows how it would have ended.'

Denzil stopped like a statue. So that was what it was! Father hadn't just stopped her in the lane and given her a talking to, he'd actually threatened her. Got hold of her and hurt her. It made Denzil's scalp prickle to think of it. He knew what Father was like when he had a drink or two in him. No wonder the poor girl was frightened.

And here Denzil had been blaming her for her change of mind. She hadn't fallen for Tom Courtney, with his clever tongue and penny ices. He might have guessed. Sprat wasn't the sort of girl to change her mind for a bit of gossip. But Father in a rage – that was quite a different matter.

The idea was so horrible that he shut his eyes. No, of course Sprat was right. She was more realistic than he was. You couldn't expect any girl to live under threats like that, even if she was fond of you. And there was no pretending Father wouldn't lay a hand on her once they were married, because he would and Denzil knew it, once he faced up to the facts.

So he really had lost her. And it was bloody Father's fault. Like everything else unpleasant in this world. Denzil found himself wishing he'd done a better job with that skillet while he'd had the chance. If he ever laid hands on Father again . . .

He was so furious that he aimed a kick at a lamp post, sending the metal ringing all the way up to the gas bracket at the top. A woman, passing with a basket on her arm, looked at him horrified, then huddled her child close to her skirts and hurried by. Denzil felt shamed. No better than his father. He had jarred his leg, too, which made him feel foolish.

The pain brought him to himself. He was still walking away from the office, and he was due at his desk already. He would have to turn back, but somehow he couldn't bring himself just to swivel round and walk the other way. People were already staring at him. He turned into a nearby shop and bought a candle he didn't need, and then hastened back to the office as fast as his legs would take him.

Four

M a was getting anxious. More than a week it had been since that awful Vargo business, and still no word from Sprat. She wanted to go up to Fairviews and talk to her in person, but Pincher had been adamant.

'You leave her be, Myrtle. You'll only make things worse, going up there and making a scene. Sprat'll be back, see if she isn't. Been a terrible shock to her – bound to be, finding out that your parents aren't your parents at all – but she's got a good head on her shoulders. She'll see we meant it for the best. Give her time to get over it, and she'll be here same as ever.'

Ma blew her nose in her handkerchief for the umpteenth time in five minutes. The necessity made her irritated with herself. Weakness, that's what it was. She said, more sharply than she meant, 'And suppose she doesn't come, what then?'

'She'll come. Snappy as a hooked eel and crosser'n two sticks, no doubt, because we never told her, but she'll be here, or my name's not Pincher Nicholls.'

But Sprat didn't come. Ma found a dozen excuses to go up on the road, but there was no sign of Sprat. Ma even sent for Peter Polmean and gave him twopence to go up to Fairviews with a message – about Mrs Mason moving out and going to Mount Misery – in the hope of learning some news without defying Pincher, but it did no good. Peter hadn't even seen Sprat. A man in uniform had come to the door, saying that 'Nicholls' couldn't be spared at present, but he would pass on the message.

Peter had been deeply impressed, but that was no good to

207

Ma. She hadn't dared to send the real message, 'Please come home'. You couldn't show yourself up like that, and anyway Peter Polmean couldn't be trusted to keep anything quiet. Not that he was a gossip exactly, just that he prattled on. Norah would have had the information out of him in no time, and then it would have been around the Cove quicker than a clockwork train.

It was all very well for Pa, he had this boat to see to, and he could forget his troubles, worrying about planking and shaping and copper-headed nails, but there was a limit to how much you could occupy your mind just dusting the hallstand or beating the mats.

Not that there wasn't a lot to do. Now that the Masons had properly gone, there had been days of disinfecting the front bedroom, scrubbing everything in sight and even taking the iron bedstead apart and washing it with Jayes Fluid but, although it made your back ache and your hands red raw, it didn't stop you from dwelling on things, the way a man's work did.

Well, at least she had been tired enough to get a good night's sleep. Other nights she had lain awake for hours, remembering: Gypsy arriving in Plymouth in floods of tears; the months of having her in their tiny house, explaining to curious neighbours how she had 'just lost her husband, poor soul' while Gypsy flaunted her shame through Plymouth, shopping and walking in the street long after her condition was obvious and any respectable woman would have stayed indoors; the dreadful, screaming, blood-stained panic of the birth and the amazing arrival of that tiny, red, shrivelled scrap, 'no bigger'n a Sprat', which had changed their lives for ever.

There! She was doing it again. Ma got to her feet heavily. Whether it was the strain of having the Masons, or the emotional upsets over Sprat, or just because she hadn't been sleeping properly, she wasn't feeling herself at all. She gathered up the tea things and went out to the garden butt for water to wash them with.

Norah was at the sea wall threading cork pieces on to freshly treated rope and handing them to Half-a-leg, who was putting new floats on his nets. The minute she saw Ma she dropped her basket and came over. The strong smell of the oak-bark 'cutch' in which she had soaked the ropes still clung to her like a cloak, and her hands were stained the same dark brown.

'Here,' Norah said. 'Terrible business up Fairviews, isn't it?'

Ma's heart sank. It had begun then, all the gossip and whispering behind closed doors. She said wearily, 'Don't know what you're talking about.'

Norah stared. 'Sprat must have said something, surely?'

Ma said levelly, 'Haven't seen Sprat, to speak of. You know what the doctor said.' Deliberate prying, she thought bitterly. Norah must know that Sprat had not visited the Cove recently. Not much escaped her twitching curtains. Well, she wasn't getting information from Myrtle Nicholls. Ma went to the water butt and ostentatiously began to fill her ewer.

Norah was not to be put off. She came and stood at the edge of the hedge. 'Daresay she's been wanted up there, anyway, with that poor man took so sick.'

Ma concealed her surprise with difficulty. Indeed, she almost let go of her jug in the water butt, but she rescued it in time. 'Mmm,' she said, hoping that it sounded like agreement. What man? Not Stan Vargo, surely. You wouldn't call his problems sickness, exactly. 'Why, what've 'ee heard?'

'That James Raeburn, or whatever they call him. Went running up the lane and had a heart failure. Proper poorly, by all accounts. I'm surprised Mrs Polmean haven't told you, with her cousin working up there and you two being so friendly.'

Ma felt a twinge of guilt. Mrs Polmean had called, the day before, but Ma had affected not to hear her knock and waited in the back bedroom until she went away. Not that she minded Mrs Polmean, just that she couldn't face her, afraid of what might have reached her ears from Fairviews.

'Haven't seen Mrs Polmean either,' Ma said. 'With this fever about.'

Norah nodded. 'Saw you talking to Peter the other day.'
Drat the woman, did nothing escape her? 'But, yes. Gennulman's poorly as can be. Got the doctor calling every day, by
all accounts, though I daresay he'll stop that, otherwise he'll
be poor as well as poorly! Months, they say, before he's over
it. His old aunt's been a Trojan, apparently, arranging a live-
in nurse for him, and arranging to go back to London to
close up her house, so she can come back and be with him
herself.'

Ma found herself saying, 'What was he doing running in the
lane? Man of his age, and a city gentleman too.'

Norah gave her a look that was sheer triumph. 'You haven't
heard? Your Sprat, it was. Got attacked in the lane by some
drunk wanting money, and started hollering for help. Mr
Raeburn heard her and came running.'

Ma's lips were dry, but she said, 'A drunk?' disbelievingly.
Was it possible that Norah hadn't heard? If there was gossip
about, Norah usually knew it before it *was* about, and she
couldn't have resisted telling what she knew. Perhaps there was
still hope, after all. Ma said, 'A drunk?' again.

'Wretched fellow got away, from what I heard. One of those
wretched old tramps, more than likely. Gentlemen of the road,
folks call them, but there's precious little "gentleman" about
them. They're around lately – I seen their marks on the stile.
You know, all the scratchings they do, telling each other who's
soft-hearted enough to give them a bit of something. Mind, I've
given a tramp stale buns myself before now, just to get rid of
him.'

Ma's mind was fixed on other things. 'And he's really ill, up
there?'

'Nearly died, from the sound of it. Went all grey round the
mouth and terrible to look at. Weaker'n a kitten still. Baker's
boy heard it when he went up with the bread. The talk of
Penvarris, it is.'

Ma nodded, still following her own train of thought. If Miss
Raeburn was going to London, Sprat would not be needed at

Fairviews full-time. She would have to come home again. For the first time in days, Ma felt her spirits rise.

Norah saw the smile. 'Yes,' she said. 'Sprat'll be thrilled, of course. Always wanted to travel, didn't she. And now she'll have a chance.'

'How come?' Ma said, not comprehending even then.

And Norah had the immense satisfaction of being able to say, casually, 'Oh, you haven't heard that either? Well, I am surprised. Miss Raeburn went to London this morning, by all accounts. Taking Sprat with her, I heard.'

Denzil had to work, whatever else he did, and at least it would occupy his mind. If he thought too much, at present, he was in danger of savagely hitting something – his Father for preference, though there was no doubt who would come off worse. He came to Bullivant's door and hurried in.

Olivia was in the front office with her father. Tom Courtney was fussing around her with a chair which she was trying to refuse without being impolite.

She looked up when Denzil came in, and her face lit up. She smiled shyly.

Denzil found himself recalling Sprat's remarks, and suddenly felt himself flushing. Couldn't be right, surely? The boss's daughter wouldn't have time for him. He glanced towards her.

She was still looking at him, her cheeks as pink as her bonnet. She was blushing. Denzil felt his own ears turning scarlet.

He had to speak. He could not in courtesy walk past her without greeting. And he was still carrying that ridiculous candle. His tongue felt too big for his mouth as he said, 'Afternoon, Miss Bullivant.'

'Mr Vargo.' She gave him another timid smile.

There was a moment's awkwardness, and then Bullivant said, 'Glad you're here, young Vargo, there's a letter needs typing, urgently. You get to your desk and Claude'll bring it directly.'

And Denzil, embarrassed and stumbling, went gratefully into the inner room. It was terrible, this happening today, when he

211

had enough to cope with. Then he pulled himself together sharply. This was nonsense. There was nothing in it. Miss Bullivant had been into the office several times recently. Nothing remarkable at all.

'Recently', his inner voice reminded him. He had worked at Bullivant's for months, and never seen Olivia. She had only started to come to the office since he had moved into the house. It was not a comfortable realisation, and Denzil was quite relieved when Claude came in with the letter for him to type, and he was able to turn his mind to his work.

Five

G one to London and never even sent word. Ma was so
shaken that she hardly knew how she got inside with the
water jug, and even then she split it all. When Pincher came in,
he found her sitting in the kitchen staring into the empty grate
with the fire out and not a crumb of tea on the table.

He came over at once. 'Here, Myrtle, whatever is it?'

She told him, not trusting herself to look at him, but staring
hard at a piece of driftwood on the hearth. She heard her own
voice, cold and steady, saying the terrible words.

Pincher heard her out. Good as gold, he was, on his knees
and already setting the fire. It made Ma feel quite guilty at her
own idleness. She got up uncertainly, but the room danced
under her feet.

'You sit down,' Pincher said. The fire was burning now and
he went out for some water to fill the kettle. When he came in
again he said slowly. 'Might be the best thing for her, you
know, in the end. Get her up there, away from those Vargos.
And she's with Miss Raeburn. Isn't going to come to much
harm, is she? Besides, what else could she do? Got to go, really,
if her employer wants her.'

Ma looked at him rebelliously. 'Might have told us, though.'

Pincher's face cleared. 'That's what Mrs Polmean came for,
you see if it wasn't. You said she came calling round here.
Penny to a shilling, that's what it was. Our Sprat wouldn't go
and never say a word.' Ma was about to protest, but Pa
forestalled her, 'And she couldn't come herself, could she,
not a second time – with this fever still in the house?'

213

Ma gazed at him. 'You think so?' But of course he did. She had to admit the justice of it. Once you had thought of it, it was obvious. She found that she was hugging it to herself like a bed-warmer. Then something else occurred to her. 'And to think I wouldn't open the door to Mrs Polmean! And now look! Whatever will Sprat think?'

'How will she know?'

He was right, again, and although she pushed his proffered hand away she felt obscurely comforted. 'I wish we'd ha' told her, Pincher, that's all. About Gypsy, and . . . oh, about lots of things. But I suppose it's too late now. Let's hope she's happy, wherever she is.'

She got up heavily and went, at last, to fry the fish for his tea.

When Denzil got home that night he was still carrying that wretched candle. He tried to smuggle it upstairs, but it was in his hand when Olivia came out of the parlour to speak to him. He found himself turning scarlet again.

'Is Mama keeping you short of light?' she was asking, anxiously. 'I noticed you had bought a candle this afternoon. I will speak to her about it, if so. She would not keep you short intentionally, I am sure.' There was surely something more than simple hostessly concern in her smile?

Bother Sprat, why had she put these ideas into his head? He mumbled indistinctly, 'No, not at all. Your mother is very kind.' That did not satisfy her and he was obliged to add, 'I had bad news, that is all, and I went into a shop to hide myself. I hardly knew what I was doing.'

She laughed, as if for a moment they shared a conspiracy. Then she said, 'Bad news? Oh, poor Denzil! Not your family, I hope.'

It was the first time, he realised afterwards, that she had called him by that name, but at that moment had been too embarrassed to notice. 'Not my family, exactly. It was a friend . . . a young lady. My father . . .' he broke off. 'No matter.'

She gazed at him frankly. 'Your father, too? Poor Denzil. Why do parents always think they know best?'

She spoke with feeling. Of course, her father was pushing her towards Tom Courtney. And yet she didn't care for him – you could tell by the way she was refusing that chair. Why couldn't Bullivant see that?

'Fathers are all the same,' Denzil said, and they exchanged smiles.

That was all, but somehow he felt strangely encouraged as he said goodnight and walked up the stairs. He'd lost contact with his mother, and now he had lost Sprat, but he was not entirely friendless and alone. They did have something in common, Olivia and he.

It took him some time to get the candle to light, but when it did, it burned softly – comfortingly – with a gentle, steady flame.

It was rather exciting, Sprat thought, settling herself into the carriage, as long as you didn't let yourself dwell on things. There was so much to look at: the sepia pictures over the seat; the little leather handles on the windows; and the netting racks for putting your luggage in. Better even than a hansom cab. She was so busy gazing at her surroundings that she didn't notice a small, forlorn figure standing at the station door watching the train pull out.

'All right, Nicholls?' Miss Raeburn said, as soon as they left the platform.

'Oh yes, Madam.' It was true, almost.

'Then will you take my gloves, and get down my travelling rug. It is in the small valise. And you may fetch my book,' Miss Raeburn said. 'I may need it later.'

Sprat did as she was bid, spreading the woollen rug across Miss Raeburn's neat knees and fetching out the novel, borrowed for the occasion from Mrs Meacham. As she did so, the book fell open, and she glimpsed a woodcut illustration of a young man and young woman, leaning together on a bridge. Just like one of Gypsy's stories. She had not read this particular tale, but no doubt it would all work out very

215

happily in the end, whatever the setbacks. It always did, in books.

Not like real life, she thought to herself, as she placed the book carefully at Miss Raeburn's side.

What was it Gypsy used to say? 'That's the thing about a story. You turn over the page and it is a whole new chapter. Anything can happen.'

Well, it seemed to have worked for Gypsy.

Sprat leaned on the window, watching the familiar Mount go past and all the life she had ever known disappearing behind her across the bay. Perhaps it was for the best. A whole new chapter.

She gulped. Then she lifted her chin, sat back in her seat and turned resolutely forward to face the future.

© 2013, Disney Enterprises, Inc.
Published by Hachette Partworks Ltd.
ISBN: 978-1-908648-85-3
Date of Printing: September 2013
Printed in Malaysia by Tien Wah Press

Tinker Bell
AND THE
GREAT FAIRY RESCUE

DISNEY
Hachette

The Pixie Hollow fairies were on their way to bring summer to the mainland.

There was so much work for the nature fairies to do that Tink was allowed to go along, too. She couldn't wait to stay at fairy camp – she'd heard it was a lot of fun!

But at the camp,
nothing needed fixing. Tink decided to
look for lost things, instead.

"Be careful," Vidia warned her. "You
mustn't let any humans see you."

Suddenly, there was a huge ROAR! Fawn,
who was painting a butterfly, was so startled
that she spattered paint all over it! The butterfly
flew off with one wing unfinished.

The roaring noise had come from a car. Tink had never seen one before, and she was so curious about this wonderful invention that she decided to follow it.

After a while, the car stopped in front of a cottage and a little girl and her father got out.

Tinker Bell flew down to get a closer look at the car's engine.

Just then, Vidia appeared. "You shouldn't be this close to the human house!" she hissed.

But Tink had found an interesting lever, so she pulled it, back and forth. And with every pull, poor Vidia was showered with water!

The humans came back outside to unload the car. The girl, who was called Lizzy, spotted the half-painted butterfly.

"Look," she said. "The fairies have painted different patterns on its wings."

"Lizzy, fairies are not real," replied Dr. Griffiths, Lizzy's scientist father.

Tinker Bell and Vidia were on their way back to fairy camp. They had to walk, as Vidia's wings were still too wet for flying.

Then Tink spotted something – it was Lizzy's fairy house. She couldn't resist going inside to explore, even though Vidia warned her not to!

Just then, Lizzy appeared – and she spotted Tink inside the tiny house! She picked up the house and raced home, where she put Tink in a cage to protect her from the family cat.

Vidia had to get help! She hurried back to fairy camp, but a sudden rainstorm slowed her down.

At last, Vidia arrived back at the camp and told the other fairies what had happened.

The meadow was flooded, so Bobble and Clank built a boat to get them to Tink. But when the boat ran aground at the foot of a waterfall, the fairies had to walk the rest of the way. What a journey!

Meanwhile, Lizzy and Tink were getting to know each other. When Tink spoke, her voice sounded to Lizzy like a tinkling bell, so Tink had to act out the answers to Lizzy's questions.

"Your name is Tinker Bell? Mine's Lizzy!"

The storm eased and Tink
was about to leave. But she saw
how lonely Lizzy was – her father
was always too busy to play with her.

Tink decided to mend the leaks in the
house, so that Dr. Griffiths would have
more time for Lizzy. As she worked, she
noticed the butterfly in a jar, so she set it free.

Just then, Dr. Griffiths found Lizzy with
Tinker Bell and tried to catch Tink
in the jar. But instead it was poor
Vidia, who had arrived to help her
friend, who was trapped!

Dr. Griffiths drove off with Vidia
in the jar. He couldn't wait to show
the fairy to his colleagues! How could the
fairies save their friend? They couldn't fly in
the rain… but with the help of a little pixie
dust, maybe Lizzy could fly them all
to the rescue!

They caught up with the car, and when Dr. Griffiths saw Lizzy flying, he finally understood that some things were not meant to be seen, just believed. He set Vidia free.

The next day, everyone went for a picnic. Tink smiled to see Lizzy so happy. Tink hadn't only fixed their roof, she'd fixed their family, too!